The Tyranny of the Fays Abolished

The Tyranny of the Fays Abolished and Other stories

by
Comtesse D.L.

Translated, annotated and introduced by
Brian Stableford

A Black Coat Press Book

Visit our website at www.blackcoatpress.com

ISBN 978-1-61227-792-9. First Printing. October 2018. Published by Black Coat Press, an imprint of Hollywood Comics.com, LLC, P.O. Box 17270, Encino, CA 91416.

TABLE OF CONTENTS

Introduction

The first of the two collections combined in the present volume of translations, *La Tyranie des fées détruite, nouveaux contes, dédiez à Madame la Duchesse de Bourgogne par la Comtesse D.L.* was published in Paris by Jean Fournil under royal privilege in 1703. The second, *Les Chevaliers Errans et le Génie familier par Madame la Comtesse D**** was published in Paris by Pierre Ribou, similarly under royal privilege, in 1709.

At some point in the mid-eighteenth century the name "Madame d'Auneuil" seems to have been attached to the two volumes speculatively, but Joseph de La Porte, the scrupulous historian of eighteenth century female authors, who published his exhaustive work in the 1760s makes no mention of the author in question, and although Charles Meyer, the editor of the *Cabinet des fées*, compiled in the 1780s, cited the name, it was only to express his doubt that any such person had ever existed. In spite of that skepticism, the name was reproduced, and it was given an official endorsement of sorts when it was included in Antoine-Alexandre Barbier's 1806 *Dictionnaire des ouvrages anonymes*. More recently, the Bibliothèque Nationale's catalogue has expanded that name to "Louise de Bossigny, Comtesse d'Auneuil," and a Wikipedia entry attached to that name adds the dates 1670-1730, although the Bibliothèque Nationale does not, and it is highly likely that the figures are purely conjectural.

In spite of the Bibliothèque Nationale's acceptance and expansion of the name, there does not seem to be any surviving evidence of the existence of a Comte or Comtesse d'Auneuil in the relevant period, and the commune of Auneuil in the département of the Oise in Picardy does not seem ever to have had such a title attached to it; although it did still have a derelict château in 1700, it does not appear to have had a seigneur. Nor does the surname "de Bossigny" seem to exist anywhere else than in the BN attribution. In view of those circumstances, I am strongly inclined to trust the judgment of La Porte and Meyer, and conclude that "Madame d'Auneuil" is fictitious. The name might have arisen as an accidental corruption of the name of Madame d'Aulnoy, one of the authors of *contes de fées* who might have been tentatively suggested as the author of *La Tyranie des fées détruite*, although stylistic analysis reveals that she was definitely not.[1] If the signature attached to that volume was an abbreviation, it suggests that the author's real name must have taken the form "de La ?" but it is also definitely not the work of Mademoiselle de La Force, the only leading writer of *contes de fées* who had names of that form.

Whoever was actually responsible for them, however, the two works in question are certainly the work of the same author; the stylistic eccentricities that they have in common leave no room for doubt about that. The collection *Les Illustres fées* (1710), credited to Auneuil in some modern sources, on the other hand, is certainly not by the same author; that confusion arose because the collection in question was reprinted in the same volume of Meyer's *Cabinet des fées*—the fifth (1785)—as a later version of *La Tyrannie* (sic) *des fées détruite*, which had been edited for republication in 1756 by Mademoiselle de Lubert.

The two volumes translated herein are part of a mere handful of collections of new *contes de fées* that appeared after 1700, although several of those produced in the initial boom of 1697-8 were reprinted frequently after the turn of the century, especially the Charles Perrault collection that had

---

[1] The title stories of both collections and one other were translated into English in a three volume collection entitled of *Novels and Tales of the Fairies written by that celebrated Wit of France the Countess d'Anois*, published in 1728, and it is possible that that misattribution made some contribution to the confusion and to the invention of the fictitious name.

started the boom in publication, although it consisted almost entirely of borrowed materials and continued to import recycled materials for expanded editions. By 1700 the clique of salon writers initially responsible for the vogue—which had formed around Mademoiselle L'Héritier, a protégé of Mademoiselle de Scudéry who had inherited her salon—had disintegrated spectacularly. Mademoiselle de La Force had been banished from court in 1697 and imprisoned in a convent, following unspecific accusations of scandalous behavior, before her collection of *contes* even appeared. Baronne d'Aulnoy left Paris in 1699 when she was suspected of implication in the murder of an abusive husband, as an accessory before the fact, although she was never formally charged. The Comtesse de Murat, who was then under investigation by the Lieutenant-General of Police, having been accused of libertinism and lesbianism, was also forced to leave Paris by the collapse of her family's finances, although it did not prevent her continued pursuit and eventual imprisonment.

Of the original coterie, therefore, only Catherine Bernard and Mademoiselle L'Héritier remained in Paris after 1700, and their association with the court appears to have been very marginal, and probably indirect. Only the latter attempted to publish any more *contes de fées* after that date, in a collection of which only one volume appeared, although two were planned and advertized. It seems that the scandal surrounding the group, especially suspicions of lesbianism—presumably encouraged by the fact that Mademoiselle de Scudéry had always liked to refer to herself as "Sapho," and the circumstance that the two members of the core group who had been coerced into arranged marriages had long since deserted their husbands, Aulnoy apparently having conspired to have hers imprisoned in the Bastille for a crime he might not have committed—seems to have cast such a dark shadow over the genre they created that it made the royal privileges required for publication of new works of that kind direly difficult to come by, in spite of their manifest popularity with the burgeoning reading public.

Against that background, perhaps the wonder is that Comtesse D.L., whoever she was, obtained a royal privilege when they were so difficult to come by, but that becomes far easier to understand when one actually reads the title story of, *La Tyranie des fées détruite* (here translated as "The Tyranny of the Fays Abolished") which is, in essence, a massive exercise in egregious flattery.

Flattery of the royal family was, of course, extremely commonplace in all the literature produced by Louis XIV's courtiers, but Comtesse D.L. went to an unprecedented and highly unusual extreme in the novella is question; the appendix to the title, "dédiez à Madame la Duchesse de Bourgogne" is no commonplace dedication, as the Duchesse de Bourgogne [Duchess of Burgundy] not only features as a character in the story but plays the role of a messianic redeemer who abolishes the seemingly-unassailable tyranny of the evil fays simply by means of her charismatic and majestic presence.

Mademoiselle de La Force had already pointed out to her colleagues that, seen as a narrative device, *fées* [fays][2] were

---

[2] The term *fée*, as employed by L'Héritier and popularized as an element in the generic label by Aulnoy, is derived from the French word *féerie* [enchantment], and could apply to any agent of enchantment, although the feminine gender of the noun was usually taken to imply that *fées* were female, and their male equivalents were generally called *enchanteurs*. The word did have an English transcription, fae, but it was rarely used and soon became obsolete, while the alternative spelling fay remained current in the name of the enchantress Morgan le Fay, as featured in Thomas Malory's standardized compendium of Arthurian romance and derivatives thereof. Contemporary translators of *contes de fées* usually translated the term into English as "fairy tales," and the *fées* in the stories usually became fairies—although nasty ones were sometimes called witches—but the term fairy, which already had a complex literary history in English, largely thanks to spectacular exemplars provided by William Shakespeare and Edmund Spenser,

simply a modern substitute for the *deus ex machina* of ancient Greek drama. Comtesse D.L., who must have been aware of that remark, was consciously employing a real person as a *deus ex machina* in order to abolish others of a different breed, tacitly declaring the end of an era, and perhaps of a genre—although the author might have spoiled that effect slightly by continuing to write more *contes* in which *fées* have not only been abolished but are represented in the full glory of their empery.

Because the tales popularized by Perrault have become a subgenre in their own right, and nowadays seem to be the cardinal exemplars of what their initial English translators chose to call "fairy tales," it is easy to overlook the fact that they were by no means representative of the genre as it had been constituted by the salon writers, and bear no trace of the rapid and spectacular evolution that the genre underwent in the hands of its original practitioners. Perrault's versions of his mostly-recycled materials are short, supposedly adapted for reading to children, with the addition of simple, explicit and supposedly (but rather unconvincing) educational morals. The trend within the genre as the salon writers developed it was, by contrast, toward longer and more complex stories, frequently designed as portmanteau works, which often dispensed with explicit morals or deliberately subverted conventional morality, while ostentatiously—and, one strongly suspects, sarcastically—paying lip service to it.

That pattern of development is clear if one tracks the development of the salon *contes* from the pioneering exemplars of L'Héritier through the prolific and substantial body of work produced by Aulnoy and the tentative complications and subversions of La Force to the bold and brilliant innovations of the Comtesse de Murat's 1699 collection *Histoires sublimes et*

---

usually implied some kind of supernatural being rather than a human enchantress, more closely equivalent to the beings called *nymphes* [nymphs] in *contes de fées*, who function there primarily as the handmaidens and assistants of *fées*.

allegoriques par Madame la Comtesse D*** dédiées aux fées modernes, especially the two novellas "L'Isle de Magnificence (tr. as "The Isle of Magnificence") and "Le Turbot" (tr. a "The Turbot").[3] Those works are the authentic core of the salon genre as devised and sophisticated by its originators, and they provided the principal models and exemplars to the writers who revived the genre and continued its evolution, after a generation in the doldrums, in the 1730s.

Comtesse D.L. had obviously read Murat's collection, and although she was not nearly as polished a writer and not as vividly imaginative as Murat, she was certainly trying to take over the trend that Murat had bought to a new level of sophistication, particularly in terms of a method of story-construction developing portmanteaux of interconnected takes. That narrative strategy soon became known as the "Galland method" because Antoine Galland made such extravagant use of it in *Les Mille et une nuits* (1704-1717), but it was Murat who actually did the initial groundwork. Comtesse D.L.'s adaptation of that method in "La Tyranie des fées détruite" is crude and tentative, but in "Les Chevalier errans"—which is her most impressive story, in spite of a certain clumsiness and disorganization—it is carried forward very extravagantly. The latter story benefits from Galland's example as well, but Comtesse D. L. was fully aware of Murat's earlier endeavor.

Another significant innovation introduced by Murat in her 1699 collection was that in three of the four stories she introduced datable references establishing that the stories are

---

[3] More elaborate accounts of the evolution of the genre in the context of salons hosted by Louis XIV's female courtiers can be found in the introductions to *The Robe of Sincerity and Other Stories* by Marie-Jeanne L'Héritier de Villandon, *The Land of Delights: Tales of Enchantment* by Charlotte-Rose Caumont de La Force and *The Palace of Vengeance and Other Tales of Enchantment* by Henriette-Julie de Murat, all published, like the present volume, by Black Coat Press, with more to follow.

not set in a pseudohistorically distant "time of the fays," as previous contributions to the genre had been, but in the present day, so that the imaginary world of the fays become a kind of parallel world coexistent with, and occasionally overlapping, our own. In two of the three stories, those datable reference refer to a single specific event viewed at a distance by the characters in the story, with the aid of fay magic: the wedding at Versailles on 7 December 1697 of Louis XIV's grandson, the Duc de Bourgogne, then fifteen years old, and his cousin Marie-Adélaïde de Savoie, a result of the Treaty of Turin, by virtue of which Savoy switched sides in the Nine Years War and became France's ally. The marriage was preceded by several days of magnificent fêtes and was the high point of court life during the brief boom in *contes de fées*—a genre whose imaginary world is, in effect, Versailles and its cultural satellites as seen through a distorting mirror. Murat was present at those celebrations and so, presumably, was the Comtesse D.L. Murat diplomatically does not mention in her references to the event that the bride was just eleven years-old, and neither does "La Tyranie des fées détruite," in which the advent of the young princess has an effect that is, from the point of view of the hypothetical fay imperium, apocalyptic.

Presumably, the young duchess, who was several years older by the time *La Tyranie des fées détruite* was published, and must by then have come into contact with *contes de fées*, appreciated the role she played in the story; the royal censor must surely have checked with the Duc's household before granting the privilege for its publication. She was not to know, of course—and neither were Murat and Comtesse D.L.—that her tenure at the Château de Marly would not last long. Shortly after her husband became the Dauphin of France, following the death of his father in 1711, the duchess died of measles in February 1712; he insisted on staying by her bedside throughout, caught the disease, and followed her to the grave within a week, followed in his turn by his eldest son, leaving the younger one to succeeded to the throne as Louis XV after the death of Louis XIV in 1715. Nobody has ever suggested, even in jest, that the fays might have been striking back in response to the insult, but what is certain is that after 1711 new *contes de fées* virtually disappeared from the French literary scene for a generation, until they made a spectacular comeback in the context of a boom in publications whose authors and printers simply decided to do without the royal privilege and publish anything for which there was a public demand—an inherently perilous strategy, as it put a huge sector of the publishing industry outside the law, but one that had an enormous impact on French culture and literary history.

Les Chevaliers errans was one of the last volumes produced in the first phase of the history of *contes des fées*, when the genre already seemed decadent. It is by no means one of the finest, in terms of its literary quality, but it is one of the most adventurous and enterprising, still attempting to push forward a pattern of progress that, when it was eventually taken up again, continued to lay important groundwork for modern fantasy fiction. The title novella (tr. as "The Knights Errant")—the closest thing to a novel published during that first phase of the genre's development—not only attempted to take Murat's narrative strategy of interwoven portmanteaux to a new extreme, but deliberately attempted to reconnect *contes de fées* with the their most important precursor genre, that of twelfth- and thirteenth-century prose romances.

It is not an accident that the best and most adventurous writer active in the renewal of *contes de fées* in the 1730s and 1740s, Mademoiselle de Lubert, not only took her principal influence from the same novellas by Murat that provided Comtesse D.L. with her inspiration, but edited a version of *La Tyranie des fées détruite* for republication, attempting to tidy up some of the clumsiness of its composition. That version remained the only practically accessible version for the next two centuries and more, until Google Books and *gallica* recovered the original, as well as the long-lost *Les Chevaliers errans*. It is only now that the nature of their contribution to the evolution of the genre can be clearly seen and properly evaluated.

The subsidiary stories in the 1703 collection are not particularly distinguished, although "Agatie, princesse des Scites" (tr. as Agatie, Princess of the Scyths") is interesting in its attempt to connect "the time of the fays" to actual history and geography, introducing a dose of *realpolitik* into its story-line. "La Princesse Léonice" (tr. as "Princesse Leonice") is more typical of the genre, and benefits in coherence in consequence. "Le Prince Curieux" (tr. as "Prince Curious") begins as a robust attempt to reconnect the genre with its roots in chivalric romance, but is interrupted and aborted, perhaps because the author realized that her hero had fallen into the same moral trap as many other possessors of rings of invisibility, from Gyges onwards, and had lost any possible pretention to being a model of knightly decency. It is not surprising that she began that particular quest again, with a much more robust model of post-Quixotic knightly perfection, in Elmedor of Granada, and although one or two of the fellow knights errant he picks up along his way are considerably less perfect than he is, he is careful to tell them to stand back and look after the ladies and the horses when the time comes for his climactic confrontation with the forces of evil.

The second portmanteau in the later collection is interrupted, like the final story in the first collection, and rudely aborted; the mock-Oriental frame narrative containing the interpolated stories is simply abandoned, as if forgotten. Nor does "La Princesse Patientine dans la forest d'Erimente" (tr. as "Princess Patientine in the Forest of Eerminte"), the interpolated story that actually concludes the printed text, fit that pseudo-Gallandesque frame, seemingly having been transplanted from an alien fictional world, that of the allegorical sector of the classical *conte de fées*. It is, however, a striking work in its fashion, and perhaps the most brutally honest work produced within the coterie, once decoded.

The story's representation of contemporary marriage as a matter of innocent young women barely out of childhood falling into the brutal hands of disgusting Ogres who abuse them horribly is, of course, only par for the course, but what is unusual is the conclusion of the tale, in which Prince Courageous, eager to do battle against the monsters protecting the cave where his beloved princess is being held captive is sternly told to put away his unnecessary sword, this particular rescue being women's work. When the rescue is complete, the prince is graciously permitted to continue adoring the princess, provided that he never lays a finger on her, while she enjoys a perfect bliss with her steadfast female best friend, under the tutelage of their benign protectress, the fay Clementine.

Tales produced at Louis XIV's court, whether in writing or in action, were not usually allowed to end like that, because it was not an ending to which royal and legal privilege was usually granted, but that one sneaked in under the radar, in disguise. Comtesse D.L./Comtesse D*** then disappeared from view completely, censored out of history, if completely not out of print, and to this day, she has only been replaced in the official record by a phantom who probably originated as a spelling mistake. In her own peculiar fashion, however, she was a heroine.

The translations of the two volumes were made from the copies of the Fournil and Ribou editions reproduced on the Bibliothèque Nationale's *gallica* website. The spelling of the names of the characters is sometimes inconsistent within the stories; I have unified it, usually employing the first spelling used.

Brian Stableford

THE TYRANNY OF THE FAYS ABOLISHED

The power of the fays had reached such a high degree that the greatest people in the world feared displeasing them. That accursed breed, of which no one knows the origin, had made themselves redoubtable by the harm that they caused those who disobeyed them to suffer. Their fury was only satisfied by changing the most amiable people into the most horrible monsters, and if they did not give you a prompt death, it was only in order to make you languish for longer in a more wretched condition than the death they refused you. The impossibility of exacting vengeance upon them rendered them more imperious and cruel, but of all the people they took as the object of their rage, none had ever been as unfortunate as Princess Philonice. Her supernatural beauty gave them a desire to marry her to one of their kings.

With that in mind they abducted Philonice one day when she was walking with her mother, the princess, without being touched by the screams of the mother or the daughter. She was about twelve years old. At that age, so hardly advanced, she was a masterpiece of nature in body and in mind. To console her for the violence they had just done her, they transported her to a charming place. It was a palace built between two hills, from which one could see a valley filed with everything that could please the eyes; the Tempe praised by the poets was never so beautiful. An eternal spring reigned in that delightful place; the gardens were filled with canals and fountains, and the orange trees formed a shade there that provided protection from the most ardent sun. In sum, everything that nature and the art of fays had of the most surprising was found in that enchanted abode.

The young princess was not sensible to so many marvels. She was in a melancholy state of mind that would have softened the heart of anyone except the pitiless fays. They put her under the guard of the least barbaric among them, whose name was Serpente; but they recommended, above all, that she should not be able to communicate with anyone.

In order to carry out that order, Serpente caused a magnificent pavilion to emerge from the ground in an instant at one end of the garden, to which she took Philonice. In order to keep her company she gave her a girl name Elise, who had been abducted at the age of two. She gave her all sorts of rare animals to divert her, and enabled her to work with golden and silken fabrics for part of the day in order to occupy her. Magnificent garments, diamonds and pearls were not spared in her regard. All in all, everything that she believed might please a young person, the fay gave her in profusion. She refrained carefully from talking to her about the monster whose wife she was destined to be.

The time had not yet come when she had resolved to make that scarcely suitable marriage; they wanted to accustom her to their manners before announcing her misfortune to her. Sometimes Serpente took her for a walk in the beautiful places I mentioned, and, inviting her to admire so many beautiful things, she told her that if she was obedient to her will, she would one day be mistress of them, but that she had to be careful not to merit her hatred, because she would be able to punish her in recompense.

While the fay was saying that, Philonice saw on the bank of the canal two turtle-doves that appeared so tame that they did not flee from their presence; she desired them, and asked for permission to capture them in order to take them to her room.

"I cannot grant you that," the fay said to her. "The destiny of those birds is not to quit this canal. They have not always been in this condition; they were once a handsome prince and a beautiful princess, whom we took in affection. We destined them for one another and they loved one another tenderly, but in the time when we were only thinking of their happiness they encountered one of our sisters who was bathing in the canal, all of whose body was covered with turtle-dove feathers, which she concealed carefully. The chagrin of being discovered made her desire that those who had seen her could not say so, and that they became turtle-doves themselves. At that moment she threw water over their faces, which had no sooner touched them than they changed their nature and became the birds that you see. Since that time they have not quit one another, and, conserving their tenderness in that new form, they spend their days lamenting their common misfortune.

"There are many other examples here of our power," the fay continued. "All the statues that you see along these terraces were once subjects of a neighboring prince. These gardens were not yet made; we had not made our residence here, but the beauty of the valley sometimes attracted us here. One evening, when we were dancing in the moonlight, we were perceived by those men. They made fun of our different postures. Irritated against those insolent fellows, we made them remain motionless in the positions they were in, and since them we have converted them into statues."

That speech only augmented Philonice's dread. She promised the fay that she would always be submissive to their will and would never merit their hatred, although that seemed very difficult to her.

Meanwhile, her beauty was augmented every day; she was the delight of all the fays. With pleasure, they saw her succeed in everything that they showed her; they heaped her with caresses and presents. They reached such a point of amity with her that she had the liberty to go everywhere without the fay Serpente. If she had been able to forget her homeland, she would have led a happy enough life. She loved Elise passionately; the girl merited it; she had so much mildness in her character that was difficult to avoid liking her.

One day, when it was very hot, they were walking in the evening in a citrus wood some distance from their pavilion. The beauty of the night charmed them so much that they were unable to resolve to retire, when they saw a woman coming toward them who was holding a handkerchief in her hand, with which she was wiping away tears that were flowing from her eyes in abundance.

Such a sad encounter excited the pity of the two young persons; they both advanced at the same time to ask her what was wrong, but they were prevented from doing so by the fear caused to them by a dragon of enormous size, which emerged from a bush and came to hurl itself upon the neck of the woman, without her giving evidence of any fear. On the contrary, she returned its caresses, and when she sat down on the ground, it lay down next to her, with movements so tender that Philonice could not doubt that there was some mystery concealed under that form.

With that thought in mind, she was drawing nearer, in order to try to learn more about an adventure that excited her curiosity, when she heard the afflicted woman say to the dragon, while redoubling her tears:

"My dear Philoxipe, until when shall I see you so different from yourself? Will the barbarity of our cruel enemies never weary of persecuting us? Ought they not to have been sated by my tears since the time when our misfortunes drew them from my eyes? Or rather, when will the adorable princess that the solitary told us has been born for the happiness of the world, come to break our chains by destroying the detestable fays, whose tyrannical power extends all the way to our hearts?"

Philonice could not help uttering a sigh at the woman's discourse, which the latter heard. She turned her head to see where it came from, and perceived the princess. She was afraid that she might be one of the fays, and that made her get to her feet in order to flee her presence, but Philonice, recognizing her fear, approached her and said: "Have no fear, Madame; we are unfortunates, like you, retained in this place. Veritably touched by the laments you have just made, if we can help to soothe your woes, we will do anything in our power to do so."

"It's a great deal, Madame," the woman replied, "to find someone in this place capable of compassion, and this is the first time in the five years that the fays have been retaining me with the deplorable Philoxipe"—she indicated the dragon—"that such a thing has happened to me."

"I wish to Heaven," said the princess, "that I had the power to end your woes; you would see that I would not stop at lamenting them; but since that is all that is in my power, do not refuse that sad pleasure, and tell us by virtue of what cruel fate you have been brought here."

"It's a discourse too long to make this evening," said the stranger. "Our implacable enemies would take our absence badly. They only grant me one hour in the entire day to see this lovable dragon, and it is only after many tears that I have obtained that mercy from the fay Serpente, the only one who sometimes allows herself to be touched by pity; but tomorrow, at the same hour, I will satisfy your curiosity.

Philonice agreed to that, and left her to employ the little time that remained to her with her dear dragon.

That object had so touched the young princess and her companion that they did not sleep that night. When the fay Serpente came into her room she found her very dejected; she asked her the reason, but Philonice refrained carefully from telling her, and after having told her that she felt ill, she went with her to the palace, where the fays were assembled. She spent the day there, impatient for the hour of her rendezvous, which finally arrived.

She took her leave of her imperious mistresses in order to go and find the afflicted beauty, with her dear Elise; but destiny had prepared another adventure for them. Instead of taking the path to the citrus trees they took, without noticing it, a route that led them on to a large terrace overlooking the valley, from which one discovered all the beauties of nature that enchanted the eyes.

They were surprised to have gone astray, and as they tried to recover their route they encountered a man lying at the foot of a yew tree at a bend in the path, who seemed to be asleep. That novelty made them stop; they had never seen a man in that place, and young Elise, who had not gone out since she was born, asked the princess what kind of animal it was.

She spoke so loudly that the stranger woke up. He got up precipitately at the sight of the two beautiful persons, who wanted to flee, and having advanced toward them he said, addressing Philonice, whose supernatural beauty surprised him: "Am I unfortunate enough to have caused you some fear, and will you be cruel enough to punish me for that by going away so promptly?"

"The lack of habit that we have of seeing persons like you," replied the princess, stopping, "has astonished us at such an advanced hour of the night. It might be dangerous for us to stop here. You doubtless don't know where you are, since you went to sleep here so tranquilly. The fays who are the mistresses here will not pardon you for having entered this place without their permission. Leave as quickly as possible, for fear of experiencing their dangerous wrath, and leaving us in dread of being mistaken for accomplices of your crime."

"Oh, Madame," exclaimed the stranger, "I have no fear of the powers of the fays when it is a matter of losing you; although I have only known you for a moment, I sense that I shall not quit you while I live, even if I must suffer the most terrible woes; whatever threats you make me, I cannot help praising Heaven for having caused me to stray from my equipage in order to see a beauty as accomplished as yours. But what demon fatal to the pleasure of the entire earth is hiding you in this place unknown to mortals?"

"It is for my particular misfortune," said the princess, "that I have been retained here for some years."

"Oh, Madame," said the stranger, "if it is against your will that you are here, and that such a beautiful abode serves as your prison, you have only to tell me to what place you want me to take you, and I will do it at the peril of my life, without asking any other recompense of you than that of spending the rest of my days at your feet."

"No, generous stranger," replied Philonice, "I cannot accept your offer, obliging as it is; I would be putting you in unnecessary danger. You could not remove me from their cruel hands. Only take care that they do not discover you; leave with diligence while you are free to do so. Take advantage of my advice, I repeat: flee, for the sake of your repose and mine."

As she finished speaking, she took Elise by the arm and drew away.

The man could not resolve to withdraw from that fatal place without knowing where the beautiful person lived; in order to enlighten himself on that score, he followed her at a distance and saw her enter the pavilion. He remained there for some time, gazing at the place where the amiable object of his nascent amour resided, but, fearful of being surprised by daylight, he withdrew, by the same route by which he had arrived, and without being perceived by the guards who were posted around the gardens.

The princess had forgotten the afflicted beauty; the encounter with the stranger occupied her all night long in spite of herself. Daylight appeared without her having slept, the generosity with which he had offered to extract her from captivity having evoked her gratitude.

In fact, a violent passion had taken possession of her heart without her being aware of it; she spent the day as she had spent the night, in anxieties that seemed entirely new her.

When the evening arrived, Elise reminded her of the rendezvous of the previous day, to which she allowed herself to be led without paying any attention. The presence of the afflicted beauty, whom she found beside her dear dragon, drew her out of her reverie.

The princess apologized for having missed the appointment that she had promised her, sat down beside her and begged her to satisfy her curiosity.

The stranger, without having to be begged further, commenced her story in these terms, addressing Philonice.

The Story of Cleonice

I was born to parents who held a considerable rank at the court of the greatest king in the world, who made it a pleasure to merit by their actions the glory of being born his subjects. It was a good fortune envied by the entire world; no king was ever more beloved by his people and more feared by his enemies. His victories had no sooner given him new provinces than he had troops to guard them; his new subjects, only too glad to live under his power, would have sacrificed their lives to maintain themselves there. Master of our hearts as well as our fortunes, he was the pleasure and the terror of all Europe; quickness in recompense, slowness in punishment, and ease in forgiveness are the least of his virtues; but how far can my zeal go for a prince so worthy of praise that one wrongs his merit by daring to speak of it?

I will tell you, therefore, Madame, that I was my mother's only child, that my name is Cleonice, and that I was brought up with all possible care. The facility I had in learning everything that was taught to me gave pleasure to those near to me; I made myself loved by my parents tenderly.

My mother was originally from a region neighboring this deadly place. One day, when she was walking with me, she had a desire to go and consult a solitary, very knowledgeable about future things, regarding my fortune. We went there, and after having examined me with application, he told us that I would endure an unfortunate fate until a moment when a princess that Heaven had caused to be born for the welfare of the realm would destroy the power of the Furies who, under the name of fays, made themselves feared by everyone.

We returned, scarcely satisfied by my horoscope, and some time afterwards, my father had the design of giving me in marriage to one of his brother's sons. He was a very well made gentleman, accomplished in every way one could wish.

Our inclination had anticipated our parents' choice; we loved one another tenderly; our joy was great when we were commanded to regard ourselves as soon to be united, and we awaited the moment with impatience. When the happy day arrived, we believed that nothing could any longer trouble our felicity.

Alas, it did not last long, and what mortal chagrins we have experienced since! Scarcely had we spend four months together when someone came to tell Philoxipe—that is my dear husband's name—that a monstrous dragon was desolating our lands by the murders of people and livestock that it carried out every day. Philoxipe commanded his men to be ready the following day, in order to go in person to aid his subjects by killing the monster. I did what I could to turn him away from it, but my pleas and my years were futile. He departed at daybreak, and although he had tried to forbid me to follow him, I accompanied him on the ill-fated voyage.

We soon arrived at the dragon's abode; it was a frightful lair in the densest part of the forest. All the men of our retinue launched arrows at it, but in vain; they only irritated its rage. It came straight toward Philoxipe, hissing horribly, and deploying its wings, it took off in order to fall upon him with more violence. My husband, taking his time, without being frightened by such a great danger, waited for it to come down, and plunged his sword into its heart. As it fell, the monster knocked its conqueror down, and covered him with its poisonous blood.

But gods, imagine my surprise when, approaching that dear spouse, I saw him in the same form as the monster that he had just destroyed, crawling on the ground and taking the route to this region. I followed him, along with all his subjects; he came into these gardens, and, of all our retinue, it was only permitted to me to follow him; an invisible power repelled the others without my knowing what had become of them.

As for me, a troop of fays received me, making terrible threats to avenge themselves on us for the death of a monster that had been dear to them. Without wanting to permit me to see the innocent victim of their fury again, they constrained me to enter this pavilion you can see, where they abandoned me to my despair. How many tears I have shed since that fatal moment!

After four years of imprisonment, the fay Serpente, whom they had given me as a guard, being more sensible to pity than her sisters, and touched by my unhappiness, finally permitted me to come for one hour a night to the unfortunate Philoxipe, who spends his unfortunate days under this bush, waiting for the moment when it is permitted for me to join my sighs to his frightful hissing. If it were in our power to kill ourselves, we would have put an end to our woes a long time ago, only seeing an end to them in the faint hope of the solitary's oracle.

Cleonice finished her discourse with a flood of tears that emerged from her beautiful eyes.

"How sensible I am to your misfortunes," Philonice said to her, embracing her, "and how much pity I have for poor Philoxipe! If only I were able to render you both happy, what a pleasure it would be for me to see you returned to your initial wellbeing and to go and enjoy with you the presence of your king. Although I was not born his subject, you have inspired me with an infinite respect for him."

"It is not one of my least woes, Madame," said Cleonice, "to be distanced from his court and not to be able to witness the conquests that he makes every day. He will soon be the master of Europe entire, in spite of the jealousy of the kings, his neighbors, who are all in league to stop that hero in his rapid course; their efforts will be in vain; his victories are marked by his days, and unless he wants, by virtue of his generosity, to make peace with them, their crowns will not be secure on their heads.

"But I am only thinking that the time of my retreat is imminent," the sad Cleonice continued. "Serpente, chagrined by my disobedience, would punish me for it severely."

"I would be very sorry to augment your woes instead of soothing them," said the princess.

After that they separated.

Meanwhile, the stranger had found his men at daybreak, and he had lodged in a town not far away from the palace of the fays, in the hope that he would be able find a means of reentering the gardens and seeing Philonice again.

With that design, he mounted a horse after dinner, and, in the company of a single squire, he made a tour of the enchanted place. He recognized the princess's pavilion.

"There," he said, sighing, "is the prison that hides the greatest beauty in the world."

After that reflection, he continued his route, having remarked a place where a river served as a wall, and which was not guarded, in the belief that Nature defended it sufficiently herself. Knowing perfectly how to swim, he understood that he would be able to cross the river easily. Content with his discovery, he returned to his lodgings and went to bed, with a little less anxiety, in the hope that he would see his princess again.

The next day, as soon as night fell, he advanced in the direction of the river; he had sent his squire via the bridge to have his garments ready. He passed over swimming, and, having dressed, he quit the confidant of his passion, with orders to wait for him at that place. Marching diligently, he soon arrived at a wide road that led him to the door of Philonice's pavilion, but, not daring to enter, he hid in a little clump of trees.

He had not been there long when he saw her emerge with Elise and they began walking straight toward him. He advanced to meet her precipitately, and was at her feet before she had perceived him.

"What!" she said, taking a few steps back. "You've come back again to risk the misfortunes that I predicted?"

"Oh, Madame," he said, "there are none greater for me than not seeing you, after having seen you once in my life. Gods, how I have suffered since the day before yesterday, in the dread of not encountering you! Do not deprive me of the pleasure of your sight, charming person," he continued, "my amour demands it with all the ardor with which my heart burns. Have no fear that anyone will discover me; I have found a safe place. If you had any feeling for me; if my presence gave you as much pleasure as yours gives me, I would be able to see you every day, and tell you all that the most powerful tenderness generates in a heart as tender as mine. But you aren't replying, adorable person; perhaps you have not even heard me?"

"In truth," the princess finally replied, "I was so occupied with the difficulty in which we find ourselves here, and so conflicted by the desire to grant you what you as of me, that I don't know what decision to make."

"That of listening to me, Madame," he said, "and banishing the fears that occupy you."

"It is necessary to believe you, then," she said to him, extending her hand to lift him up.

She plunged into the thickness of the boscage, and made him enter a cabinet[4] with Elise, the door of which she closed on them. They sat down on a crimson velvet sofa with a golden lining. The moonlight was bright enough to permit the stranger to see the magnificence of the cabinet, but he was so beside himself in being next to Philonice and understanding that he might one day be loved by her, that he could not see anything but her.

The princess desired to know who he was, and what had brought him to the abode of the fays. In order to satisfy her, the stranger told her that his name was Anaxandre, that he was the son of a very powerful prince, that since his childhood the

---

[4] The word *cabinet* is very versatile in French, used to refer to all kinds of enclosures; in the context of a garden it would normally refer to an arbor, and it is odd that this one has a door and furniture. The gardens at the Château de Marly and Versailles, however, were extensively landscaped and embellished, and did contain very elaborate furnished arbors.

latter had destined him for the daughter of his sister, who was married to a prince not far from his Estates, but that at the time when the alliance in question had been planned, the young princess had been abducted while out walking with her mother.

"Alas, you are looking at her," cried Philonice, unable to hide herself from the prince. "I am that unfortunate princess, whom the fays transported to this place without ever having told me with what design they snatched me from the arms of such a tender mother."

"What!" said Anaxandre, astonished. "You are that Philonice, who has always been destined for me, and whose loss was so sensible to me?"

"I am, undoubtedly," she said.

"Oh, my princess," cried the prince, "I am not astonished by the effect that you have had in my heart since the first moment I saw you; it was only the admirable Philonice who could have touched me; the protective gods of my race have brought me to this place, solely in order to enjoy the pleasure of seeing you and adoring you."

"I am no more astonished than you are," said Philonice, blushing, "by the esteem that I could not help having for a man that I had only seen for a moment; blood was speaking in my heart without my knowing it."

"Oh, Madame," the prince said to her, "what you are telling me is cruel, in letting me think that only your penchant carried you away."

"We will examine another time whether I am not mistaken," said the princess, laughing. "But give me news of the princess, my mother."

"The princess your mother," Anaxandre replied, "in despair at your loss, not being able to console herself for it during the long years since you were abducted, is leading a very languid life. As for me, Madame, seeing my father at peace with all his neighbors while all of Europe is at war, I obtained his permission to come and learn my métier under the greatest king in the world.

"With that design I departed toward him. Having traversed all of this realm, I arrived, on the evening when you found me on the terrace, in a large forest pierced by a hundred thousand paths. I marched very rapidly, leaving my men behind, and, having taken a route directly contrary to the one I was following, they were soon distanced from me.

"I only perceived that I had gone astray when night fell, but, seeing in the moonlight a gate at the end of the path that I was on, I advanced toward it. I found no guard there. I dismounted from my horse, and after tying it to a tree I entered these gardens. Their beauty enchanted me. Having arrived on that terrace, I admired the diversity of the landscape of the valley for some time, and fell asleep, due to weariness.

"O gods, how agreeably I was woken up by your presence! And how touched I was when you quit me. Determined to see you again, no matter what the cost, I followed you as far as your dwelling, and having withdrawn I rejoined my men.

"Since that moment I have only been occupied by the care of searching for you. I have found you again, thank Heaven; my happiness no longer lacks anything, provided that my adorable princess wants to listen to me favorably. Everything obliges you to do that, charming Philonice: the will of our parents, who destined us for one another in our earliest childhood; that of the gods, which seems to be explained by that miraculous encounter; and the ardent amour to which you have given birth in my heart, which merits some recognition."

"I confess," said Philonice, "that the princess, my mother, had commanded me to receive you as the man she destined for my husband. But Prince, my fortune has changed greatly; I no longer depend on a good and tender mother; I am in the hands of the fays, who will not allow me to follow my penchant. If I respond to your tenderness, you will only be more unfortunate; rather think of forgetting me. Follow the first design that brought you to this realm, and don't come to this misfortunate place again."

"Quit you, my princess!" said the princess. "Forget you! Oh, what advice are you daring to give me? Do you think that

I am in a condition to follow it? No, my dear Philonice, don't think that I have any other occupations than those of seeing you and adoring you. It is in vain that you want to frighten me with the power of your fays; they cannot prevent me from seeing you, if you think it good; it is only up to you to find yourself in that clump of trees every evening, with this amiable person...." He indicated Elise. "Don't worry about what might become of me; I shall be able to hide from all other eyes, provided that you permit me sometimes to see yours."

"You can settle that tomorrow at the same hour," said Elise, seeing that Philonice was not making any reply. "For tonight, it's time for us to retire, for fear of arousing suspicion of our conduct."

"But Elise, to what are you engaging us?" said the princess, swiftly.

"Oh, Madame," said the prince, "don't refuse me the favor that the charming Elise is granting me, "or I can no longer acquit you of a few misfortunes that might befall me."

"Well," said Philonice, getting to her feet, "let tomorrow be the last time, then."

After that, she left, without Anaxandre daring to reply to her, putting off until the next day the matter of obtaining a further delay to such a cruel sentence. He went to find his squire.

On the other hand, Philonice, when she went back to her apartment, found the fay Serpente there.

"Why are you so late," the latter said to her, in a severe tone that made the young princess tremble.

"I've just," she said, after making an effort to pull herself together, "had a encounter that touched me with so much pity that I couldn't resolve to quit that afflicted person sooner."

After that, she told her the story of Cleonice, and, continuing her discourse, she begged her to be good enough to allow her to go and spend her evenings with her.

Serpente, touched by that person's misfortune, said that she would allow it, provided that she was able to hide it from her sisters well enough for them not to perceive it.

Philonice embraced the fay, in order to thank her, and, after wishing her a good night, she went to bed, not without having spoken to Elise about the scare they had just had.

The next day they spent the morning searching for means to hide the prince, which appeared to them to be very difficult; they feared that one of the fays might encounter him entering or leaving the garden. They concluded that if they could not persuade him not to come back again, it was necessary that he did not leave the cabinet.

After having thought that they had taken all their safety measures, they went to the rendezvous in the evening. They found Anaxandre there, whom the princess told about the fright they had had on finding Serpente in their apartment. On that note, she took the opportunity to tell him that it was necessary for them no longer to expose him to the risk being discovered, and that he must not come again to such a dangerous place.

Anaxandre listened to that speech impatiently, and started speaking as soon as she had stopped.

"I can see, Madame," he said, "that you are repenting of the generosity that you have had for me, that you are hardly touched by the woes I am suffering and only want to abandon me to the most frightful chagrin. Well, cruel person, deprive me of seeing you freely, you can do that; but you cannot prevent me from living in the same locale as you, of breathing the same air and sometimes seeing you pass close to me. Perhaps the charming Elise will be less harsh than you, and will be willing to listen to my laments and receive my last sigh."

"The princess," said Elise, with a simplicity that gave the prince great pleasure, "has so little design of not seeing you again that we have resolved that you will no longer leave this cabinet; I will take care of furnishing you with all that is necessary to life, and we will come as often as we can."

"Oh, my dear Elise, how obliged I am to you," said Anaxandre, "for giving me certain proof of the generosity of Philonice. Why is it, then, lovable Princess, that you made me such a cruel speech? Did you want to test my tenderness and see whether your presence was dear to me?"

"In truth," said Philonice, "I am so troubled by the fear of being discovered that I have no sooner made a resolution than I repent of it. The ever-present idea of the implacable anger of the fays frightens me to such a point that I believe that I will see you at any moment become a wolf, a lion, or something more frightful, and spend my life following you, as the sad Cleonice follows her dear dragon."

"Oh, my princess," exclaimed Anaxandre, "let the fays do with me as they wish; after what I have just heard from your beautiful mouth, dying no longer matters to me. What, Madame: you love me enough to follow me in a frightful form, if the wrath of your Furies reduced me to one?"

"Doubtless I said more than I intended," she said, blushing, "but since my heart has expressed itself with so much tenderness, I do not repent of it, provided that you merit such advantageous sentiments."

Anaxandre swore a hundred times that he would always adore her with the same ardor, whatever difficulties he found in consequence of his passion.

After that they decided that he would remain in the cabinet for a few days, and that, for fear that Cleonice, having not been warned of what they had said to the fay Serpente, might spoil things, Philonice would go to find her the following evening, and that when she returned she would come to fetch Elise, who would be with the prince. After that, they retired to their pavilion, where, having no desire to sleep, they only went to bed after having talked for a long time about what occupied them most.

They did not know that among the animals that the fay Serpente had given them there was a she-monkey that had not always been one. She was a young person who had beauty and a humorous and malicious mind, but who excelled above all in the art of mimicry. One day when she was in company, she saw in the distance a woman whose slow pace had something indolent about it. The young woman began to imitate it in such a natural manner that the entire company laughed loudly—but against whom was it directed? It was a local fay, who had turned her into a monkey to punish her for her temerity, and had transported her to this place.

In her new form she retained her envious and malicious nature. The fay Serpente, in giving her to the princess, had ordered her to take note of everything she did and to inform her of it; she returned speech to her whenever she had something to say.

That malevolent she-monkey had conceived a mortal hatred for Philonice; she had been waiting impatiently for her to give her an opportunity to exercise her tongue, so that when she had heard the conversation of Elise and the princess, she believed that she had found the wherewithal to satisfy her envious rage.

She waited impatiently for the fay Serpente to arrive. As soon as she came into the room she signaled to her that she had something to tell her. The fay approached her; she told her that she knew many things, but that she could not say them in front of Philonice.

"I'll come back this evening when she has gone out," Serpente told her, "but be careful not to lie to me, for fear that I might punish you more severely that the fay Tante.

After that, she approached Philonice; having her secret design, she withdrew.

Evening having come, Elise took the prince some food, and the princess took the path to the citrus wood, while the fay, curious to know what the she-monkey wanted to tell her, went back to the pavilion.

The accursed beast rendered her an account of everything that she had heard the two young women say, and said that she had seen Elise charged with things good to eat, who had told Philonice that she would taken them to the prince, and that she would wait for her there to return from seeing Cleonice.

The fay went out, very angry with the princess. She went to the citrus wood in order to see whether the monkey was lying, determined to discover the mystery. She found her there as she was quitting Cleonice, and followed her to the cabinet in the boscage.

She soon knew what she wanted to discover. The prince had no sooner seen Philonice than he told her that he was dying of impatience to see her again, that he could not live under such harsh constraint, that if it were true that she was kindly disposed toward him she would consent to him taking her out of the hands of the barbaric Furies in order to take her to her mother, the princess, who had been languishing for years in the chagrin of having lost her.

"For myself," said Elise, "I can't see that you ought to hesitate to go with a prince for whom you are destined by the people who have the right to dispose of you, since he is promising to put you back in your mother's hands, and that he assures you that he can get you out of this wretched prison."

"But Elise," said Philonice, "do you think that I like this misfortunate abode enough not to accept what Anaxandre is proposing to us, if I thought it possible?"

"Oh, cruel person!" the prince interjected. "You only think it impossible because of the repugnance you have for me, and I have flattered myself in vain that I have a small place in your heart; you have acquired with time the barbarity of your demons with women's faces; you would see my death with joy, since you do not want to consent to such a just design."

"Well, then," said the princess, "It's necessary to go with you no matter what might happen, but when the lightning strikes you, remember that it wasn't left to me to protect you from it."

The fay, unable to listen any longer to what was being said against her kind, showed herself as the princess finished speaking. The latter thought she would die of fright, as did Elise.

"What has made you so bold, audacious youth," the fay said to Anaxandre, "as to come into this place without permission, and to have the temerity to think of taking this princess away from us? Do you think that we have brought her up with so much care for you? You're mistaken if you thought so; in spite of your fine plan, you will never see her again. Get out of my sight, for fear that I'll punish you more severely."

"Oh, cruel fay," said Anaxandre, "What more frightful punishment could you give me than that depriving me of the sight of my princess? If you had any sensibility, you would allow yourself to be touched by pity and, favoring two hearts that amour unites, you would return Philonice to me."

"I confess to you," said the fay, "that if I were the mistress of the destiny of this princess, I would do what you say; my heart, more sensible to pity than to offense, would easily pardon you for the insult that amour has caused you to make us, but I am only a guardian, Anaxandre; she is a deposit that my sisters have made me; I know the design that they have for her, and I must conserve with care those they have confided to me. Once again, go away; leave this princess alone, if you do not want to be the cause of all the misfortunes of her life."

"Oh, Madame," said Philonice, finally emboldened by the fay's generosity, "fear none for me if you deprive me of seeing Anaxandre."

"But Philonice," replied the fay, "do you not fear my anger when you make me such a confession? What has become of your obedience to my will?"

"I confess, Madame," said the princess, "that I merit all your indignation; I know my fault, it is not in my power to repent of it. The orders of a mother I respect, and a penchant stronger than me, which draw me toward this prince, would perhaps serve as an excuse with regard to you, if you wanted to follow the impulses of your heart. Oh, Madame, all the unfortunates that are in this place only find pity in you; will I be the only one that you render unhappy?"

"It is not in my power," said the fay, "to give you to this prince; you are destined or another, who, I confess, is not as lovable."

"Me!" cried Philonice. "Destined for another? Oh, Madame; he will be presented in vain. You are the mistress of making me suffer the cruelest torments, but you cannot be the mistress of my will."

"Oh, my dear princess," said Anaxandre, "What prayers of thanks I owe you for so much generosity? It is up to me, my princess, to deliver you from this tyranny, and I will kill the one for whom you are destined, even if he is guarded by all the Furies together."

"We do not fear you," said the fay, laughing. "The one who will be Philonice's husband has no fear of death, but he gives it easily."

"Let him give it to me then," said the prince, "for he will only possess Philonice by ending my life."

"Alas," said Elise, who had not yet spoken, "what is the point of amusing yourself making threats that only serve to irritate the fay? Rather implore her omnipotent aid; she is only waiting for your obedience to soften all your woes. If she cannot render you completely happy, her heart cannot be exempt from an impulse of tenderness for this beautiful princess. Profit from it, and trust the word that she gives you that you will not go for long without feeling the effects of her compassion."

"Adieu, Anaxandre," said Philonice, holding out her hand to him. "Let us believe Elise; she is wiser than us, and let us yield to her design, since we cannot do otherwise.""

The prince took the princess's hand, which he kissed with such a tender fervor that he completed disarming Serpente. She hid her sentiments carefully, however; only Elise perceived them, which obliged her to take Philonice by the arm violently in order to make her emerge from the cabinet.

The poor prince remained in a deplorable state. He followed his dear princess with his eyes as far as he could, but

Elise made him a sign to stay where he was, and made him understand that he would have news of her.

Meanwhile, the fay Serpente took Philonice back to the pavilion. She forbade her to leave it until she returned, and, without saying anything about what she had decided to do, she withdrew,

O Gods, in what state was the poor princess left! Elise could not console her, and the mere idea of being married to some monster put her in despair; tears and sobs scarcely gave her time to draw breath. She spent the night in that sad occupation.

At daybreak the fay came back into the room.

"Philonice," she said, "I have done all I can to make my sisters consent to set you free. I have praised the merit of your lover; I have tried to make them understand that it would be good to return you to your mother, heaping you with all the gifts that are in our power; that you have never given anything but subjects of joy; and that it is not just to constrain you, if your inclination does not lead you to remain among us; but all my remonstrations have been in vain. They have told me that they only abducted you in order to give you to the King of Monsters, and that I should dispose you to marry him."

"Oh, Madame," Philonice said to her, "You would more easily dispose me to death than that evil marriage. What will become of poor Anaxandre if he does not see me again?"

"I can enable you to see the prince once more," said the fay, "but, not being able to give you to him, my indulgence would only serve to render you more unhappy. Rather make the resolution to obey my sisters than to love a prince to whom you will never belong, unless our power is destroyed."

"It cannot last much longer!" cried Philonice. "Heaven, weary of so many injustices, will not always abandon unfortunate mortals to the cruel tyranny of your barbaric sisters." She continued, in a prophetic tone:

"I can see her, I can see the adorable princess whom the gods have promised us, though the mouth of the savant solitary, ready to come to break our chains and reduce your sisters only to be able to use their power to embellish this place. I can see those Furies, I say, on the river bank, reduced to making wheels of a prodigious grandeur turn, in order to furnish water to this enchanted palace.[5] Their despair will constrain them to utter cries similar to those unfortunates who are metamorphosed into the most ferocious beasts, which will make those who pass by this place believe that Hell has opened here.

"As for you, Madame, who have never consented to the evils that your pernicious sisters have done in the world, you will not be of that number; the princess will know how to recompense as well as punish; she will distinguish you from all the fays, and will give you the guard of this beautiful place; you alone will enjoy its august presence, glorious in the caresses that you will receive, you will spend happy days, while your sisters repent, but too late, of their cruelties."

Serpente listened with astonishment to the princess's speech; she saw clearly that some divinity was inspiring her, all the more so as that prophecy had been written since the commencement of their Empire, without the time being marked other than that it would arrive during the reign of the greatest king ever to occupy the throne; but although they saw that victorious prince perform actions every day so splendid that they could not be misunderstood, they had flattered themselves that it was not him to which the oracle referred, and that the princess fatal to their empire had not yet been born. But

---

[5] This is a reference to the famous Marly Machine, an extremely ambitious and absurdly costly hydraulic system built in 1684 to pump water from the Seine and deliver it to the Palace of Versailles, although it was never sufficient for that purpose. It consisted of fourteen giant water wheels, more than eleven meters in diameter, and must have made a terrible racket. When Mademoiselle de Lubert revised the present story for republication in 1756 she added the subtitle *ou l'origine de la machine de Marli*.

the fay, seeing it confirmed by Philonice, saw clearly that their ruination was imminent.

She resolved to warn her sisters, in order that they could decide collectively what remedy to bring to it, and, not repenting of having been sensible to the unfortunate, she told the princess that she was not afflicted, but that she did not mistake for a prophecy what only her animosity had inspired in her; that their power had been eternal through the ages, and that it would only end with the world; that she promised to make one last effort to render her happy; and that, if she could not obtain anything, she would give her the means to see the prince, so long as she was under her dependence .

After that, she quit her, in order to go and tell the fays what had just happened.

They were frightened by it, all the more so because the fay Envious told them that, having tried to change a prince who had offended her into a bear, she had not been able to do it. The fay Rancor also complained that she had not been able to do all the harm she had wanted to do. In the end, in fear of seeing their Empire overturned, on going to consult the Magic Book, they found Philonice's prophecy veritable.

In despair at a cruel fate that they saw so imminent, instead of listening to the advice of the fay Serpente, they redoubled their rage against the unfortunates who were in their power. Philonice was not exempt from that, no matter what the prudent fay could say. They sent for her immediately, and, heaping her with insults, they told her that she should be ready to marry the following day the husband that they had destined for her.

"But in order that she know him, sister," they said to Serpente, "take her into the Hall of Mirrors."

For fear of irritating them further, Serpente took the princess by the hand and took her into the room where the Monster was waiting for her.

He was like the Polyphemus of the poets, except that he had a snout more frightful than a pig's, which rendered his voice so horrible that poor Philonice nearly died of fright

40

when he approached her and asked her whether she really did not want to be his wife.

"I would rather marry Death than you," the sad princess replied.

"You will, however, tomorrow," said the Polyphemus, "without me caring about your tears; I feed on the suffering that I cause, so do not think that you can make me feel pity with your tears; rather dispose yourself to obey me without difficulty."

After that, he drew away, without having been touched by her dolorous cries, any more than the detestable fays had.

Serpente took her back to her apartment, more dead than alive. Unable to do anything else for her consolation, she had the prince come, whom she covered with a dense cloud.

"I have brought you Anaxandre," she said to her, unwrapping him from the cloud, "in order that you can make your decision with him."

Having said that, she quit them. The prince, transported by joy at seeing his princess, could not understand why she was not as sensible to it as he was, and why her only response to all his urgent attentions consisted of tears. Elise accompanied her in the lugubrious exercise without him being able to get a word out of either one of them.

"Why," said Anaxandre, finally, "are you not telling me what is causing your tears? I flattered myself that my presence might soften your chagrins, that the pleasure of knowing all the love that you inspire in me might suspend your dolors. Do you believe that I sense them less than you? Charmed, however, by being at liberty to swear an eternal constancy to you, whatever woes it might be necessary to suffer in order to merit you, the joy of seeing you prevails over my chagrins. If you loved me, Philonice, as I love you, my presence would have the same effect on your heart."

"Cruel prince," said the princess, "don't finish crushing me by means of your reproaches. You know only too well how sensible I am for you; but you don't know all our misfortunes. The fay Serpente has tried to make these barbaric fays consent to our happiness, but they were inflexible to her pleas. They want to give me tomorrow to a frightful monster that they recognize as their king, and you can ask me the cause of my tears? Oh, my dear Anaxandre, the source will never dry up; I am going to lose you forever, and those infernal Furies, nourishing themselves on my tears, will not permit me to end them by my death. The compassionate fay has explained that she can do nothing to help us but give us the sad pleasure of lamenting together, for the last time."

"Oh, Madame, you do not merit all these kindnesses if you do not take advantage of them," cried the prince. "I understand well enough what her last words meant to know the misfortunes that are in preparation for us. 'I have brought you the prince,' she said to you, 'in order that you can make your decision with him.' And do you know, Madame, what the decision that I will aid you to make will be? Do you think that, knowing all the love that I have for you, she hopes that I will advise you to give yourself to the King of Monsters? No, Madame, she wanted to make you understand that you must follow the advice I gave you in the cabinet, that while you are free, since your guardian has opened our prison, you can get out of it. Beware of making that decision too late. Take advantage of the moments that her generosity has given us; they are passing quickly, and will never return."

"Oh, Madame," said Elise, seeing the princess uncertain, "Why are you delaying in leaving this place? The fay will doubtless hide us in our flight, and we will not find any obstacles in returning to your mother."

"Alas, you are flattering yourselves in vain," said the desolate princess, "in thinking that it will be so easy to avoid the misfortune that is pursuing me."

"But can you be any more unhappy," persisted Elise, "And what are you risking in following our advice?"

"Well, then, let's follow it," said the princess, finally, "but know, Anaxandre, that I am doing more than I ought to do in taking you for a guide of my conduct."

"Oh, Madame," said the prince, "you have no subject for repentance; my amour will answer to you for that."

After that, Elise went to fetch all the jewelry they had. All three of them left the pavilion, with the design of hiding in the boscage until nightfall, but they were very astonished when they found themselves enveloped by the same cloud that had served to hide the prince; they did not doubt that the fay Serpente wanted to favor their retreat, and, having no more need of darkness, they marched without fear along the path that Anaxandre showed them.

It was the one to the river; it was not that he was not embarrassed to know how he would enable the princess to cross it, but his embarrassment ceased when he saw his squire in a boat, covered very properly, who was waiting for them. What joy for the princess and the amiable fugitives! They climbed into it urgently, and, having passed diligently to the other bank, they descended to the ground.

Anaxandre turned round in order to command his squire to go in search of the fastest horses he could find, but he found neither the boat nor the squire. Elise told him that the fay Serpente had given them that aid; that she had said as she left that they should travel all night; that they should make as much haste as they could, and that if they could set foot on their own land, it would no longer be in the power of the fays to harm them.

As Elise finished speaking, the prince saw horses coming toward them, with numerous people; that worried him, but his fear was soon dissipated when he recognized his men, with his veritable squire at their head. He asked him who had ordered him to come to that place.

"A man on your behalf," replied the squire, "who bought me this note."

Again they recognized the cares of the obliging fay; wanting to profit from her advice, they mounted horses, and, quitting the high road, they went to wait for night at the first habitation, where, for fear that Philonice's beauty might attract curiosity, the prince advised her to put on masculine attire, in order that her beautiful face would be hidden under the armet. Elise did the same, and as soon as night fell, all of them mounted up again, and rode with all possible diligence.

They did the same all along their route; the princess resisted a rude fatigue by virtue of the haste she was in to reach a place of safety. Anaxandre would have liked to spare his dear Philonice all those difficulties; he was in a mortal apprehension that she might fall ill with lassitude. However, they had made such rapid progress that they were no longer more than a day away from their homeland. The hope of finding repose gave new courage to the entire troop; they had never been more cheerful; they only talked about the happiness they were about to experience.

"What a satisfaction for me," said the princess, to see such a good and tender mother again. Gods, we shall have such happy hours! I can already see the fires that are lit on the towers every night as lights for ships. Finally, we are approaching the happy moment when we will no longer have anything to fear."

"May the gods will it," said Elise, "but I don't know what noise I can hear behind us. The desire to arrive has made us march longer than usual; here's the daylight, which has been forbidden to us by Serpente."

As soon as the prince had heard marching he had turned his head. He heard a great noise of men and horses; that made him anxious. He told the princess to advance with a few cavaliers to defend her, and took the rest of his men with him. Philonice did not want him to leave, but he protested so many times that he would rejoin her as soon as he knew who the men were that he could hear, she consented to it.

Scarcely had the princess gone than the prince saw a host of monstrous men; at their head was the King of Monsters, who, having learned that the princess had run away, had followed diligently in order to punish her for the scorn she was showing for his alliance. The fay Rancor was by his side, who was taking great care to stimulate his anger against the lovable person.

The prince had no sooner perceived that horrible troop than he prepared to forbid its passage. The fay Rancor, seeing his action, advanced first. "This is apparently Philonice's lover," she said to the King of Monsters, "whom my sister Serpente tried to persuade us to prefer to you. See the vengeance that I shall exact for that."

So saying, she touched Anaxandre with her wand, but her design was futile; her magical charms proved powerless, and the prince was no less in a state to fight the frightful monsters, who only had human bodies bearing the heads of wild boar.

Swollen with rage, the fay quit the prince, heaping him with maledictions, and, rising up into the air, she flew after the princess, whom she knew to have gone on ahead. She reached her before the time when she no longer had anything to fear, and, taking hold of her by her beautiful hair, she lifted her up into the air. When she was above the place where she had left the monstrous troop battling Anaxandre she stopped, and raised her voice.

"See, prince, that my power is not always devoid of force. Cease a combat that is useless to you, and come and snatch this fugitive princess from my hands. That would be more glorious for you." She continued: "And you, King of Monsters, leave that wretch; you will avenge yourself much better by giving him life than terminating his misfortunes by a quick death."

As soon as the fay had made her voice heard, the combat ended. At the arrival of Philonice, the prince fainted, overwhelmed by the dolor of being unable to help her.

When he recovered from his weakness he no longer saw any of the monsters; they had all disappeared as soon as they saw that the fay Rancor had Philonice in her power.

She transported her to the abode of the fays and, taking her to the palace, had her enter a vaulted hall where all the fays were assembled.

"Here, my dear sisters," said Rancor, "is this criminal fugitive, who quit us to follow a reckless youth, whom I have been unable to punish for his insolence. It is necessary that she serve as an example to those who dare to displease us, in order that they tremble merely at the story of her punishment."

"We abandon her to you," said all the fays, in unison. "She is your conquest; it is for you to avenge yourself on this unappreciative princess."

"She is mine before being hers," said the King of Monsters. "I was ready to be master of her destiny. You gave her to me at the age of twelve, when you snatched her from her mother's arms."

The fays agreed that the king was right, and that they could no longer dispose of the princess. Rancor consented to that with difficulty, but she consoled herself with the hope that the monster would be no less cruel than her. The poor victim was therefore delivered to him, without pity for the tears of her despair.

He took her to a frightful lair, and as soon as she had entered it, he told her that if she agreed to marry him, he would pardon her for her flight, that she would be queen of all the monsters of Europe and all the treasures that were in his power.

"If I consented to marry you," said the princess, "it would only be to discover by what means I could liberate myself from you, so do not make me a proposition that horrifies me; content yourself with rendering me unhappy, without requiring me to give my consent to it."

"Well, since that is what you wish," he replied, furiously, "So it shall be. Come and commence your torment."

As he said that he made her descend into a place even lower than the first she had entered, and, opening a door, he showed her a great plain filled with fresh grass, irrigated by a steam as clear as crystal. A rock limited that plain. He had the princess attached to it by a chain long enough for her to be able to walk all around it, and, having monsters of every species emerge from sheds, he said to her that since she had not wanted to be their queen, she must spend her life guarding them; that she must take care that they did not go astray; and that she had only to touch them with a crook that he gave her.

After that, he left the unfortunate princess, so full of fear that she would have awakened pity in any heart other than that tiger's.

As soon as she saw the horrible herd approaching, she uttered frightful screams and, with her back to the rock, she made use of her crook to drive them away.

Meanwhile, the unfortunate Anaxandre was in despair, not knowing what to do in order to follow his Philonice, when Elise, who had retraced her steps as soon as the princess was abducted, arrived in his presence, shortly after he had recovered consciousness.

"Oh, my dear Elise," he said to her, where can I find my princess?"

"It's necessary to return to the abode of the fays," said Elise. "It's doubtless there that he's taken her. Perhaps, by means of the fay Serpente, I'll be able to see her, and let her know that you haven't been killed in the battle with the monsters."

"Alas, my dear Elise," said the prince, "it would be better for me if I had died therein than to remain on earth useless to Philonice."

"Just follow me," said Else. "I hope that we'll be able to see the lovable princess again."

After that they mounted their horses again and, making incredible diligence, they arrived on the bank of the river in a matter of days.

It was night when they dismounted, and they had no small difficulty knowing how they were going to get across, but the person who had furnished them with the means of getting out of the abode of the fays came to their aid once again, in order to enable them to reenter a place that had become so dear to them in the hope of seeing Philonice again. She enabled them to find a boat, and served as their boatman; they had soon made the short journey. What thanks they gave her, and with what haste Anaxandre asked her for news of the princess!

"She is in the power of the King of Monsters," replied the fay. "My barbaric sisters delivered her to him as soon as Rancor had returned her to their cruel hands."

"Oh, compassionate Serpente," cried the prince, "will you suffer that such a charming person should perish, and will you not give me the means to die at her feet if I cannot extract her from her woeful fate?"

"I cannot change the destiny of the princess," said the fay. "A time will come when she will be more fortunate, but that will not be by means of your help, nor mine. All that I can do is to take you to the place where she is spending her misfortunate days, while disguising you and Elise in the form of monsters, for fear that the king of the subterranean realm might recognize you."

So saying, she touched them with her wand, and they appeared half human and half horse, similar to the centaurs of fable. After having given them a herb, with which they had only to touch themselves in order to recover their true form, she took them to the abode of the King of Monsters.

They descended into the plain where the unfortunate Philonice was guarding the monstrous herd day and night. They found her lying on the rock, her crook in one hand and her head leaning on the other, with large tears flowing from her eyes over her beautiful breasts, which were partly uncovered.

Dawn was breaking when they approached her. The noise they made in walking extracted her from her reverie; she shivered in the dread of seeing new monsters, but he prince did not want to leave her any longer in the deplorable state in which he saw her.

"Since it is only permitted to monsters to approach you, divine princess," he said to her, "do not be astonished to see Elise and me in this hideous form. Nothing appears impossible to love and amity in combination. The fay Serpente, compassionate, as usual, has transformed us thus in order to give us the pleasure of spending our days with you.

"Alas, Anaxandre," said the princess, finally, after having recovered from her astonishment, "what demonic enemy of our days has brought you both here? Did I not have woes enough without the dread that the cruel tyrant who has me in his power might discover you and make you pay very dearly, with horrible tortures, for the pleasure of seeing us? Oh, my dear Elise," she continued, "You would not have brought the prince if you loved me, and would not have prepared me by your imprudence for the sad spectacle of having caused his death."

"Cease to fear for the charming Elise and for me," said the prince. "In telling you that it is the fay Serpente who brought us here, I am telling you that we have nothing to fear."

As he finished speaking, the sun having continued rising, the monstrous herd woke up and filled the air with terrible howls. Unaccustomed to such cries, Elise fled in terror to the other side of the rock, and, finding a concavity there, she entered into it precipitately.

She was astonished to find a chamber therein, hung in mourning; there was a coffin in the middle of the lair, illuminated by two rock crystal lamps. A young woman clad in black was beside the coffin, whose beauty, in spite of the tears that were flowing from her eyes in abundance, appeared to Elise to be one of the most accomplished on earth.

The surprise that she experienced at such a novel spectacle caused her to utter a cry so loud that the princess heard it, as well as Anaxandre, who had followed her. Accelerating their pace, they entered the tomb.

The presence of so many people drew the afflicted beauty from her ordinary occupation, and she made an effort to stop the sobs that were taking away the usage of speech. "What unfortunate destiny brings you here?" she said, addressing Philonice. "Is it hazard or the barbarians who possess this place that constrains you to come and mingle your tears with mine?"

"A similar destiny constrains us, as well as you, to inhabit this infernal place," said the princess. "So, Madame, if your dolor can be soothed by the company of persons as unhappy as you are, we offer you that sad consolation."

"My dolor is of a nature," the unknown woman replied, "never to be able to end. All that the gods made perfect on the Earth, and everything that was able to please me, is contained in this tomb. I spend my unfortunate days wanting to give him a futile aid. I see," she said, seeing that Philonice was astonished by those last words, "that you do not understand how the person I regret can be in a condition to be in need of aid, after having told you that he is contained in this tomb, but Madame, it would be necessary in order to enlighten you regarding that adventure to tell you the cause of my torture, which could only renew my dolors with more vivacity."

As the princess was about to reply to her, a plaintive voice that she heard emerging from the tomb stopped her, and the unknown woman, redoubling her tears, made incredible efforts to open the sepulcher. Philonice, the prince and Elise joined the afflicted beauty, but all their efforts were futile.

"Don't fatigue yourselves in vain," the plaintive voice said to them. "Leave me to conclude my destiny in this sad dwelling; a day will come—and that day is not far off—when it will be permitted to me to see the light again, and to tell you, oh my dear Melicerte, that the chill of the tomb can have no effect on my amour. Enjoy, in the meantime, the consolation that Heaven has sent you, by means of the presence of a prince and a princess as unfortunate as you.

The plaintive voice fell silent after those words, and Melicerte threw her arms around Philonice's neck. "Oh, Madame," she said, "What joy your presence has brought me! I have heard my husband promising me a happier time; I can hope to see him again one day." She let herself fall on to a bed, from which she had got up. "But is this not a dream? Oh, doubtless my mind, troubled by the length of my misfortunes, is making me believe impossible things!"

"No, Madame," said Philonice, "You are not deceived in what you have just heard; we heard it as you did. Doubtless Heaven, weary of the torture of so many innocent victims, will soon give us an aid proportionate to our woes; it is not only through the mouths of the dead that we are promised that; the living have predicted it as well.

"Oh, Madame," said Melicerte, "what do I not owe you for confirming what I dared not believe?" She looked around. "But where, then, is the prince of whom my husband spoke? Can it be this amiable centaur, who aided me with so much urgency to relieve the unfortunate Yphidamente?"

"Yes, Madame," said Anaxandre, "it is me, whom a cruel fortune obliges to hide beneath this extraordinary form."

"I confess to you," said Melicerte, "that I am seeing things so surprising that I cannot help being curious to learn your adventures, with the promise that I give to this beautiful person"—she indicated the princess—"to satisfy hers whenever she wishes."

"That would be right away," said Philonice, "If I were not obliged to quit you for the rest of the day, for fear that the King of Monsters, who often comes to see whether I am acquitting my duty, not finding me, might take away the scant liberty that he gives me. As for you, generous prince," she continued, "remain with the amiable Melicerte, and, quitting your disguise, enable her to see that you merit her esteem, while my dear Elise, delivered as well as you from that metamorphosis, will make it known to this beautiful person, by telling her my story, that she is not alone in her misfortune."

"But my princess," said Anaxandre, "do you think that I can quit you so soon, and that, satisfied with having seen you for a moment, I do not still have a thousand things to say to you."

"As soon as night has fallen," said Philonice, "I will come to listen to you gladly, but Anaxandre, be kind enough to me not to show yourself before my Argus; the agitation that he would see on my face would tell him what we have so much interest in hiding."

After that, she went out, without wanting to permit anyone to follow her. She arrived at the tip of the rock just in time; the frightful king appeared at that moment.

"You're very cheerful today, Philonice," he said as he approached her. "I don't see, as I usually do, the tracks of your tears on your face. Is your torture no longer one for you, then, by dint of suffering it, or, content with your fate, have you made the decision to marry me?" Wanting to soften her, he continued: "Speak; my generosity is still ready to welcome you; but be careful not to irritate me further by your refusal; everything that you have suffered thus far is nothing in comparison with the woes I have in store for you if you do not resolve to obey me."

The princess trembled at that speech, but, making the resolution in an instant, she said to him: "I can see that I will be constrained in the end to surrender to such a long constancy; I only ask you any longer for the time until the return of the new moon, in order to make a sacrifice to that goddess."

"I grant you that," said the Polyphemus, with a contented expression, "provided that you are not deceiving me, although a month is a long time for my impatience. I will inform all my subjects, as well as all the fays, to be ready to celebrate my marriage with the pomp due to my grandeur."

With those words he separated from the princess. She would have liked to return to the tomb of Yphidamente as soon as she saw him leave, but, fearing that he might return before the end of the day, she waited until night had closed the eyes of her terrible herd.

Elise had just finished her story when she appeared in the chamber. Melicerte expressed to her how interested she was in all her misfortunes; the prince told her a hundred times, with transports that no other lover had ever felt, that he could no longer bear her absence, and that she ought not to ask again for such cruel proofs of his obedience. She responded to her Anaxandre with tenderness and addressed herself to Melicerte:

"It only depends on you, Madame," she said, "to satisfy my curiosity now that I can listen to you without the fear of being disturbed by my cruel tyrant."

"That is just, amiable princess," said Melicerte, "and such precious moments ought not to be wasted."

The Story of Princess Melicerte

I will tell you, Madame, that I am the daughter of a prince who is the sovereign of a great country beyond a river known as the Rhine. I had two brothers, whose courage was signaled in all the occasions of a war that occupied all Europe for several years against the king of a realm, who, to the shame of several crowned heads, could never be defeated on any occasion, whatever forces they armed against him.

While my father and my brothers were employed in defending their provinces from the conquests of that great conqueror, I spent my days with the princess, my mother, learning everything that could improve a young woman; but winter brought our warriors back and filled our court with all the great lords of the province.

Rumor of the little beauty that Heaven has given me attracted others from neighboring Estates, but among all those lords, Prince Yphidamente appeared to be so far above the others that I could not help feeling a penchant for him, which I perceived with chagrin. Everything he did had a grace that I did not find elsewhere; the attentions he rendered me seemed so urgent that it was easy to understand that his heart was touched by a violent passion. He had not yet been able to reveal it to me; what I felt for him made me avoid opportunities to speak to him; I was afraid that he might realize that I loved him as much as he wanted to persuade me that he loved me.

In that constraint the winter passed, and, when spring took him back to the war could not resist bidding him adieu in such a way that he perceived the movements of my heart.

With what transports of joy he received that evidence of my tenderness, and how many protestations of eternal amour. He would never have wearied of reiterating them had he not been told that my father and my brothers were waiting for him in order to depart. I was glad that the absence of so many persons who were dear to me gave me a pretext to hide the mortal chagrin with which I was filled.

I spent the entire campaign in unbearable anxieties, and if winter had not come to calm my irritations I would not have been able to resist them any longer. We went a long way to meet my father; the prince, on seeing me, after having saluted my mother, came to me with such an urgency that it was remarked by the entire court. The entire time of the journey we had to make to return to the city he employed in saying the most tender things to me. I listened to them with pleasure; it seemed to me that he was even more amiable, and my heart could not refuse to admit its defeat to him.

In one such tender conversation we arrived at the palace. From that time on, every day only served to augment our amour, and the prince, finding himself master of a considerable Estate, asked me to give him permission to ask those who disposed of me for my hand. I permitted him to do so without difficulty, and, not wanting to delay his happiness, he spoke to the prince, my father, that very evening.

He was received with all possible kindness, but although he was promised that I would never be given to anyone but him, my father did not want to permit our union until there was peace, telling him that it was not just to celebrate marriages while all Europe was languishing under the weight of the war.

Yphidamente came to repeat that conversation to me, and the chagrin he had in seeing that his happiness depended on public repose. I tried to make him understand the reasons my father had for acting thus.

From that day in we spent our lives is the most pleasant society; we saw one another all the time; everyone approved of our amour. How happy we would have been if that time had endured! But the good weather arrived to commence our misfortunes; it was necessary to separate. What despair for hearts as tender as ours! It nearly cost me my life; I was carried to my bed unconscious, while my brothers dragged Yphidamente from my chamber.

Alas, we sensed what was going to happen to us; a secret presentiment warned us that our absence would only be limited by death. My faint was followed by a violent fever that reduced me in a short time to the brink of death. My mother was inconsolable; she did not quit me for a moment; but my youth brought me through that evil pass. When I was in a state to emerge from my room, I begged my mother to allow me to go and spend the rest of the summer in a country house a few leagues from the city. I employed the time thinking about my dear Yphidamente: I counted the days, the hours and the moments that I had to pass without seeing him.

One afternoon, more urgent in my tenderness than usual, I was walking in a nearby forest. I had few people with me. I was walking quite slowly along a very beautiful but very gloomy path. A location in such conformity with my mood caused me to walk further than I thought; I felt weary and I sat down at the foot of a tree and went to sleep; but O gods, what became of me when I woke up to find myself n a frightful lair and the same tyrant who now holds you under his law beside me. He was accompanied by the fay Rancor and her sisters, Cruel and Envious.

I did not know whether I was dead or still among the number of the living. I was about to open my mouth to ask where I was when the fay Rancor said to me: "Praise Heaven for your good fortune, Melicerte, for having enabled us to pass through the forest where you were asleep. Your beauty has surprised the King of Monsters; he was so touched by all the grace that you possess that we carried you away immediately in order to make you queen of all that that powerful king possesses. Receive such a great honor as you ought to, and merit our amity by your obedience."

"I believe," I said to her, "that that I only ought to obey those to whom I owe birth, and I cannot understand what right you have to command me, nor what justice you find in the action that you have just carried out."

"We have," Rancor replied, "the rule that we make of our will; everyone recognizes our power over the Earth; fortunate are those like you who have obtained our favor; profit from it, if you are wise, or fear our anger."

"And what could you do to me that is worse," I said, "than to take me from the arms of my family in order to deliver me to this execrable monster? Oh, render me my liberty or take away my life."

"Go," said that charming lover, finally. "Don't worry about the repugnance that she testifies toward you; I shall be able to reduce her to obeying me. Leave me alone with her."

"Oh, Madame," I cried, throwing myself at Rancor's feet; "if ever you have bee sensible to pity, don't leave me alone with your king, if you don't want me to die of fright."

For the first time in her life, the fay was sensible to my dolor. She told the monster that she would take care of disposing me to obey him, but that she thought that it was necessary to win me over by a feigned mildness. The king consented to what Rancor said; I was put into her hands. She took me to the abode of the fays; she showed me all the beauties of the place, and took me after that to her pavilion. It is, as you know, the one that stands in a large wood; everything there was glittering with gold and precious stones; I was given magnificent garments, and the fay did not neglect anything to make me forget the insult that had been done to me; but all of that could not dry up my tears. The separation from my father and mother was very sensible to me, but the idea of not seeing Yphidamente again put me in despair.

Meanwhile, the King of Monsters became impatient in not seeing me disposed to marry him, and Rancor, wearying of a mildness that was not natural to her, said to me one day that

I was abusing all her generosity, that I had to dispose myself not to resist her any longer, or to prepare myself for the cruelest torture. My tears and my sighs could not again any purchase on her irritated heart; she brought me to this misfortunate abode and, abandoning me to all my despair, she left me here more dead than alive.

I called her back as she was about to draw away. "Oh, Madame," I said, "how can you expect me to marry the King of Monsters, since I am promised to Yphidamente? It is not in my power to break oaths so piously sworn."

Rancor did not like my excuses, and without listening to me any further, she left me with that accursed tyrant, who is a hundred times crueler than he is frightful.

I remained without sentiment when I found myself alone with him; a long weakness succeeded my tears, but I finally came round, without him giving me any help. He told me that I did not merit that he should show concern for my life, that he no longer wanted to marry me, that the fays had abducted a beautiful young princess—who was doubtless you, Madame—but that I would not be any happier; and that, since I was only sensible for Yphidamente, he would bring him here to share the punishment that he was preparing for me.

The entire night passed in that sad conversation, and daylight had no sooner appeared than I saw Rancor. "Follow me," she said, in a severe tone that made me tremble. I followed her, with a mortal pallor, into this sad location, where I found this coffin in this chamber, covered with a black drape, which she removed in order to show me Yphidamente lying unconscious in this tomb.

No dolor was ever equal to mine; at that fatal sight, all that the most tender amour can make one say and do, I said and did to excess. I wanted to die with that dear object of my tenderness. Anyone but the cruel Fay would have been touched by the unhappy state that I was in, but, as if the sight of that deplorable prince might have been some consolation to me, she replaced the black sheet that covered it. Having circled the coffin a few times, she quit me, after having said to me in a mocking tone that I ought to be content, because she was leaving me with everything I loved.

As soon as I saw that she had gone I ran to lift the veil that hid my dear husband from me, but gods, how astonished I was to find the tomb sealed. I had redoubled my tears, when I heard a voice from the coffin, which was uttering great sighs. Imagine my despair; I made incredible efforts to open the sepulcher; I appealed to the gods and men to help me, but it was too heavy for me. In the meantime, the voice ceased to make itself heard. I thought that my dear Yphidamente had stifled.

I had spent the entire day and the entire night in agitations that put me beside myself when my ears were struck by the same voice. I ran to the tomb; I tried to release him, but it was as futile as the first time.

Ever since that fatal moment I have not failed, at the same time, to hear my husband lamenting, and without remembering that it is not in my power to end his troubles, I make the same efforts to extract him from the tomb that you have witnessed.

Melicerte stopped, pressed by dolor, at that cruel point in her story. Philonice did what she could to enable her to hope that her troubles might end soon. The prince and Elise joined in with the princess in order to console her, but, Yphidamente's laments recommencing as usual, she ran to the tomb with the same urgency as she was accustomed to do, without wanting to listen to what those amiable persons were saying to her.

In the meantime, the King of Monsters had returned to the rock, having given the fays orders to assemble everyone that was dependent on their powers to celebrate his marriage with Philonice, to tell her that nothing as fine had ever appeared in the empire of the fays as everything he had ordered for his wedding; and that, while waiting for that happy day, he had come to conduct her to a magnificent apartment that he had had prepared for her.

Astonished not to find her, he looked to see the direction in which the chain by which she was attached to the rock extended, and by following it, he arrived in Melicerte's chamber just as Yphidamente's laments ceased.

What a fright for the lovers! They remained motionless, listening with a mortal fear to all the insults that the King of Monsters vomited against Philonice. Passing from insults to actions, however, he took her by the arm and pulled her out of the cavern violently. Anaxandre tried to snatch the princess from his hands, but, looking at him with scornful eye he said: "Reckless youth, learn to know your strength, in order to augment the pains of this infidel woman, come and share her torments.

At the same time, Anaxandre found himself bound to the same chain as Philonice and constrained, with her, to follow the tyrant. If it had not been for the despair of being unable to help his princess, it would have been a consolation for him to bear the same chains.

In that wretched state he took them to an obscure prison.

Poor Elise was inconsolable. Melicerte's sobs were redoubled. Even the unfortunate Yphidamente made it known by new laments that he was sensible to the situation.

Meanwhile, the King of Monsters went to see the fays, who had assembled from all parts of the world in order to be present at their king's marriage. There was not one of them who had not prepared an extraordinary gift with which to endow the princess. They were quite astonished by the news that the Polyphemus announced to them. They hastened to invent new tortures with which to torment Philonice and her lover, in order to prove to the king the zeal they had for him. He thanked them for that, and told them that he knew one crueler than all those they had just suggested to him; that he had resolved to marry her and to kill Anaxandre in front of her on the same day. They all praised him for knowing so well how to avenge himself, and prepared to watch that terrible spectacle.

The next day, the cruel tyrant went to see the illustrious couple in order to announce that terrible sentence. No dolor was ever equal to the one they both felt.

"Again," said Anaxandre, "if I could render you happy by my death, I would suffer it with joy, but leaving you prey to all that nature has of the most frightful is a despair a hundred times more frightful than death.

"Oh, Prince," said the sad Philonice, "if the King of Monsters would give me your life, I would marry him without reluctance, but the barbarian knows full well that he can only punish me by your death."

They spent the whole night lamenting thus, and daylight had no sooner appeared than the fays Rancor, Cruel and Envious came to collect the princess in order to take her to the palace. The King of Monsters came to join them there, and without being touched by the pitiful state in which he saw her, or listening to the ardent prayers she made him to spare the life of the unfortunate Anaxandre, he conducted her to the Temple.

A scaffold was set up there, and the prince was attached to a stake, ready to be immolated in order to serve as a nuptial victim. What a sight for the tender Philonice! She threw herself at the feet of the cruel tyrant and, recommencing her tears, she begged him once again to grant the prince his life if he did not want to see her expire under the same blow that struck him. He was as deaf to hr prayers this time as the other, and the mortal knife had already been raised when a clap of thunder was heard, accompanied by lightning that made the vault of the Temple tremble. At the same time, the sound of a thousand resounding trumpets struck the ears of the King of Monsters and the fays, and they ran to the door of the Temple urgently in order to discover what was causing that military din.

The fay Serpente, however, ran into the Temple precipitately. "Courage, Philonice," she shouted, "your woes are about to end; the divine Princess whom the oracles have predicted, is advancing; all of Heaven, in order to announce such great happiness, is on fire; my barbaric sisters are about to receive the punishment of their crimes."

All the fays trembled at that news; they wanted to flee in order to avoid her presence, but at the same moment the Princess appeared, with a beauty so majestic that those Furies commenced their torture in gazing at her.

"Go, execrable monsters," she said to them, in a menacing tone, "and suffer the punishment that you merit; be reduced to suffering, for as long as the world lasts, all the evils that you have done to so many illustrious unfortunates, with which this place is filled, and, seeing you forbidden to employ of the magical arts of which you made use to overwhelm them and invent new torments for them, they will recognize that Heaven is just to punish you for so many crimes. Go, then," continued the irritated princess; "like new Danaides, fill monstrous water machines endlessly, without ever being able to have drawn enough."

The Princess had not finished when the King of Monsters and all those Furies, all uttering different screams, fled in the direction of the river, and, working to prepare their own tortures, they filled the current of the water with huge beams, to which they attached wheels of prodigious size, and, making them turn by the force of arms, they filled great vessels with the water they drew, which, conducted by pumps, rose up to the enchanted gardens.

Such a new torment caused them to utter screams so piercing that the entire neighborhood was frightened by them; they reached all the way to the ears of the Princess, who was occupied in delivering the unfortunate Anaxandre. He and Philonice threw themselves at her feet to thank her for having saved their lives. She lifted them up kindly, and turned to the fay Serpente.

"Since we are liberated from all those infernal Furies," she said, taking Serpente by the hand, "Conduct me to the palace. I know that you have never contributed to the evils that your pernicious sisters have wrought in the world. I like the science that you have; make use of it, as you ordinarily do, to embellish this fortunate place by the presence of the greatest king in the world, who, having given peace to Europe, is coming to relax from his great labors in these enchanted gardens; find new inventions every day to please his eyes; combine with nature all that the art of Enchantment has of the most beautiful; I make you the mistress on his behalf; but above all, do not leave unfortunates where all the Pleasures ought to make their abode. Go, prudent Serpente, take all those innocent victims from their chains and bring them to me.

As she said that, followed by Philonice, Anaxandre and all her brilliant court, she arrived at the palace, where she made a thousand amities to our unfortunate princess. Everyone looked at her with admiration; her beauty and her grace charmed them, and if Serpente had not come into the hall, that praise would not have ceased for a long time. She was holding Cleonice by the hand, followed by her dear dragon. The fay presented her to the princess, saying that she merited her protection, and told her the story of her adventures, which touched her with so much pity that she did not want to delay for a moment drying up the source of her tears. She touched poor Philoxipe with her beautiful hands; immediately quitting the horrible form that he had retained for such a long time, he appeared to everyone's eyes as he had been when he made the conquest of the heart of his charming wife. She thought that she would die of joy at the feet of the Princess, and if Philonice had not stepped forward to sustain her she would have fallen.

The two turtle-doves followed, who found themselves in a state to thank the Princess; they made it evident by the polite way in which they made their compliments that they were not unworthy of the aid that Heaven had sent them. At the same time, the statues on the terrace found themselves animated by the same life that the malice of the fays had taken away from them all came to make the hall resound with the praises due to the adorable Princess who had caused their happiness.

Princess Biche Blanche, who had been a white cat for such a long time; the queen who had languished for so long under the tyranny of the fay Geanne; Princess Lionne, with her amiable husband; and Leonisse, conducted by the charming

Levrette, came to augment the triumph of the Princess.[6] All those amiable persons, although from different countries, found themselves speaking the same language in order to recognize such a charming sovereign.

Only Melicerte did not appear; she was still weeping in the midst of such general joy, as well as the sad Elise, whom the King of Monsters had constrained not to accompany Philonice. They were both unaware to such an astonishing change; but the incomparable Princess, whom the fay Serpente had informed that Yphidamente's enchantment could not be lifted except by her presence, arrived at the moment when, in despair of their fate, they had both resolved to die. Such a sad subject, and the beauty of the person who was occupied with it, touched the great Princess keenly. Waning to end their woes promptly, she approached Yphidamente's tomb; she lifted the veil that covered it, and he emerged instantly.

The astonishment of Melicerte and Elise when they saw the Princess was redoubled when they saw Yphidamente alive. Without looking at the person who had withdrawn him from the abode of the dead, Melicerte ran to embrace the dear object of her tenderness. Elise did the same to Philonice, and it was only after a long time that, ashamed of their fault, they came to beg the pardon of their amiable benefactress. She pardoned them easily, but, never weary of doing good, she asked the fay Serpente whether there were any more unfortunates who needed her help.

"All sense your divine presence," said the fay, "and the unfortunate cannot exist where you direct our steps; you ought to be content with all the good that you have one today; all these illustrious persons will not forget this fortunate moment."

---

[6] The first of these references appears to be to Madame d'Aulnoy's "La Chatte blanche" and the fourth to another story translated in the present collection "La Princesse Léonice" (the Comtesse D.L.'s spelling of the names of her characters is often inconsistent). The other two are a trifle enigmatic.

"Let us go, then, to savor the repose that we have given to the others," said the Princess. "Let us get out of such a sad place; I do not think that Melicerte wants to occupy it any longer."

As she said that, she did indeed leave the frightful lair, and she arrived at the palace in the company of all those unfortunate beauties. Their happiness was so rapturous that they were not quite convinced that they had nothing more to dread. When the time came to retire, however, and having taken their leave of the Princess, they found themselves free to converse with one another. What pleasure they obtained from that, how animated their conversation was, and how short the evening seemed to them after unhappy days they had had.

The tender Melicerte, most of all, never wearied of asking her dear Yphidamente how he had been conducted to the tomb, and how he had been able to make such a long sojourn within it without dying.

"It is not in my power, charming Melicerte," he said, "to tell you by what enchantment I have been able to live and die every day since the fatal moment when I returned from campaign with your father the prince and no longer found you. You can easily imagine my despair, and I retired to my apartment resolved never to see our common homeland again while I did not know in what place you were living. I went to bed in those sentiments, and without knowing how I was transported into the tomb from which the Princess has just extracted me, returning every day as if from a profound slumber, I was astonished to find myself in that abode of death. I strove to emerge from it, I uttered sighs, I heard yours, and, falling back into my mortal lethargy, I became insensible. You know as well as I do how long that lasted. I have no more to tell you except that in those moments of life, my heart burned with the same fire that your eyes had ignited within it."

Yphidamente finished his discourse thus, and, Melicerte having told him that it was late, he retired immediately, as well as our other lovers. How different that night was for our amiable dragon, and how content he was to spend it with his amiable Cleonice.

The next day, the fay Serpente prepared garments covered in gold and gems for that adorable sovereign, which she accepted gladly, and mounted a triumphant chariot that the fay had arranged to have at the gates of the palace; she arrived followed by her illustrious slaves, before the king, the conqueror of Europe; with a charming grace, she presented to him all those witnesses of her glory, and he received them with the grandeur and mildness that were so natural to him. So many beauties surprised him, especially Philonice; he attached his gaze to her, and the good looks of her lover made him desire that he might remain in his court. The sovereign Princess decided that she would also be very pleased if Philonice did not quit her; she told her very obligingly in the evening that she could not bear her to leave her so soon.

"Oh, Madame," exclaimed Philonice, "I am very happy that you have so generously anticipated my wish to attach myself uniquely to you. I know from the fay Serpente that I have lost the princess, my mother. For that misfortune, nothing can console me except sacrificing the days that you have returned to me to your service; so, Madame, order my destiny."

"It can only be happy, my dear Philonice," she said to her, embracing her tenderly, "while it depends on me."

Meanwhile, everything was prepared for the marriage of the sovereign Princess; never was anything more magnificent and elegant seen than everything that appeared at that superb celebration; all the foreign princes signaled their skill there in tourneys and horse races; the princesses appeared there with garments so rich, and so prettily designed, that no one except the fay Serpente could have made them. She had chosen the colors that she had given to each one so expertly that they were even more beautiful; but among all those beauties, that of our amiable sovereign shone with such a vivid and piercing splendor that no one could look at it without admiration. The Prince, her husband, was, among all our Princes, what she was among all our princesses. The celebration lasted nine days, and everything that the power of a great king and the art of our amiable fay, in combination, could display appeared during those fortunate days.

After that time, the blissful Yphidamente, speaking for all his companions in fortune, took his leave of the sovereign Princess, and assured her that they would never lose the memory of her benefits. Melicerte made her the same compliment on behalf of her companions. The fay Serpente, who never failed in anything that could give pleasure, provided them with equipages proportionate to their birth, and promised them always to be their affectionate friend.

It was not without tears that Philonice separated from Melicerte and Cleonice, although the latter did not have such a long journey to make. The moment of departure having arrived, however, all those amiable persons embraced one another for the last time.

They arrived in their principalities without any inconvenience, and returned joy to their subjects by their presence. The amiable Philonice remained with the Princess, with her charming Elise. Prince Anaxandre, pressed by his amour, demanded the recompense for it with so much urgency that she could not refuse him. Her wedding was honored by the King and the sovereign Princess.

The fay, loving that beautiful person tenderly, heaped her with all the gifts that could make her adorable mistress love her, and succeeded in that so well that she could not live for a moment without her; she often told her all the tales she knew about the art of Enchantment, and the latter, finding the manner in which she told the stories elegant, ordered her to write them down.

Anaxandre, content with his lot, spent his days happily in the service of the greatest King in the world, and, while fulfilling all his duties, conserved for his wife all the ardor of a nascent amour.

AGATIE, PRINCESS OF THE SCYTHS

The Scyths, who live on the banks of the Araxes, were once governed by a queen, the granddaughter of Tomyris, well-known to history by virtue of the death of Cyrus the Great.[7] She had the same name as that cruel princess, and was no less proud. She had married a very accomplished prince who died in a battle against the Issedones, a people who, although Scythian, had large cities and were very civilized. He left the queen pregnant with a daughter, to whom she gave birth shortly after his death, and whom she named Agatie.

That child was a masterpiece of nature. From the moment of her birth, the fays, who amused themselves greatly among those bellicose peoples, heaped her with all the gifts that could render her perfect. Her mother, the queen, never wearied of embracing her; the child resembled her father, the king, so strongly that she was even dearer to her in consequence.

However, as soon as she was able to suffer the fatigues of war and had repaired the disorders that the death of the king had put into her army, the queen thought of avenging him, and, leaving the young princess in the royal tents, she set out on campaign. No one is unaware that Scyth women are scarcely less valiant than the men; the wars that the cruel Tomyris

---

[7] Tomyris was actually said to be the queen of the Massagetae, who lived, according to Herodotus, "beyond the Araxes," but they were a Scythian tribe, neighbors of the Scyths and the Issedones. The story that Tomyris had Cyrus the Great beheaded and then stuffed his head into a wineskin full of human blood is only reported by Herodotus as one of several legends surrounding that king's death, but because it was the most gruesome it became far the most popular and secured Tomyris' posthumous fame, even though it never happened.

sustained against the conqueror of Scythia are famous enough for it not to be astonishing that her granddaughter wanted to fight herself, at the head of her army, in order to avenge her husband's death.

The King of the Issedones, who had suspected that his enemies would not leave him in peace, had advanced toward his frontier, in a great plain. A little stream separated the two armies, which was fordable in many places, and did not prevent them engaging.

The violent transports that agitated the heart of Tomyris only gave her the time necessary to arrange her troops in battle order, and having made them a short speech on the obligation they had to fight well, to appease the shade of their king by the death of his enemy, she was the first to pass over the stream; her example was followed by the whole army. The king of the Issedones received them like a prince accustomed to victory.

The battle was long, and bloody on both sides; victory seemed to be leaning toward the Issedones, but the superb queen, remarking the disorder of her left wing, raced there and reanimated her soldiers by means of the great deeds that they saw her perform; ashamed that a woman was teaching them how to vanquish, they rallied, and, charging those who had defeated them, constrained them to cede victory to the Scyths.

Disorder became general throughout the army of the king of the Issedones, who, in order to avoid falling into the hands of his implacable enemy, retreated with a few men into a city on the frontier.

The queen did not savor the pleasure of her victory, by virtue of the chagrin of not having her enemy in her power. All the blood that she had shed could not satisfy her irritated heart, if she had not shed that of the King of the Issedones. She knew that the Scyths fought with a great deal of valor, but they did not know how to lay sieges, and she did not doubt that her enemy would retreat to his capital city.

She held a council of war with her generals on the battle-field, in order to decide whether to pursue the King of the Issedones. They represented to her that, although her army was victorious, it needed repose, and that it was necessary not to advance into enemy territory without knowing it.

All those arguments were not to Tomyris' taste; she only respired for vengeance, and everything that delayed it rendered her desperate. She therefore replied to them that the gods were too just not to side with her; that it was necessary not to give the enemy time to reach Issedones, which was an almost impregnable city; and that it was necessary to surprise them in Ispanis, where the king still was, which, being not very strong itself and defended by soldiers half-defeated by fear, would not resist them.

In the end, it was necessary to render to such insistent arguments. At daybreak the next day, the army marched through dangerous passes and arrived before Ispanis after three days.

It is not my design to recount exactly what happened in that bloody war; it is the story of Agatie that I am writing, not that of Tomyris; so I shall content myself with saying that the vindictive princess, after a long siege, constrained Ispanis to surrender, but, not finding the king there, she put its unfortunate inhabitants to the sword and, pushing her fury and hr victory all the way to the capital she laid siege to it for two years after her emergence from Scythia. Finally, Issedones followed the destiny of the rest of the realm; she entered it triumphantly, after twelve years of war.

The king was captured and taken before the proud queen, who had him laden with chains. Wanting to sacrifice him on the tomb of her husband, she had him taken to the palace. She found his wife, the queen, there, accompanied by a young princess. She consigned them to the same prison as the unfortunate prince, and only stayed in Issedones for as long as it was necessary to allow her army to rest.

After having left governors in the city and the realm to conserve her conquests, she resumed he road to Scythia, taking with her the king, his wife, his daughter and two young princes, his nephews.

The joy of the royal tents was great at the return of such a glorious princess. Agatie came to meet her with the entire court. The road was bordered with people eager to see their sovereign. The young princess threw herself at the feet of the queen, her mother, who lifted her up immediately. Gods, how content she was to see her so beautiful! Nothing could equal the beauty of her figure or that of her face, such as Venus is deputed when she wanted her advantages to prevail over the other goddesses. The entire army could not weary of uttering cries of admiration on seeing their princess so accomplished.

She saw with dolor the crowned victims laden with chains following the queen, especially Menalipe—that was the name of the enslaved princess—who softened her heart so much that she turned her head away in order to hide the tears that such a touching spectacle drew from her beautiful eyes.

The whole numerous court arrived at the royal tents, where the king of the Issedones and his family were to be carefully guarded until the day destined for his death; it was to be the one on which the king had been killed, which would only arrive in six months. The Scyths, who were accustomed to immolate to their cruel gods the strangers who passed through their land, awaited that day with impatience.

Only Agatie mourned the unfortunate prince, and could not help testifying it to the queen. She asked for the mercy for him that he be treated as a king, and that she be permitted to have Menalipe with her. That was granted to her, with difficulty. The young princess no sooner had that permission than she ran to the queen of the Issedones and told her that she would employ all her credit with Tomyris in order to save her husband's life.

Menalipe did not want to quit her mother, the queen, but the latter made her understand that it would have the consequence for them of conserving the amity of the princess. She therefore went with Agatie, shedding tears, and went to thank Tomyris for that indulgence. From that day on the two princesses became inseparable. They loved one another tenderly; their age and beauty was similar, and their minds, in such early youth, had nothing reminiscent of childhood. They often went riding along the river.

One day, when they went further than was customary, Agatie's horse got the bit between its teeth, and, running a top speed, it was soon far away from her retinue. Her fear was extreme; she uttered cries with which the river bank resounded. A young shepherd, who was guarding his flock, heard them and, running in front of the princess's horse, he presented the iron tip of his crook to it; then, seizing the bridle, he stopped it. That gave her the time to jump to the ground, where, lying down on the grass, half dead of fear, she did not have the strength to thank her benefactor. However, the court arrived at that moment. Menalipe ran with open arms to embrace Agatie, who returned her caresses.

"Without this handsome shepherd," she said, "I'd be dead, my dear sister."

Everyone hastened then to the young man, whose manners and beauty inspired respect, in spite of his shepherd's costume. He made no response at all to anything anyone might say to him; he was motionless, his eyes attached to the princess. But when she stood up in order to go away, and looked at him with the charming mildness that was so natural to her, she told him that she would inform her mother, the queen, that she owed her life to him, and that she would make his fortune.

"What I did, Madame," he said to her, "does not merit any recompense. I am sufficiently repaid by the pleasure of having been of use to you."

After that the princess returned to the royal tents, where she told the queen about the adventure that had happened to her. She did not neglect to praise the service rendered to her by the shepherd, his good manners and the air of grandeur that emanated from his person.

Tomyris commanded that a search by mounted for the shepherd, but it was fruitless; he could not be found. The queen expressed annoyance at that, but Agatie was veritably chagrined. The thought of him often returned to her mind; amour hiding under the mask of gratitude occupied the heart of the princess without her being aware of it. She became more pensive than usual; she sought solitude, and only Menalipe was the confidant of her anxieties.

Meanwhile, the time destined for the death of the King of the Issedones drew nearer. Agatie had implored the clemency of Tomyris in vain; she could not obtain mercy for the unfortunate king. Believing that the more blood she shed, the more she would satisfy the plaintive shade of her husband, she also wanted to sacrifice the two young princes; she only yielded the queen to Menalipe's tears.

That poor princess was inconsolable. Agatie forgot the handsome shepherd for a few days in order to comfort her friend.

Finally, the fatal day arrived, and a huge pyre was built outside Tomyris's tent. All the troops surrounded the square. There were platforms at the four corners to accommodate the entire count; the queen's was covered by a rich awning, and as soon as she had taken her place there, the High Priest emerged from the tent of the King of the Issedones. That unfortunate prince appeared, covered in all his royal garments; the young princes followed him, so little touched by the dire state that they were in that their barbaric enemies could not help feeling a sentiment of pity. The cruel Tomyris , triumphant, her eyes avid for the blood of those crowned victims, gazed at them with a malign joy.

The king arrived at the pyre and, not deigning to lament his fate, mounted it without waiting for the High Priest to constrain him to do so. His nephews did likewise and, taking the torches from the hands of the cruel ministers themselves, they set fire to it. An action so heroic caused all the people to utter cries of admiration, and made all the court think that princes who were so well able to scorn death merited living forever. The vindictive queen saw with an extreme pleasure the flames ready to devour those illustrious victims.

Suddenly, a chariot drawn by four flying dragons was seen in the air, which settled lightly on the pyre, and a tall woman emerged from it dressed as Pallas Athene is depicted.

Her armor was covered in precious stones; her helmet, the visor of which was raised, allowed the sight of a visage full of noble pride. She approached the three princes and, enabling them to climb into her chariot, she placed herself beside them. The dragons took off again and were soon lost to sight in the sky from which they had just descended.

A spectacle so novel had rendered the people motionless. Tomyris uttered screams of rage, and one of Agatie's domestics ran to tell her about such a surprising adventure. Menalipe nearly died of joy, and the Queen of the Issedones could not believe in such a great good fortune. As they were in those first transports, they felt themselves lifted up, and the tent they were in was split in two to let them through, at the moment when the queen, desperate at seeing her victims snatched from her, arrived with the design of killing them with her own hand.

What a redoubling of rage for that pitiless princess! She directed it against the protective gods of her empire, and swore not to offer them any more sacrifices, but that was not the end of the misfortunes that were to overtake her on that day, which she had thought so appropriate to satisfy her vengeance. Scarcely had the pyre died down than a monster was seen born from its ashes, so frightful that everything the poets have told us about the chimera that Bellerophon vanquished so gloriously had nothing so terrible. Whirlwinds of flame emerging from its eyes and nostrils made a new fire visible.

The fearful people fled as far as the banks of the Araxes, and the queen, hearing the screams uttered by the unfortunates it devoured, commanded all the troops assembled to guard the camp to kill it. All the arrows that they launched at it, however, unable to pierce the hard scales by which it was covered, only served to irritate it. Cutting through the army, it burned and flattened everything that was presented to it in its passage. It went to find a retreat in a forest behind the royal tents, from which it came every day to desolate the regions by the murders it committed. The crops of the soil were not exempt from its fury, the flames that emerged from its nostrils consuming them.

The desolation was general throughout Scythia; those brave people, finding themselves overwhelmed by a superior power, recognized too late that the cruelty of their queen had attracted misfortunes to them that were going to destroy their land. Nothing was exempt from that public calamity. The monster devoured old men, and even children, and women were not spared by its murderous teeth.

Tomyris sought in vain for a remedy for such great evils. She offered prayers to the same gods whose sacrifices her anger had made her swear to abolish; they were deaf to her voice. The princess mingled her own prayers with those of her mother incessantly, but they were not heeded, and the cruel monster redoubled its depredations every day.

To complete the despair, it was learned that the fay Amazone had taken the King of the Issedones and the whole family to Issedones, that she had enabled an uprising of the people, who had surprised Tomyris's garrisons and cut them to pieces, and had replaced the king on the throne. He was preparing to come and take vengeance on the Scyths, accompanied by the fay Amazone.

That last stroke of misfortune was all that was needed to overwhelm Tomyris. No longer knowing which way to turn to extract herself from the labyrinth into which she had fallen, she resolved to have recourse to a powerful fay who had a palace near the Araxes, and who was one of those who had heaped Princess Agatie with gifts.

The fay received her affectionately, but told her that she could not put an end to the misfortunes into which the bloody vengeance she had wanted to take upon the King of the Issedones had plunged her; that the fay Amazone had sworn her doom; that the monster thirsty for royal blood demanded her daughter; that it was up to her to sacrifice Agatie's blood in order to conserve the rest of her unfortunate subjects; and that she could only foresee an end to her woes by way of her greatest enemy.

Such a bleak response put the queen in the utmost despair. She could not hide it; the entire court that had followed her had witnessed it, and she had no doubt that the cruel people would constrain her to deliver Agatie to the monster rather than see themselves perish.

She returns to the royal tents in a consternation that nothing could equal. The entire court was in the same state. Agatie was so generally beloved that her death was regarded as the greatest of tragedies. That princess was unaware of her fate; she had not gone with Tomyris to see the fay; coming to met her, she asked her urgently whether there was any hope of a remedy for the public misfortune.

"Oh, my dear daughter," Tomyris said to her, embracing her, with a torrent of teas, "let our woes last eternally rather than see them ended by your death."

The princess shivered at the queen's speech, and without daring to ask for a fuller explanation, she awaited her sentence.

Tomyris repented of what dolor had caused her to say, but, seeing that she could no longer hide it from her, she told her what the fay had predicted, swearing that all Scythia would perish if it required such precious blood to save it.

"I do not merit such tender marks of your generosity, Madame," the beautiful princess said to her, after wiping away a few tears that such a frightful fate had drawn from her beautiful eyes. "If the gods want my death in order to protect your subjects from the murderous teeth of the dragon, I will give it without any other regret than that of quitting you."

"No, my daughter," cried the queen, "it is in vain that the cruel gods ask me for your life; I shall be able to protect such a dear head."

"It would be futile," said the princess, "to want to extract me from their orders; they would punish me for it without my death being useful to your unfortunate subjects; so, Madame, don't render me more criminal than the monstrous dragon. Between the time that the fay announced their will to you and the moment of my death, I shall be culpable of all the murders it commits."

Everyone admired the constancy of Agatie in such great youth, and, such noble sentiments redoubling the tenderness of the queen, she forbade her so absolutely to say any more that she dared not do so.

However, the monster's fury increased; it seemed to come every day to demand its victim, by means of the murders that it committed at all hours around the royal tent. All the people demanded in loud voices to be delivered from such a cruel enemy, and threatened to take the princess by force if the queen was not willing to deliver her to the monster, since there was no other means of lifting such a frightful yoke.

Agatie threw herself at the feet of the queen to beg her to yield to such an urgent necessity, representing to her how shameful it would be for a princess to be dragged to execution. She finally obtained that she would be delivered to the monster the next day, and, having retired to her tent, she spent the night preparing herself for that cruel sacrifice.

The people no sooner knew of the queen's resolution than they calmed down, and as if the monster had already commenced to feed on such fine blood, it retired to its retreat without doing any more harm to anyone.

Daylight had no sooner appeared than the princess emerged from the royal tents, conducted by the tearful queen. The entire court admired the strength of the young person. Never had she appeared so beautiful; it was necessary to be as cruel as the monster not to be touched by her fate.

They arrived at the fatal place. The queen thought she would die of dolor when she saw the monster approaching. On seeing it, the princess embraced Tomyris for the last time, and, tearing herself away from her arms she advanced toward it; but the gods, protectors of innocence, sent her help.

The same shepherd who had already saved her from the ardor of her horse, came again, to extract her from such a great danger or to lose a life that he found insupportable without her. He appeared before her just as the monster was about to devour her, and, striking it with the iron of his crook, he was so well able to find the mortal spot that it fell, drowned in its own blood.

What joy for the queen when she saw that dear daughter delivered from such a great danger! She ran to her with open arms, and, turning to the shepherd, said to him: "What demon favorable to this empire has sent you to my aid, and what shame for my infidel subjects that a foreigner should come to extract their princess from the execution to which they had condemned her!"

"Oh, Madame," said Agatie, recognizing the shepherd, "this is not the first time that he has saved my life; it's him for whom you have already searched with so much care; doubtless he's some god; a mortal man could not have done what we have just seen."

"That is saying too much, Madame," he shepherd said to her, "about an action that does not merit such praise. I thank Heaven, which has preserved me until this day in spite of all my misfortunes, that I have been able to be useful to you."

"Oh, I shall never forget such a great service," said Tomyris, "and if it is fortune that you lack in order to be happy, I will place you at a rank at which you will have no reason to complain of it."

After that, the queen resumed the road to the tents. Nothing was heard resounding anywhere but cries of joy; everyone hastened so see the miraculous shepherd. The courageous people, who had not been able to vanquish the monster, wanted the shepherd to be the realm's tutelary demon, in order to save their glory.

With that thought in mind, respects were rendered to him little different from those rendered to the queen. The army that the King of the Issedones had raised throughout his lands and the help of the fay Amazone no longer frightened them. All the generals begged Tomyris to give him command of the troops; which she was only too willing to do. Thus, the shepherd became the general of the army; he assured the queen that he would sacrifice his life in order to acquit the honor that she and all Scythia were doing him.

Although the princess felt joy at seeing her benefactor heaped with so many benefits, she had some chagrin in feeling that her gratitude went further than she wanted; the baseness of his birth made her disapprove of the sentiments that she had for him. Sometimes, in order to flatter her dolor, she told herself that it was not natural that the young man could be what he appeared to be.

One thing that confirmed her in that thought was that she had perceived that he had a scepter on his hand; she could not believe that the gods would have given that royal mark to a man of such low rank. Meanwhile, the queen, who wanted to heap him with benefits, did so with an enthusiasm parallel to hers, and, sending him garments similar to those that princes wear, she ordered that he be served as one henceforth.

How handsome he was in that magnificent attire! It appeared so natural to him that it was difficult to believe that he had not worn it all his life. The signal services that he had rendered to Agatie gave him free access to her tent at all the hours when she was visible; he was able to profit from that so well that he no longer quit her. Constrained as he was, his eyes spoke only too clearly of the violent passion that he had felt for her since the fatal moment when he had seen her on the bank of the Araxes; he was consumed by such an ardent fire that if he had not followed her instantly, it was because a supernatural force had prevented him from doing so.

The young princess had enough interest in the handsome shepherd—whom we shall henceforth call Agatrice, a name that the queen had ordered him to bear—to perceive that she was making him suffer; but, still remembering that he had not been born a prince, she hid her sentiments so well that her unfortunate lover did not believe himself heeded. He knew that he had been born in a condition equal to hers, although he did not know the name of those who had given him birth. That knowledge gave him the boldness to love the princess, but he was unable to provide any proof of it, and, fearing to be considered temeritous, he contented himself with sighing in secret.

That constraint put him in mortal chagrin. The queen, who loved him passionately, often asked him the cause of it. If Agatie had made him the same request, I do not know whether he would have been able to refuse himself the pleasure of telling her.

Meanwhile, Tomyris received news every day that the King of the Issidones was ready to set forth on campaign. She wanted to anticipate him; she gave the necessary orders for the army to be ready to march in a matter of days. The Scyths, ashamed of having constrained their princess to surrender herself to a cruel monster, wanted to repair their barbarity by as many fine deeds in the war, and that the infamy should be washed away in the blood of their enemies.

Agatrice was waiting impatiently for opportunities to make the princess see that he was not unworthy of the honor that the Scyths had done him. It was only the fear of dying in the war without making his sentiments known that augmented his melancholy.

The day destined for the departure arrived; Tomyris said adieu to the princess. Agatrice could only take his leave of her in the presence of the court. In the end, he had to follow the queen, and the pleasure of seeing himself at the head of an army composed of brave men enabled him, to some degree, to forget the passion that he had for Agatie.

After a few days' march they arrived in a great plain, where they discovered the army of the King of the Issidones. The queen's design was to give battle as soon as possible, having learned from spies she had in the enemy camp that the king was waiting for a reinforcement of ten thousand men, who would only arrive in two days. That obliged her, even though her troops were fatigued, to want to fight the next day.

She gave her final orders, and as soon as daylight appeared, Agatrice put the army in battle order and marched straight toward the enemy. They did not refuse the combat, even though they were weaker, the fay Amazone having told them that that day would decide the war.

Agatrice performed supernatural feats there; the queen could not praise Heaven sufficiently for having sent her that miraculous man; alone, he opposed himself with prodigious courage to Amazone; he had almost defeated the entire enemy army, and was near to immolating the unfortunate King of the Issedones to the vengeance of the queen when the fay retained his arm.

"Stop, reckless youth," she cried to him. "Do you want to cause a prince who gave you life to perish?"

Agatrice stopped at such a surprising discourse, and the queen, who was not far away from him, approached and made a sign to those who were fighting in that vicinity to suspend their victory momentarily.

"Cruel fay," she said, "are you not content with all the harm that you have done to me without wanting also to retain the victorious arm of my defender by means of something so far from the truth?"

"Excessively vindictive princess," the fay said to her, "the misfortunes you have suffered ought to have taught you that the gods do not approve of your vengeance; but, far from punishing you, I want to render you happy, without anything being able to trouble the rest of your days. Know, Tomyris, that this prince really is the son of the King of the Issedones, whom I have brought up carefully with the design of making an eternal union between the Issedones and the Scyths, who will live under your power, by means of the marriage of Agatie and him." She turned to the king. "See, wise King, the royal mark that the gods have given him, and receive this glorious present from my hand."

Having recovered from the initial astonishment that the fay's speech had caused him, the king looked at that extraordinary mark, and, recognizing the prince, his son, he threw his arms around his neck tenderly. "Oh, my dear Agatrice," he said to him, "what enemy demon made you combat to take my life?"

"Sire," the prince said to him, throwing himself at his feet, "the ignorance of my birth in which I was cannot serve to excuse my crime."

All that the queen suffered in such a surprising adventure was indescribable; the desire gripped her a thousand times to pierce the King of the Issedones with her sword while he was embracing the prince, but the affection she had for the son retained her arm.

While she was in that uncertainty, Agatrice turned toward her. "Madame," he said, "to what extremity will you reduce me if you do not allow yourself to be flexed by such a novel spectacle? Can I fight an unfortunate king who has given me the light of day? Can I be in the party of your enemies after the honor that you have done me and the violent amour hat I have for Princess Agatie? No, Madame, if you do not grant me the favor that I ask of you, I shall pierce my heart with this same sword that nearly took the life of my father, the king."

"You have vanquished, too generous prince," cried Tomyris, extending her hand to him to lift him up. "I cannot be the enemy of the father of a prince who has rendered me such great services."

The fay Amazone, delighted to see that the queen had yielded, came to embrace her, and made her swear between her hands an eternal peace. The King of the Issedones did the same, and the victors and the vanquished embraced one another tenderly before returning to their camps.

By the command of the king, Agatrice did not quit the queen. The next day, the Queen of the Issedones and her daughter, the princess, who were in Ispanis, arrived in the camp. They fay took them to Tomyris, who received them admirably, and, presenting the prince to them, she said: "Madame, this is the knot of our amity; I hope that it will be eternal."

The Queen of the Issedones responded to such an obliging speech as she was bound to do, and, asking for permission to embrace her son, she took him in her arms. The princess, his sister, wanted to have her share of that dear brother, but the fay, who wanted to complete a work that she had conducted by such an extraordinary path, told Tomyris that, in order to render joy to the two realms, it was necessary to give Agatie to the Prince of the Issedones, which she could not refuse without ingratitude, since he had saved her from the murderous teeth of the monster.

"I consent with joy," replied the Queen of the Scyths, "and I cannot make known too much to my generous defender how grateful I am to him."

"Oh, Madame," cried the amorous prince, "How far that prize is above my services!"

The fay, who wanted to advance Agatie's happiness, departed immediately in her chariot drawn by dragons, and, descending to the royal tents, lifted up Princess Agatie and, placing her by her side, returned to the camp.

They soon arrived at the tent of Tomyris. The sight of the princess surprised all those royal persons agreeably, but nothing equaled the joy of the prince.

"Madame," he said, after Tomyris had told her daughter the design that she had, "will you be more inexorable than the Queen? May I hope that you will not regard me as having emerged from a blood that has always been odious to you, and condemn the unfortunate Agatrice to death?"

"I am too submissive to the Queen's orders," said the princess, blushing, "and too grateful for the services that you have rendered me, to allow the Prince of the Issedones to die."

"Oh, my dear sister," Menalipe said to her, "how obliged I am for the generosity you have for my brother. Who would have thought when we encountered him on the bank of the Araxes that that shepherd would be your husband?"

"If we were not in the Queen's chamber," said the princess, "I would ask him by what enchantment the shepherd has found himself the son of a king."

"I will tell you," the fay said to her.

The two queens also wanted to be informed. The fay told them that, knowing by her science that the prince would kill his father, she had stolen him from his cradle and taken him to the home of a Scythian shepherd of whose goodness she was aware, and given him to his wife to nurse, recommending him to take care of him.

"I had no need of pleas," said the fay, "for them to grant me what I asked of them. The extreme beauty of the prince prejudiced them to an amity so strong that I was assured in that regard.

"I let some years pass without seeing my nursling again, and he might have been fifteen years old when I did so. I was charmed to find him so well made and to know that he had all the sentiments of a great prince under the costume of a shepherd. It was about that time, Madame," she said to Tomyris, "that you brought back the King of the Issedones as a prisoner, and all his family, and Princess Menalipe became dear to Agatie; all their pleasures were, as you know, in riding on horseback along the bank of the Araxes. You have not forgotten that without my shepherd, the Princess would have been doomed, but you do not know that the Prince was struck as if by a thunderbolt by Agatie's beauty.

"He listened to all the thanks that were given to him for the services that he had just rendered to all Scythia in the person of the Princess, without taking his eyes off that charming object; when she left he wanted to follow her, and he had already taken a few steps to do that when he felt himself lifted into the air, from which, after having traversed rivers and mountains, he was set down in a magnificent palace. Everything he saw of the beautiful and surprising did not console him for not having followed the Princess, although, in the condition into which he believed himself to have been born, he knew full well that it would never be permissible for him to reveal what he felt for her.

"He lived thus during the imprisonment of his father, the King, and until the moment when Agatie was exposed to the cruel monster; but, my design being to render him dear to you, Madame, in order to be able to make a solid peace between two realms that I loved, I went to find him. 'Generous shepherd,' I said to him, 'the beautiful Agatie is going to be the prey of a frightful dragon; her cruel subjects are constraining her to that; run to deliver her, and have no fear that it can avoid the death that I will give it by your hand. Finally, do not fight as a shepherd who only knows how to protect against wolves, but as a great prince, since Heaven has caused you to be born as one.'

"Having said that, I opened the doors of the palace, and enabled him to see the Princess, ready to be swallowed. He ran to help her without responding to me. You know how he killed the monster, the acclamations of the people, your joy, Madame, and how Agatie recognized him as the same shepherd who had rescued her on the bank of the Araxes. I no longer have any need to tell you that the passion she had inspired in him the first time he saw her was augmented with so much violence that he fell into a melancholy of which he would surely have died if the desire that he had to perform feats worthy of his princess in the war on the Issedones had not sustained his life."

The fay finished her discourse thus, and the two queens thanked her for the trouble she had taken.

"You will only be able to recompense me," she told them, "for having raised such a perfect prince by consenting that I make him happy."

Although Tomyris would have liked the marriage to be accomplished in the royal tents, she replied that the fay only had to command, and what she wanted would be done.

The fay told her that she would take care of everything, and that she had only to agree that she be taken with the beautiful Agatie to the place that she would have prepared.

After that the Queen of the Issedones withdrew, conducted by her son. Menalipe remained with her dear Agatie.

The day after, at sunrise, martial music was heard in the two camps, which woke the princesses agreeably. The fay Amazone had all the troops take up arms, and having set up a magnificent altar in the middle of the great plain she conducted Tomyris and her illustrious daughter there. They found the

King and Queen of the Issedones there. Having taken the hands of the King and Tomyris, the fay made them swear an eternal peace again.

After the High Priest had concluded the marriage, they returned to Tomyris's tents, to the sound of a thousand instruments and the cries of delight of the two armies. They found a delicious meal there. In the afternoon, the entire royal party had all the pleasures for which they could have wished in the most tranquil court, and when evening came, the fay took the two charming spouses to a tent glittering with gold and precious stones. It was illuminated by a hundred rock crystal lamps. Leaving the blissful lovers, she went to prepare everything necessary for the departure the next day.

It was not without some chagrin that the King and Queen of the Issedones separated from the prince, their son; as for Menalipe, she went with her brother, and, the fay having made them mount magnificent chariots, they soon arrived at the royal tents. There, after heaping them with all the gifts that could render them happy, the fay left Agatrice the placid possessor of his dear Agatie.

PRINCESS LEONICE

There was once a king who was the model of other kings for the great qualities that he possessed. He had lost his wife, the queen, very young, of whom he had had a handsome and well made prince; that was his only consolation, and he merited it fully, for no prince ever had as many perfections. As the king was already advanced in age he thought of marrying him.

The kings of that realm not suffering foreign blood on the throne, he cast his eyes upon a young princess of his court, named Florinice, who was the sovereign of a province dependent on him. She was beautiful but very ambitious, jealous of everyone near to her; she had a sister named Leonice whose beauty surpassed hers by far, whose mild and obliging character made her loved as much as her sister's imperious airs made her hated.

The prince had not been able to see Leonice without being touched by her; she had charmed him, and he had already felt a violent amour for her for some time, to which she was not indifferent. They hid their passion carefully; no one at the court had yet received it, except for one of Leonice's maids, named Cephise, who was dear to her mistress.

Those two young hearts savored a happiness all the more perfect because it had been untroubled thus far. However, the king having formed the design that I have just mentioned, sent for his son in order to command him to dispose himself to marry Florinice. No dolor was ever equal to that of the prince.

To that cruel order he replied to the king that he begged him not to think of establishing him so soon, that he had a natural aversion for marriage, but that it might perhaps diminish at a more advanced age. The king replied, however, that the beauty of the princess would cause him to lose that unfounded aversion, that princes like him did not follow their inclinations, and in sum, that he must obey him. He had already spoken about it to Florinice, who was powerful within the realm because of the large province of which she was mistress, and could cause a great deal of trouble if he did not deliver what he had promised her.

All those arguments were not to the liking of the prince; the amour he had for Leonice rendered marriage to her sister a frightful torture; but, not daring to irritate the king by an obstinate refusal, he contented himself with saying that he begged him to grant him some time in order to dispose himself to obey him. The king granted it to him on the condition that he commenced that very evening to attach himself to the princess. After that, he dismissed his son.

He had no sooner quit the king than he ran to find his dear Leonice in order to tell her about their common misfortune. What a thunderbolt for the young princess! She nearly died of dolor. Cephise hastened to console both of them, but after many lamentations, sighs, tears and protestations that they would always love one another, they resolved that the Prince must make a semblance of obeying his father, and must give his attentions to Florinice.

There was a ball that evening at the palace; the two princesses were adorned with all they had of the most magnificent. The prince, in order to commence what they had agreed, only talked to Florinice, who, believing herself to be queen already, received him with an insupportable arrogance. That scarcely touched the prince, The king, who was watching them attentively, thought that very bad, and said so to Florinice.

The next day the entire court went deer-hunting. The ladies were on horseback, dressed as amazons. Leonice seemed so beautiful to the prince's eyes that he suffered a rude constraint in accompanying her sister.

The hunt was very agreeable for the ladies; the deer ran for a long time; it often passed before them. As it was hot, Princess Florinice felt thirsty. She saw two springs that were emerging from the foot of a rock, which formed a stream that ran alongside the path they were on. She went to quench her thirst; the prince followed her with the same intention, and after he had assisted her to descend from her horse, she drank abundantly from one of the two springs. The prince did the same thing, but not from the same spring. He did not know the virtue of the two springs, one of which inspired amour and the other hatred.

The princess had drunk from the one that caused tenderness; she felt its effects. Immediately, her heart, which had never been touched by anything but ambition, found itself sensible to another passion. She saw the prince with other eyes; he appeared much more lovable to her, and she deemed herself very fortunate because he was destined for her. While she was conceiving such tender sentiments, however, the prince felt his hatred for her increasing with so much violence that he could scarcely constrain himself to stay with her. In such different states of mind, they went back to join the hunt.

No longer being master of himself, the prince drew near to his dear Leonice, in spite of everything that she could say to him, and did not quit her for the rest of the day.

The proud Florinice saw the prince's urgent attentions all too clearly. At that cruel moment a thousand things came back to her mind to which she had not paid attention, which convinced her that they had loved one another for some time. Jealousy took possession of her heart with as much violence as amour; torn between her two passions she retired to her apartment so beside herself that she no longer recognized herself.

Leonice was no more tranquil; she knew full well that the prince loved her tenderly, but the king's orders frightened her; furthermore, she dreaded her sister's imperious humor, and trembled that she might perceive her lover's sentiments.

He had no repose either; amour, hatred and the dread of displeasing his father tormented him equally. No night had ever passed as sadly for those three persons, and daylight only augmented their woes.

Florinice, having resolved to discover whether it was true that the prince was in love with Leonice, said that she felt ill and that she did not want to see anyone. She had no sooner given those orders than she got up. She knew that there was a cabinet that opened from her apartment into the space behind her sister's bed, which was very dark and only served as a place to put clothes that the young princess no longer wore. She hid herself there, not doubting that the prince, knowing that no one would be allowed to see her all day, would take advantage of those fortunate moments to be with Leonice, if it was true that he loved her.

She was not mistaken. Having been to her apartment, the prince came into her sister's, and, having found her alone with Cephise, he knelt down.

"My beautiful princess," he said to her, "I shall have the pleasure of seeing you today without constraint; Florinice is ill, and I've been told that she doesn't want to see anyone."

She invited him to sit down next to her, and he continued: "What a pleasure for me to be able to tell you everything that I have suffered since the fatal moment when you ordered me to deceive my father. I am no longer master of doing it; I hate Florinice too much, and I love you with too much violence to hide my sentiments." He knelt down again. "Yes, my beautiful princess, it's necessary that you permit me to declare the love that I have to the king and to beg him not to contradict me in the choice that my heart has made of you."

"Alas," relied Leonice, sadly, "that impulsive action would only serve to render us more unfortunate. The king has his reasons, as you know, for preferring my sister; whatever tenderness he has for you, politics will prevail over his heart; furthermore, I depend on the proud Florinice, by virtue of the death of my father and mother; how do you think she would receive such an affront? No, my dear prince, don't make such a bad decision, I implore you; it would only serve to separate us forever."

"But what do you want me to do?" said the prince. "Is it necessary for me to marry Florinice?"

"I don't have the strength to advise you to do that," said the princess. "Rather continue to make the king hope that you will obey him, and try to constrain yourself in the company of my sister; above all, she mustn't find out that you love me."

"What is the objective of all that constraint?" said the prince.

"To give us time," replied Leonice. "That's all that we can hope for in our misfortunes."

The proud Florinice listened with a mortal displeasure to such a tender conversation. No longer able to bear it, she retired to her apartment for fear of no longer being mistress of herself.

Gods, what did she not say when she was at liberty to express herself! All the most violent resolutions against the prince and Leonice passed through her mind; iron and poison were too mild to punish their perfidy in accordance with the sentiments of her irritated heart An agitation so violent rendered her really ill, but whatever need she had to be alone, she had no sooner returned to bed than she summoned her maidservants and ordered them to go and tell her sister to come and see her. A fit of jealousy made her want to have her, in order not to allow her the pleasure of being with the prince any longer.

He was still there when the young princess received the order. She went to see Florinice tremulously; she told her as she approached her that the prince, having known that she was ill, had come to see her in order to have news of her.

"I'm much obliged to him for his concern," said the elder princess, with a disdainful laugh, "but he must have consoled himself with you for my illness and my absence."

Leonice blushed at her sister's response, and made no reply.

That worried her for the rest of the day; their conversation was sad.

The next day the prince came to see Florinice with his father, the king, who only stayed for a moment. The prince would have liked to follow him by leaving, but he dared not do so; he therefore remained alone with her, which distressed him to such a extent that he did not say anything for a long time.

The princess, however, not wanting to waste such a good opportunity, seeing that he was not returning from his reverie, said to him, her eyes inflamed with amour and anger: "Admit the truth. Your heart begrudges the moments that the king's orders force you to give me; the excessively fortunate Leonice occupies you even when you're with me."

At the name of Leonice the prince came out of his reverie. "Why, Madame, are you making me that reproach?" he said. "Am I not guilty enough for having forgotten for a moment that I was with you, without accusing me of loving Leonice, knowing that the king has ordered me to attach myself to you?"

"Can you deny to me that you love my sister," said Florinice, "after the conversation that I heard yesterday?" No longer in control of herself, she continued: "Yes, traitor, I was in a place where I did not lose a word of all the protestations you made never to love anyone but her. I was a witness to everything tender that the two of you said, but the ingrate Leonice will not triumph over me with impunity; I shall sell her the pleasure of your conquest very dear; she will answer to me for all the woes that the amour I have for you is making me suffer. I shall reduce her to cursing the day when she received your heart; and if I cannot make myself loved I shall have the pleasure of avenging myself on the person who is dearer to you than me."

Until then the prince had been so surprised to see that he had been found out that he had not known what to do, but, seeing that it was futile for him to disguise anything, he could not suffer any longer the threats she was making against his dear princess.

"Of what do you have to complain, Madame," he said, "if I love Leonice, being master of her destiny? Mine gives me to your lovable sister. When the king ordered me to love you, my heart was no longer my own; I dared not tell him. You did not love me before that fatal order; I am even more convinced now that it is the crown that pleases you in my alliance. I consent that the king gives it to you and leaves me my lovable Leonice; all three of us will be content."

"It would be necessary," said Florinice, "for me to neglect my heart in order to make that division, but in the sentiments that I have for you, the crown, without you, would be a frightful present. What! Am I so unlovable that you would cede it to me rather than want to share it with me? Think about it, charming prince; foresee the misfortunes that you will cause in your realm if you continue to scorn me; take advantage of a moment of tenderness that I cannot retain; abandon Leonice, give yourself to me, and I will forget all the woes you have caused me, but it is time to decide."

"Since I have gone so far," sad he prince, "as to admit to you the love I have for your sister, you must understand that I can never change my sentiment for her. All your threats do not frighten me, and you can make me the object of your vengeance without me paling."

"I will be able to strike you in such tender places that I will make you feel it," she told him.

"Oh, it's my princess that you mean!" exclaimed the prince. "But remember, Florinice, before attempting it, that I can cause to fall back on you anything you might do against a head so dear."

"Go on, go on," she said to him, in a scornful tone. "I don't fear you. The woes that you have made me suffer have taught me not to fear any others."

A conversation so angry could not fail to be overheard by Florinice's maidservants. Cephise, who was with them, having heard it like them, ran to inform Leonice of it.

The latter was in mortal chagrin at such sad news; it was what she feared most in all the world. She knew that the princess was capable of anything when she was offended. In that apprehension, she went out immediately, and, not wanting to expose herself to her sister's violence, she went to retire into a Temple of Vestals that was near the palace. Only Cephise went with her; the young princess's other maids ran to warn Florinice.

She was still with the prince; that suspended the anger of both; the prince was thunderstruck; Florinice did not know whether to be glad or annoyed, for if that took away the means the prince had of seeing her so often, it also prevented her from making her suffer all the woes she was preparing for her. The prince, however, carried away by his passion, left her to sort out her sentiments and ran to the Temple where his mistress was enclosed. He demanded to see her so insistently that the Grand Vestal, fearing to start a quarrel with the prince, who would probably soon be king, constrained the sad Leonice to come and talk to him in her presence

As soon as the prince saw her he cried: "What, my princess, you're abandoning me to the fury of your sister? Is that what your protestations of loving me as long as you live are worth? What do you think will become of me if I do not see you again? With what design are you retiring to his sacred place? Do you think that I cannot defend you against the anger of Florinice?"

"I know your amour and your courage," said Leonice, "but Prince, it would not be kind to me to make use of me against my sister, who is supported by the orders of your father, the king. I can see the fire that my unfortunate tenderness is about to light. It is up to me to apply the necessary remedy to it. It is me who ought to be sacrificed. Marry the proud Florinice in order to bring peace to your kingdom, which she would fill with trouble and confusion. Obey your father; forget me, if you can, and let me spend the rest of a life that will not be long in the service of the goddess. You will only have her for a rival; since I was not born for my dear prince, no mortal will ever touch my heart."

"No, my princess," said the desolate prince. "You do not love me any longer, since you are capable of giving me such advice. Do not expect that I can follow it. I will never adore anyone but you. The furious Florinice has power on her side, the king is in her party, but they will never be the masters of my heart or my hand. If you will not promise me to conserve yourself for me, and always to be my lovable Leonice, I cannot answer for the mastery of my wrath."

"O gods, who see my innocence," cried the sad princess, giving free rein to the tears that she had held back until then, "help me in such great misfortune!"

The Grand Vestal, who had listened until then, intervened in the conversation to beg to the prince to think of what he owed his father, the king, but it was futile; she was obliged to take Leonice away without having been able to obtain anything.

Meanwhile, the king had been informed of all that great disorder. He ordered that the prince be found and brought to him; he was found as he emerged from the Temple and was told that the king was asking for him. He went to find him immediately.

"Sire," he said, throwing himself at his feet, "when you commanded me to love Florinice, I had adored her sister for a long time; the dread of displeasing you caused me to hide my passion. Florinice, having perceived it, being proud of your authority, there are no threats that she has not made against the lovable Leonice, who, in order to avoid them and give you proof that she is not culpable of my disobedience, has gone to imprison herself in the Temple in order to spend the rest of her days there. But Sire, I cannot live without her; my amour is redoubled the moment when I find myself deprived of her. I have come to beg you, if you want to conserve my life, to withdraw her from a place so fatal to my repose and to defend her against the fury of her sister."

"I ought to punish you more severely for your disobedience than I am going to do," said the king, "but prince, you can still merit your pardon and see Leonice at liberty again."

"Oh, Sire, what is it necessary for me to do?" cried the prince, precipitately.

"Go find the princess, swear to her that you will no longer love her sister, that you are submissive to my orders, and be ready to give your hand tomorrow. I will guarantee the

Florinice will give her amity to her sister again, and that she will have nothing to fear from her."

"Oh, Sire!" cried he prince. "Once again, if the liberty of my princess is at that price, I understand that I shall not see her again for as long as I live. I shall never marry the detestable Florinice, and whatever might happen, I shall always love her adorable sister."

"Well, then," said the king, "I shall marry her in your stead; I shall disinherit you of my crown without your ever being able, in consequence of that, to see this Leonice, who is making you defy my orders with so much insolence. I give you until tomorrow to think about it; that is all the grace you'll get from me."

After that he dismissed the prince, who retired to his apartment in a despair that had no equal. He spent the night in frightful agitations, and as soon as he thought that Florinice was visible he went to see her.

"Madame," he said, "you see a prince whose life only depends on you. The king wants me to marry you, or he will do it himself; in order to keep the word that he gave you to put you on the throne, he will deprive me of it forever, assuring it to the children born to you and him. I consent to that gladly; I will see you in that place without chagrin, if you obtain from my father that he will only avenge himself partially and will return my princess to me. I will even consent not to marry her, provided that I know that she is happy and that I can see her sometimes. Is that too much to ask, Madame," he continued, "for a crown: a few moments in which I can tell Leonice that I have sacrificed my glory and my life for her?"

"O gods," said the princess, "how have I been able to suffer a speech so outrageous for so long? How do you think, Prince, given the tenderness that I have for you, that I will receive the offer you are making me of your crown? Did I not tell you yesterday that I do not want it without you? Does your beauty blind you to the point of thinking that I can render her to you—I, who wish at the price of my blood that you might never see her again, and that, forgetful of those pernicious charms, you might render me the smallest part of the care that you have for her? You want me to return her to you in order to make me see the scorn that you have for me in ceding me to your father? No, traitor, don't expect that, since I can gain nothing over your heart by all my tenderness, I will abandon myself to all my fury, and I will accept the king's hand, but it will be on the condition that I will always be my sister's mistress. Gods, what a pleasure it will be for me to make her share the woes that you will make me suffer, and to render your Leonice so unhappy that she will be constrained to renounce life!"

"Oh, cruel princess," said the prince, interrupting her. "You are driving me to the ultimate chagrin, but you'll answer to me for your sister's life; there is no extremity to which I will not go if she is in danger."

Having said that, he got up to leave, but the king, who came in at that moment, stopped him.

"Stay, Prince," he said to him, and tell this beautiful princess and me whether you are ready to render her the justice that is due to her."

"Sire," he said, "you know what I said yesterday, that I cannot live without Leonice. It is for you to give me death or life."

"Go," replied the king, angrily. "You have rendered yourself unworthy, by your obstinacy, of anyone taking care of it." Turning to the princess, he went on: "Madame, may I, in order to repair my son's blindness, offer you my hand and my crown, and promise you that your sister will only ever emerge from the Temple on your orders."

"I am confounded by Your Majesty's generosity," replied Florinice, "and submissive to anything that it pleases you to order me to do."

What a blow it had been for the unfortunate prince, when he heard the resolution of the vindictive Florinice. But it was not in his power to prevent it. It was necessary to suffer seeing her as his father's wife that very evening, the king not having wanted any preparation for that marriage.

The entire court was sorry about it; the humor of the princess was well known, and no one doubted that the king, who was already old, would allow himself to be governed by that malevolent woman. Most of all, they felt sorry for the prince, who did not merit such ill fortune.

He wanted to go to console himself with his dear Leonice, but the queen had given orders so absolute that he was refused that pleasure no matter what pleas he made.

The poor princess was inconsolable when she learned of her sister's marriage; she saw quite clearly that it was in order to have more power to torment them that she had decided to marry the king, and that she would never see the prince again. What lament did she not make regarding her unhappy fate to her dear Cephise? The maid tried to console her, but she could see so clearly that she was right that she could only weep with her.

Meanwhile, the new queen savored a pleasure mingled with chagrin; she had no sooner married the king than she understood that it would no longer be permissible for her to gaze at the prince. She repented of having put herself in eternal opposition to what she wanted most in all the world. Her vengeance fell back upon her with more violence than she had imagined, and whatever effort she made to find satisfaction in having rendered the objects if her hatred and her amour unhappy, she found herself even unhappier. She could not even prevent herself from fearing that the king, repenting of the injustice he had done to his son, would eventually permit him to marry Leonice in order to console him for having given him a stepmother.

She had no sooner been struck by that thought than she thought of remedying it while she was omnipotent over the mind of her husband. There was a prince named Ligamon who had been in love with Leonice for a long time, for whom the young princess had a mortal aversion because of the bad qualities she knew him to have, in addition to the fact that he was very ugly and ill made. She sent for him, and she told him that if he wanted to abduct her sister, and marry her, she would give him the means; that he need not fear the anger of the prince; that she would give him the authority to take her to the province where she was mistress, and where he would be absolute master.

Ligamon accepted offers that were so much in conformity with his sentiments; he did not have the delicacy to want to be loved; provided that he possessed Leonice, it did not matter to him how; and the queen, content to find him disposed to obey her, dismissed him, telling him to assemble secretly as many men as he could, and leave the rest to her.

In order to succeed in her design it was necessary to take the princess out of the Temple, from which it was not possible to abduct her. For that she went to see the king one day and, throwing herself at his feet, she asked him for mercy for her sister, and that he suffer that she could be with her, guaranteeing that she would prevent her from having any communication with the prince. The king, who could not refuse her anything, and who had conceived a powerful tenderness for her since his marriage, consented to that.

The queen no sooner had that permission than she sought out the prince urgently, to whom she had not been able to speak since she had become his stepmother, and she told him that, repenting of the woes that she had caused him, she wanted to return Leonice to him; that she had received the permission of the king, her husband; and that she was going to take her out of the Temple.

The prince did not know whether he ought to believe it, and how such a great change had come about. She perceived his irresolution, and tried to persuade him of her sincerity. "I can see," she said, "that you don't believe me, but Prince, be witness to it; give me your hand and come with me to a place where everything that can be dear to you is contained."

"Oh, Madame," said the prince, receiving the hand that she offered to him, "how thankful I will be to you if you are not deceiving me. My life is too little for what you are doing for me today."

After that they went to the Temple and the queen, showing the king's orders to the Grand Vestal, ordered her to bring out her sister. She replied that she was ready to obey the king if the princess wanted to do it, but, the Temple being a place of sanctuary for anyone who had chosen to put herself under the protection of the goddess, she could not force her to quit the refuge she had chosen.

The queen listened to that speech impatiently, and turned to the princess. "Well, Leonice," she said, "do you want to remain here for the rest of your life? Do you not want to obey the orders of the king, who has commanded me to take you to the palace? Do you hate me enough to prefer a prison to being with me? Speak, since your consent is necessary."

"Oh, Madame," said the prince, seeing that she was still uncertain as to what she ought to do, "what is delaying you in emerging you from a place so contrary to the repose of the prince who adores you? The queen, touched by the woes that I am suffering from your absence, has wanted to soften the king, my father. Will you be more inexorable than him?"

"I do not doubt the generosity of the queen," said Leonice, finally, "but prince, although I am disposed to obey her, I cannot resolve without difficulty to quit this sacred place."

After those few words, she took her leave of the Grand Vestal and all her amiable companions, but it was not without shedding tears; and she went to the palace with the queen, who presented her to the king. He received her rather coldly, but the entire court hastened to express the joy they felt at her return. The queen heaped her with caresses. When she was in her apartment she swore to her that she had forgotten the past, that she would try to make the king consent to her marriage with the prince; that in the meantime, they could see one another with all liberty, provided that it was not in his presence; that she wanted to repair with so much service the evil that she had done to them, so that they would be constrained to give her their amity again.

The prince did not know how to thank her; he believed that everything she said was sincere, but the young princess could not be convinced; she was more retained in her joy. When the queen had conducted her to a magnificent apartment she had prepared for her, she told the prince, who was with her, about the suspicion she had of Florinice's caresses. The prince was unable to approve of that suspicion; he was in inconceivable transports of pleasure at seeing his dear Leonice again.

Everything that the most tender amour can inspire was in those two hearts, but the princess only responded to it with tears. Whatever the prince could say to overcome her apprehensions, he could not persuade her that the queen did not have some hidden design in what she was doing, and that she was selling the pleasure she was giving them very dear. And she was not mistaken.

The malevolent woman had no sooner retired to her cabinet than she sent for Ligamon to tell him that he should be ready the following night. Her rage could not wait any longer for satisfaction; the sight of the prince's love for that innocent victim of her fury had redoubled her amour and her jealousy; she could not bear the moments that they were spending together and although, for political reasons, she had resolved to let a few days pass, she changed her plan. She organized everything with the minister of her hatred so that it could not fail, and gave orders for him to be sustained in all the places where he would pass.

After that he took his leave of her and went to post his men, all ready to execute their design as soon as everyone in the palace had retired.

The queen had deliberately given her sister an apartment distant from her own, which overlooked the gardens, in order that she could be abducted without any noise via a door to the park that she had kept open. Everything had been so well prepared that the queen appeared full of joy all evening; she said a thousand tender things to her sister, and, the time for retirement having come she embraced her in order to wish her goodnight.

The prince, who could not quit her, offered to give her his hand, but she begged him to let her go for fear that the king might perceive his urgent cares. He therefore let her go, reluctantly, but, unable to resolve to go to bed without having found a means to see her without witnesses, he thought that when she was alone in her apartment he would be able to enter without her thinking it bad. With that design he promptly went into the gardens and, hiding in an arbor that was under her windows, he waited impatiently until there was no longer anyone but Cephise with the princess.

After having placed his men, Ligamon came almost to the same place as the prince in order to execute his pernicious design, and, seeing very little light in the palace, and knowing that there was nothing to fear from Leonice's guards, he thought that it was time. He therefore gave is men a sign to advance; at the same signal, the princess's doors were opened. Ligamon entered with a party of his men before the prince had perceived him, because the night was so dark, and it was only the screams of the princess and Cephise that drew him out of his reverie. He ran to that dear voice as Ligamon was trying to force her to go with him.

At that sight he became like a furious lion and, drawing his sword he cried: "Stop, wretch, if you do not want to pay with your life for your insolence,"

Ligamon turned his head and went pale with fear, believing that he had been discovered, but, seeing that the prince was alone, he did not deign to respond to him and, making a sign to his men to prevent the prince from approaching, he tried to take the princess; but the prince, having run through the man who had advanced first, laid him dead on the ground, leapt lightly over his body, shouted to the perfidious individual to defend himself, and struck him on the arm with which he was holding Leonice, forcing him to let her go.

Meanwhile, the screams of the princess's maids woke everyone in the palace; guards who were not in the confidence of the plot ran to see what was happening and arranged themselves alongside their prince as he was about to be overwhelmed by the large number of men who were with Ligamon. The latter tried to run away as soon as he saw them coming, but the prince struck him so furiously that he fell dead on the floor.

During all the disorder the poor princess was in a pitiful state; she implored Heaven to aid her dear prince, whom she saw in danger of being killed at any moment. Her joy was great when she saw the guards arrive and Ligamon fall, drowning in his blood. As soon as his men saw that he was dead they fled with so much haste that, in the confusion, no one ran after them until they no longer had anything to fear.

The queen, however, was transported by dolor at knowing that her plot had failed and that her plan had only served to render her sister to her lover. That thought put her in despair, but, not wanting anyone to know her evil intentions, she got up and went into Leonice's apartment with all her guards in order to give her help that she knew to be unnecessary. She found the princess half-dead with fear, her room filled with blood and dead bodies, with the prince, on his knees before her, holding one of her beautiful hands, trying to help her recover from her fear.

She nearly died of rage, but, constraining herself, she was trying to tell her sister how sorry she was about the accident when the prince, interrupting her, made her aware that he knew only too well that it as the work of her hands, and that henceforth, he would serve as the princess's guard, in order to protect her from her evil designs. The princess denied it vehemently, and, having said to the princess that she ought not to remain in a place so full of horror, she ordered her to go with her.

Daylight appeared in all that confusion, and the prince went to complain to the king about the insult that had been offered to the princess, and to tell him that the queen was complicit in it. The king did not listen to him with regard to the queen, but he promised to give Leonice such good guards that she would no longer be exposed to such misfortune.

All that did not reassure the prince; he went to find the princess and swore to her that he would not quit her again.

His precautions were futile; the queen, seeing that all her power could not separate those two hearts, addressed herself to a fay whom she knew to be an enemy of the royal family because of a few displeasures she had received therefrom. She told her that she had come to implore her aid against the prince, her son-in-law, and her perfidious sister, and that in avenging her she could satisfy her own hatred. Delighted to find that opportunity, the fay told the queen that provided that she brought the princess into the palace gardens, she need not worry about the rest.

The queen, without returning fully content, hoped to be rid of her rival forever. For that design, she went for a walk in the gardens in the evening with scant company, and took her sister with her. The prince, who no longer quit her, went with them in spite of the queen, to whom he was constrained to give his hand. The princess was walking behind them, leaning on Cephise's arm, when she felt herself being lifted into the air without being able to see those who were lifting her. She uttered a scream so frightful that it made the prince stop.

He dropped the queen's hand in order to run to help the princess, but he only found Cephise. He could still hear her, and, following her voice, he drew away from the palace in a short time, but, no matter what efforts he made to arrive at the place where he heard the voice, he could not reach it; it faded away in the air and he collapsed as if dead, of lassitude and despair.

Meanwhile, the fay transported the poor princess to an old castle built on the tip of a rock so steep that no mortal had ever been able to climb it, and, having set a dragon with three fiery tongues to guard her, she returned to the desolate prince. Taking on the form of an old woman she said: "What are you doing, unfortunate Prince? You're reposing while someone has abducted your princess?"

"Alas," said the prince, making an effort to speak, "I followed her for as long as I could hear her voice, but the cruel gods did not wish me to hear it any longer, for fear that I would snatch her from their hands."

"Come, she said, touching him with her wand. "I'll take you to the place where she is."

He followed her with a lightness similar to that of a bird. They soon arrived at the foot of the rock, and the fay showed him the castle. "That's the place where your princess is; I'll enable you to see her so that you'll have no doubt of it. Get her out of such a frightful place if you can.

So saying, she left the prince overwhelmed by dolor, and, entering the castle, she took Leonice by the hand and led her to the tip of the rock. "See that what I say is true," she said to him, showing him the princess's hand. "Take her out of my power if you can." And without giving either of them the time to speak, she took her back into that horrible prison.

The prince remained in a cruel consternation when he saw his dear Leonice go back inside. The impossibility of getting her out of such a frightful place drove him to despair. He tried vainly to climb the rock, but always fell back as soon as he had taken a step. He wanted to return to the palace in quest of men to help him carve a path in the rock, but, fearing that he might no longer find the princess there, he could not resolve to leave.

He spent the night in that irresolution, lamenting without any hope that the day would render him more fortunate.

For her part, the queen was very glad to be rid of her sister, but she was not happy at not seeing the prince again, and the king was anxious for his son. He sent men everywhere to look for him, but it was in vain; they could not find him, no matter what trouble they took. That redoubled his chagrin; he held it against the queen, and spoke to her bitterly. He repented, but too late, of the woes that he had caused his son. He no longer had anything but aversion for his wife. That did not worry her much; by virtue of her intrigues, part of the kingdom was hers, and the king was no longer anything but a pictorial king. The absence of the prince was more sensible to her than the coldness of her husband.

She went to find the fay in order to ask her where he was and what she had done with her sister. The fay replied that she would give her the pleasure of seeing both of them in the pitiful state to which her hatred had reduced them. The queen begged her to do so urgently, and in a moment the fay transported her to the castle where the unfortunate Leonice was. She found her chained to the foot of a column from which she could see the prince without being seen. A frightful dragon was beside her, which never slept.

The barbaric queen was rapturous with joy at seeing her in that sad state; she heaped her with reproaches instead of consoling her; to which the princess did not deign to reply; nor did she take her eyes off the prince, whom she could see making efforts to climb the rock. The queen, turning her eyes to follow the direction in which her sister was gazing, saw that object of her hatred and her amour, at the moment when, having circled the rock many times, he had finally found a path less steep; he began to climb it, with a great deal of difficulty. She uttered a scream, in the fear that he might liberate her rival, but the fay told her that she had nothing to fear, that the dragon would prevent him from doing so, even if he reached her.

Meanwhile, the prince was still climbing the winding path. The hope of seeing the princess gave him strength. He perceived a greyhound bitch attached to a fragment of the stone that composed the mountain, which seemed to be choking. That awoke his pity; he approached the animal and, taking the chain in a powerful grip, he broke it, with difficulty. What was his surprise to see the greyhound become a woman as soon as she was free. He took a step back, but the beautiful person took him by the hand.

"Unfortunate Prince," she said, "have no fear of the enchantment that you have just broken. I am of the race of fays, and I have several gifts that I will give you, but my power is limited, and the envious fay that is holding your princess prisoner attached me to his rock in his hideous form some years ago to punish me for having loved several princes who scorned her. I awaited your coming impatiently; I will serve you with all my power, out of gratitude, and to avenge myself on her." She showed him an opening carved into the rock. "Go into this cavern, put on the arms you find there, and have no fear of the fury of the dragon; you will vanquish it easily. I shall wait for you on the edge of this stream, which you can see running among these pebbles."

Having said that, she quit him, and the prince picked up the fatal arms, in order to continue his route all the way to the gates of the castle. The fay, seeing him climbing, detached the dragon from beside the princess and set it to guard the entrance where the prince was.

Without being frightened by such a horrible monster, he advanced in order to strike it with the lance he was holding, but the monster, uttering a horrible hiss, launched itself into the air in order to cover him with its body. On seeing that, the prince took few steps back and, choosing his moment when the monster extended its belly, he struck it with his sword so adroitly that it fell dead at his feet.

The fay had no sooner seen it laid low than she seized the princess, in spite of her screams, and lifted her into the air for a second time, as she had done the first.

Meanwhile, the prince, victorious over the dragon, entered the room precipitately in order to deliver his princess. O gods, what was his despair when he only found Florinice! The bloody sword fell from his hands, and he was as if insensible for a time. The presence of the malevolent woman reanimated him, however, and he ran straight toward her.

"What have you done with my princess?" he said to her, in a menacing fashion. "It's necessary for you to return her to me, for fear that I will punish you for all your crimes."

"She is no longer in my power," said the queen, without seeming astonished by the prince's threats. "As soon as she saw you victorious over the dragon, the fay Envious took her away from this place, of which she saw that you were about to be the master by virtue of your prodigious valor. Gods, how I trembled for you when I saw you exposed to all the fury of that horrible monster. I love you with even more violence than your Leonice. I watched her attentively during your combat with the dragon; nothing appeared in her but the joy that hope gives, without the fear of seeing you succumb causing her to pale for a single instant. Will you never know your error? You believe that you are loved by her, but you are not; it is in my heart that you will find the inflamed tenderness that would be worthy of yours."

The prince would not have suffered such an irritating speech for so long if the dolor that had gripped him on learning that the princess was not liberated had not made it impossible for him to respond to the queen. He was more unhappy than he had ever been, Leonice had been snatched away from him at the moment when he believed her delivered from all her misfortunes, without him knowing which way to turn in order to rescue her.

In that deplorable state, he was only thinking about what to do, and without paying any heed to what Florinice was saying, he was occupied in seeking a means of rediscovering his princess. Eventually, he remembered that the fay Levrette[8] had told him that she would wait for him by the edge of the stream; he thought that she might help him, as she had already done.

With that thought, without looking at the queen, he went out the castle with incredible rapidity and went down the mountain with the same urgency, without pausing for the cries that Florinice uttered on seeing him draw away.

She wanted to follow him, in spite of his scorn, and, running precipitately, she found a fissure in the cavern where the prince had found his marvelous arms against enchantment, and fell into it, without anyone ever knowing what had become of

---

[8] Because Levrette is used as a proper name here I have retained it rather than translating it into "greyhound bitch" as I have when it is used as a trivial noun.

her thereafter. Heaven had determined that the death of such a wicked woman should be unknown to humans, and that, deprived of a sepulcher, she only had the belly of the ferocious beasts of which that lair was full for a place of rest.

The prince, continuing his path with so much promptitude, soon arrived at the stream. He found Levrette there, waiting for him. "Well, generous prince," she said to him, "you are victorious over the monster."

"How does my victory serve me, alas," he replied, "if I have not delivered my princess and not know where to look for her?"

"We will find her," replied the compassionate fay. Having said that, she drew away from the prince, told him to wait for her, and, coming back a moment later, presented him with a horse that she was holding by the bridle. She told him to mount up, and that if he always to keep to the narrow path that she showed him, which ran alongside the stream, without taking any other, it would lead him directly to a subterranean cavern where the princess was. The entrance to it was guarded by several monsters, half-human and half-serpent, which would oppose his passage, but he need have no fear; he only had to present his shield to them, without making use of his sword or his lance, in order to vanquish them. After having vanquished them, he would find a furious lion, which was the princess's last guard; he must take care in approaching her to show her the shield, in order that it would no longer be in the power of the evil fay to take her away as she had done before.

The prince thanked Levrette briefly, leapt lightly on to the horse and, running down the path without pausing for an instant, he did not take long to arrive at the fatal entrance. He found it guarded as the fay had said. The monsters had no sooner seen him than they all tried to launch themselves upon him at the same time, but when the prince presented the buckler to their eyes, they remained motionless, and, losing their serpentine eyes, they became again what they had been before. They threw themselves at the feet of the prince, swearing to him that they would spend their lives thanking him for having delivered them from the enchantment in which the fay Envious had held them; that he only had to command them and they would do whatever he wished.

"I only ask," said the prince, "that you help me to liberate an unfortunate princess that your accursed fay is holding prisoner in this cavern."

As he said that, he went in first. He saw her at the back of the frightful lair, attached to the vault by a thick chain that held her by the midriff. A monstrous lion was lying at her feet, with its tail wound around her.

What a sight for the prince! Animated by the desire to save her from such a wretched fate, he uttered a cry that caused the furious lion to turn its head. It got to its feet and made ready to defend its prey with all its might, but the prince, without being astonished, approached it, and before the slaves that had followed him had reached his side he plunged his lance into the maw of the lion of the lion as it opened its mouth in order to hurl itself upon him.

Without losing any time, he struck it in the side with his sword, making a large wound. In spite of all that, the furious animal was no less strong; it was about to pounce on him and kill him with its claws when the men the prince had freed came to their benefactor's aid and belabored the monster with so many blows that it fell at the feet of the princess.

The prince no sooner saw that enemy defeated than he ran to her and presented the marvelous shield to her. The chains broke and the frightful place was changed into a magnificent palace. A large number of beautiful women emerged from several chambers, who came to rejoice with the princess for her deliverance and theirs. The men who were following the prince uttered cries of joy at the sight of those ladies; they threw themselves at their feet, expressing their joy at having found them again.

The prince, however, without perceiving all the surprising things that were happening in the place, was at the knees of his princess, where he was expressing to his dear Leonice everything that the most violent amour can make felt.

"So I see you again, my adorable princess," he said to her, "and the cruel gods must be weary of my suffering."

"Alas, my dear prince," Leonice replied to him, "I am so unfortunate that I do not know whether I shall enjoy the pleasure of seeing you again for long, or whether the implacable Florinice will find new torments for us."

"No," said Levrette, who appeared at that moment. "Your woes are ended, as well as mine. The queen has been punished for her crimes, the fay Envious no longer has any power over me, and you are the absolute mistress of his palace, which your generous lover has just returned to me by his valor. I only receive it in order to see you both happy here, without anything being able to trouble your happiness henceforth.

The princess saw all these surprising things happening so rapidly that she did not know how to respond, but the prince, who already knew the amiable fay and had already experienced her generosity, thanked her with a genuine gratitude for his dear Leonice and for himself. Until then he had not noticed the change that had made the cavern into a palace, nor all beautiful women that were surrounding him; he had only seen his princess. However, all the ladies and their cavaliers hastened to render their respects to their princess, for Levrette was the sovereign of that palace and the considerable lands that surrounded it.

Leonice could not get over her astonishment; she wanted to ask a thousand questions of her lover at once, in order to clarify the adventure, but the fay princess, taking her hand, told her that it was not time to tell her, that she needed to repose, and that she would satisfy her curiosity the next day.

As she said that, she took her to a chamber where everything was glittering with gold and precious stones; shortly thereafter a very proper supper was served. As soon as they had left the table the fay left her at liberty to converse with her dear prince. How tender their conversation was! They would have spent all night in it if Leonice, fearing to offend decency by suffering her lover so late, had not dismissed him.

The next day, the fay princess came to ask how she had spent the night, and, as she embraced her, said: "My dear princess, the obligation that I have to the prince is so great that I do not know by what benefit to recognize it, except to render him master of everything that he has returned to me."

"Madame," said Leonice, "the prince that you say has been of service to you appears to me to be so grateful for those he has received from you that I believe it is for him to render you eternal thanks, but Madame," she continued, "you promised to tell me what will make your acquaintance, and explain the astonishing changes that I have seen since yesterday."

"It is only just that I keep my word," said the fay princess. Seeing the prince enter, to whom Leonice made a sign to sit down next to her, she added: "And I am not sorry that my benefactor will be a witness to it. I am the daughter of a king who, of all the great Estates he possessed, was only able to keep this caste and the surrounding lands, by virtue of adventures that it would take too long to tell you. He had married a princess of the fay race, who had many gifts to share; she gave them all to me at the moment of my birth, knowing that she would die in giving birth to me, which happened.

"I also lost my father when I was very young, and remained mistress of this petty sovereignty. My court was elegant and full of all that was most beautiful in both sexes; the pleasures that followed us everywhere were nothing but fêtes and tourneys given to me every day by neighboring princes. Envious was my neighbor; her court was as deserted as mine as full. Jealous of my happiness, she could not suffer it; she sought means to render me unfortunate.

"One day, as we were all dressing for a magnificent ball, and I was washing my hands, I had forgotten to replace on my finger a ring that my mother had given me, which had he virtue of impeding enchantments. The fay Envious, who was in my chamber, perceived the lapse of memory, and, wanting to take advantage of it, she followed us to the assembly. Everyone danced for a long time without anyone asking her; outraged by that petty scorn, she got up in a fury and struck the floor three times with her ring. 'Accursed race,' she said, in a frightful tone, 'know the power of the one you scorn.'

"At the same time, the women became immobile, the men became half-serpent, without consciousness of what they had been a moment before, and my palace became a frightful lair. Approaching me, she took me by the hair in spite of my screams and dragged me to the rock where you were a prisoner, where she gave me the form of a greyhound bitch, attached me to the stone with a strong chain and left me there with a mocking smile. 'Serve as an example,' she said to me, 'to those who, not knowing their strength, are scornful of those who might destroy them. Remain in this unfortunate state until a prince more unfortunate than you comes in search of his princess.'

"She quit me after those words and left me overwhelmed by despair. I spent years waiting for your coming, and when I was no longer thinking of emerging from my misfortune, because of the time I had been suffering therefrom, I saw you arrive, Prince, and, touched by my unhappiness, you broke my chains. You saw my transformation with astonishment; you know the rest of what happened to you: how, by means to your prodigious valor, you rendered liberty to your lovely princess and all my unfortunate subjects.

"What rage for the fay Envious no longer to be able to harm us, and what a pleasure for me to be able to give the beautiful Leonice the gifts that my mother left me in dying: beauty and youth will only quit you in the tomb; Pleasures will follow you in a crowd wherever your feet take you; and finally, all the places illuminated by your beautiful eyes will become filled with all that can satisfy magnificence and ambition, without anyone ever being able to trouble the pleasure that amour is preparing for both of you.

"For you, Prince, the only chagrin that you will suffer in your life, I am about to give you: the King, your father, weighed down by old age and the chagrin of your loss, full of remorse at having caused your woes by marrying Florinice, died two days ago. Your kingdom has need of your presence;

depart with your amiable princess to go and occupy a throne worthy of you and her. I have prepared an equipage for you that will second your impatience."

As she finished those words she stood up and embraced both of them tenderly. She conducted them, without wanting to listen to their thanks, to a carriage made of gold and precious stones drawn by flying dragons, and, having bid them a final adieu, left them to go to their kingdom, where they soon arrived, and where they ended their lives in all the pleasures that mutual amour can cause, when it is accompanied by goodness and beauty.

PRINCE CURIOUS

In the days when the fays were in great veneration, a princess reigned among them who was named Prodigal because of the immense benefits that she lavished on her subjects. She was beautiful, young, intelligent and rich, and sought after by all the neighboring princes, which rendered her court the most elegant in all Asia; but one of its greatest ornaments was Princess Modest. Prodigal loved her tenderly; she always had her with her, she was at all her pleasures, she could not have any where she was not; which obliged all of Prodigal's lovers to make every effort to be her friend. It was only elegant fêtes to which Prodigal appeared indifferent.

One day, when Prince Ambitious held a tourney, the entire court was placed on platforms that had been set up in the grand square of the palace; nothing was more magnificent than all that appeared there; even the harness of the horses was decked with gold, precious stones and diamonds, and the princes had spared no effort in showing off their wealth.

Scarcely had a few lances been broken, however, than cries that were heard stopped the combatants and caused the eyes of the entire court to turn toward the barriers of the camp to discover the cause. They saw that it was a knight of admirable stature, whose armor was golden. What could be seen of his coat was blue embroidered with pearls; his helmet was the same metal as his armor, and in the midst of a host of white plumes, the portrait of Princess Modest could be seen. The same painting was on his shield, surrounded by diamonds of prodigious size. The horse on which the handsome knight was mounted was as white as snow, and all of its harness was gold.

Nothing could equal the curiosity that the Princess and the entire court had to know who the handsome stranger was. Modest could not be sufficiently astonished by seeing her portrait on his arms. Prodigal ordered the judge of the camp to ask his name and what he wanted, to which he replied that his name was Prince Curious, and that he had come to beg the princess to allow him to compete against all the combatants.

The judges came to render an account of their commissions to Prodigal, who was pleased to permit Prince Curious to compete, in order to sustain her friend's charms. The combat recommenced at the first signal; all the princes showed their valor and their skill, but in the end, Prince Ambitious having remained the sole victor, he prepared to combat the handsome knight. Everyone was charmed by the pride with which he entered the lists, and no one doubted that he would vanquish the vanquisher of the others. They were not mistaken, for after having done nothing in the first career, in the second, Curious dealt him a blow of the lance beneath the helmet so furious that he sent him to fall thirty paces away. His squires ran to him in order to lift him up, and carried him away full of rage and confusion.

Curious remained at the end of the career or a long time, to see whether anyone wanted to dispute the victory with him, but it was futile. On seeing that, the camp judges descended from their platforms and came to collect the handsome knight in order to conduct him as the victor to the princess, who presented him with a diamond bracelet, which was the prize of the tourney. He accepted it, after having made a profound reverence to her, and having turned to Modest, he put one knee on the ground. "Since the princess had permitted me to combat for you, Madame," he said to her, "she will find it good that I present the prize of my victory to you." So saying, he gave her the diamond bracelet.

Modest blushed and looked at Prodigal, as if to ask her what she ought to do. The princess understood her embarrassment and told her to accept it, which she did, in a rather cold manner.

After that, the entire court returned to the palace, where there was no talk of anything but the good looks of Prince Curious and the gallant manner in which he had made his present. All the princes defeated by Ambitious were delighted to see themselves avenged, and not by their rivals. Those praises would not have ceased if he had not been seen entering the hall, with an attitude so noble that everyone was convinced that he was incomparable in whatever manner one looked at him.

The princess received him with an extraordinary goodwill, and, having taken him by the hand, presented him to Modest. "Receive this knight, I implore you," she said, "as the only one worthy to serve you."

Curious only responded with a profound reverence, and, kneeling down before Modest, he said: "Will you be cruel enough, Madame, to refuse the favor that the Princess asks of you on my behalf with so much generosity, and will it not be permissible for me to name myself your knight?"

"The princess is so absolute over my will," said Modest, without looking at Curious, "that as soon as she speaks, I am always ready to obey." After that, she presented him with her hand to lift him up.

The rest of the day was spent in talking about those who had combated well or poorly; when she retired, the princess said that she wanted to go hunting the following days, and gave an order that everyone received with pleasure.

At daybreak, all the equipages were ready; the sound of horns woke Modest and she ordered her maids to bring her a hunting costume that she had had made not long before. They were very astonished that it was no longer to be found, and to see in its place one of flame-colored velvet, all of the buttons of which were diamond. Surprised, they ran to Princess Modest's bedroom; she was no less surprised than they were on being shown that magnificent attire. She was uncertain for some time as to what she ought to do, but, the time of departure approaching rapidly, she got dressed and appeared to the eyes of the princess with an appearance so brilliant that everyone as dazzled.

Prodigal praised her abundantly, and Modest, having drawn nearer to her, told her about her adventure, which neither one of them could understand. Their surprise was augmented considerably when the princess, having descended from her room to mount her horse, found Prince Curious at the foot of the staircase, clad in a similar outfit. They stepped back a few paces, and, having turned to Modest, she said to her: "There's enchantment in this adventure." At the same time, Prince Ambitious having advanced to give his hand to her, and Curious having rendered the same service to Modest, they mounted up.

The weather was fine, and it seemed that the game they chased only defended itself in order to give pleasure to the ladies. The day passed as agreeably as possible, and they only returned to the palace when night obliged them to do so. That was not without having discussed the conformity of the attire of Modest and Prince Curious.

The Princess, impatient to know the truth of that adventure, sent everyone else away and, remaining alone in her cabinet with Modest and Curious, after inviting them to sit down and addressing herself to Prince Curious, she said: "I confess that since your arrival in the court I have seen things do surprising that I can't help asking you who you are, how you came to have the portrait of my friend, by what enchantment you both found yourselves dressed in the same manner, and what demon caused that garment to be found in her wardrobe instead of the other. Speak, I implore you; don't hide anything from me.

"Since you order me to, Madame," said the prince, "I will tell you that I am the son of the King of Phrygia, and that, when my mother was pregnant with me, she was out walking one day in the company of a young woman she loved tenderly, in a wood that was at the end of the palace gardens. They had not gone very far when they were approached by a tall woman with a majestic air, who greeted her and told her that she was pregnant with a son who would obtain the adoration of peoples, but whom amour would render very unhappy, although she wanted to ensure that he would attain his goal in the end, and that she was the sovereign of the fays of Lycia. After that

117

she disappeared, and left my mother so surprised that it was some time before she could return to the palace.

"Some time later than that, she gave birth to me, and did not forget to beg the fay in her heart to remember her promises. I was brought up carefully, and the desire I had to know all things caused me to be named Curious. I spent the first years of the life like all princes of my age; the King and the Queen loved me passionately; my dominant passion was hunting all the most ferocious beasts.

"One day when I went in search of a furious wild boar that was desolating our lands, I lost my way in a forest and could not find it again; I marched hopelessly all day, and night fell without my having been able to find any of my retinue. I resolved to spend it at the foot of a tree; I descended from my horse in order to carry out my design when my eyes were struck by a surprising light, and the same fay, of whom I had heard mention many a time, approached me and said: 'I have come to your aid, Prince Curious; follow me without fear.'

"As she finished speaking she marched directly toward a magnificent palace, which I saw ahead of us. We arrived here very shortly, and I cannot describe to you everything that I saw in that enchanted abode. It is very little to tell you that the walls were gold and that my eyes could not sustain the glare of the precious stones that were glittering on every side.

"The fay conducted me to an apartment of the same beauty, and we were served a supper there in which there was everything of the most exotic. When we left the table she retired, and told me to repose all night, as I had need of it. I went to bed, and the following day I was woken up by a music so charming that only Apollo and the Muses could have made it. When I got up I found a very elegant costume on my dressing-table, and I was dressed without being able to see who as serving me.

"Scarcely was I in a state to appear than the fay came in to my bedroom. I tried to thank her for so many favors, but she told me that she had taken me under her protection since birth, that I could count on her provided that I was not ingrate, and that she would never abandon me. I assured her that my gratitude would be eternal.

"After that, she took me into the gardens, the beauty of which responded to the magnificence of the house. Of all that I saw, nothing appeared to me to be more surprising than a large avenue of orange trees, all the trunks of which had human faces. I could not help asking her what those faces were; she told me that they were all lovers that she had had, that she had turned them into trees to punish them for not having been able to please her, and that their destiny condemned them to remain in that enchantment until she found a man fortunate enough to make her love him.

"I felt very sorry for those unfortunates but I dared not say so to the fay for fear of irritating her. At the end of the avenue we went into a pavilion. She invited me to sit down on a bed, and, after having closed the door on us, she said to me: 'Prince Curious, it is time that you commenced your adventures. I shall enable you to see all the beauties of the earth; if will be up to you to make a good choice.'

"At the same time she circled the room twice with a wand she was holding, pronouncing a few words that I did not hear. Immediately, I saw the most beautiful women in the world appear in mirrors that served to decorate the walls of the chambers. I saw you, Madame, and although none of them appeared to me to be as beautiful as you, I confess that I was charmed by Princess Modest, who was with you.

"The fay did not hear that without chagrin, and she said that she would do what she could to turn me away from sacrificing my life; she could not change my destiny, she was constrained to render to my urgent pleas, but that was not without predicting to me that I could never be loved without making myself hated. I confess to you, Madame, that I nearly died of dolor at such a baneful oracle; the fay was touched by pity in consequence, and promised me her protection.

"Afterwards, we emerged from that fatal place, and as we passed along the avenue of orange trees again, all the trees inclined far enough to touch the ground and covered the path with flowers and fruits. We arrived in a great hall in the palace, where I found the armor with which I was covered on the day of the tourney; but O gods, what thanks I gave her when she presented me with the buckler and I saw the portrait of my adorable princess thereon!

"'Prince,' she said to me, 'go where your amour takes you, to the woes you are going to suffer in Modest's service; depart, since I see that nothing can change your design; you will find all your men waiting for you at the gate of the castle, and as I cannot follow you, here is a horn, of which I make you a present. When you want something of me, put it to your mouth and ask for whatever you need.'

"I threw myself at her knees to thank her for her generosity, and, having taken the marvelous horn, I mounted my horse. I will not tell you about the joy of my men on finding me; I am in too great a hurry to tell you that I took the road to Lycia, and that, having made all the diligence that my impatience to see my beautiful princess demanded, I finally arrived on the eve of the tourney.

"You know everything that has happened to me since that moment, and it only remains for me to tell you that on the day of the hunt, having wished to have a costume similar to Modest's, I was quite astonished to find on my table the attire that you have seen, and which has given you so much curiosity, but which will serve no purpose if I cannot have any effect upon the heart of my princess."

The Prince finished his discourse thus, and Prodigal spoke, saying: "I suspected strongly that there was something extraordinary in what you have done since you have been in my court, but although the fay has predicted disaster, I cannot believe that it is possible for Modest to see you poorly."

After that, Prodigal got up and went to give an audience to the ambassadors of the King of Syria.

From that day on, Prince Curious did not waste a moment in making known to the princess the violent amour that he had for her; but he experienced only too well what the fay had predicted; she received all the services he rendered her with civility, but her heart had no part in it. The entire court was astonished by that, as well as Prodigal, who had all the esteem for him that he merited, and often spoke about him to her friend.

One day when they were both walking in a wood of green oaks that was near the palace, after having walked for a long time she went to sit down on the bank of a steam that passed through the wood. The princess having made a sign to her maidservants to retire, she said: "Let's stop here, my dear Modest," she said, "And savor the fresh air on the edge of this spring."

They listened to the murmur of the water and the song of the birds for a while, but then the princess said: "In truth, I can't go on any longer without asking you whether your heart isn't touched by gratitude for poor Curious."

"I admit to you Madame," said Modest, "that like everyone else, I can see the Prince's good qualities, and that I'm obliged to him for the services he renders me, but I feel nothing more. My heart still conserves its indifference; and I would tell you more, Madame," she continued, "if I did not fear seeming ridiculous. I am annoyed that everybody finds too much merit in him and has no inclination to excuse me for the injustice that I am rendering him."

"Is it possible," said the princess, "that you can have such sentiments? Where will you find a prince more perfect, who loves you with more passion? In truth, there is caprice in your procedure."

"I merit everything you say to me, Madame," said Modest, "but it is not in my power to have other sentiments for him."

How much you have to lament, poor Prince, responded a thousand birds that were in the branches of the trees covering the heads of the princesses, *if you can only be paid in ingratitude for your amour; but Modest, a time will come when you pass from the strongest hatred to the most sensible tenderness for the unfortunate prince.*

No astonishment ever equaled that of the princesses. "What!" cried Modest. "I even hear animals talking about the object of my indifference, and I cannot have one moment without him giving me some proof of an amour that is odious to me! Oh, I'm beginning to feel hatred, and I can't guarantee that I won't banish him from my presence if he doesn't leave me in peace!"

"Be careful," said the princess, laughing at her friend's anger, "of making the oracle of the fay of the birds come true."

"No, Madame," Modest interjected. "I have no fear of hating him, and I'm sure that I shall never love him."

Don't answer for that, Modest, said a voice from the depths of the stream. *You cannot flee your destiny.*

"Oh, that's too much!" cried Modest, angrily. "Let's get out of a place, Madame, where such frightful things are predicted for me."

Prodigal got up in order to oblige her, and as they went back into the flower garden that found Prince Ambitious and Prince Curious there, who were coming to look for them. Ambitious gave his hand to Prodigal; Curious having approached Modest in order to render her the same service, she received it, and, having drawn a few paces away from the princess, she said:

"Prince, all of nature is rising against me in your favor. I even know that I am wrong not to recognize your amour; you merit an entire heart; but with all that knowledge I can do nothing for you, and if my repose is dear to you and it is true that you are only in this court for me, withdraw and never see me again. I know that I will be criticized for such an ungrateful procedure, but it is necessary that I have entire obligation from you and that you ask the princess for leave to go without speaking to me again."

In saying that, she quit the prince's hand. No astonishment ever equaled that of Curious; he took a long time to make his resolution, but in the end it was necessary to obey. Prodigal did what she could to change his mind, but it was futile. He was not allowed to see Modest to take his leave of her; he nearly died at that new cruelty, and he went back to his apartment in a mortal chagrin. He gave orders to have his equipage ready to depart the following day.

After that he went into his cabinet and picked up his horn. "Powerful fay," he said, putting it to his mouth, "Don't abandon me in the despair that I'm in; enable me to be invisible, in order that I have the means to see my princess without displeasing her."

He had not finished speaking when he heard something fall to the ground. Having bent down to pick it up, he found a ring wrapped in a piece of paper on which these words were written: *The ring you see is the one of which the King of Pontus made use to remove Mandana from the prison of King Croesus, at the sight of the army of Cyrus. Make use of it to see your princess by putting it in your mouth. Have no fear of being seen, or of doors closing before you, but beware of forgetting yourself in admiration of what you see.*[9]

After having read those words, the prince thanked the fay, his benefactress, and, putting the ring in his mouth, he left his apartment without being perceived; that gave him the boldness to enter Modest's.

He found that she was about to go to bed. Gods, what became of him when her maids had withdrawn and he saw that adorable person going tranquilly to sleep by the light of a lamp that burned all night! Forgetting the orders that had been given to him, he was trying to draw nearer in order to admire so

---

[9] The reference is to an incident in Mademoiselle de Scudéry's extremely long novel *Artamene ou le Grand Cyrus* (1649-53), in which Mandana, the daughter of King Cyaraxes and the object of Cyrus/Artamenes' amorous obsession, is continually being abducted and imprisoned, one of her abductors being Tomyris (who does not succeed in killing Cyrus in this version). The King of Pontus frustrates Cyrus more than once by means of a "heliotrope stone" that allows him to make himself invisible.

many charms at closer range when, forgetting that he had the ring in his mouth, he let it fall, and the noise it made in falling woke the princess, who uttered a scream at the sight of a man.

"What makes you bold enough," she said, on recognizing him, "to come and trouble my repose, and what design brings you to my bedroom at such an hour?"

Anger prevented her from saying any more. The prince took that opportunity to justify himself. "I came to your apartment," he said to her, "to tell you that, far from your eyes, I will make a sacrifice to you of my life, since you do not want to be witness to it."

"Shut up," interjected Modest. "Go so far from this place that I never hear your name pronounced in my presence again. I forbid you to take your life; your torture would be too mild. It is necessary, to satisfy my hatred, that you are unhappy for a long time. But above all, never appear before my eyes; after your insolence, I cannot see you without horror."

Modest could have said more, but she would not have been heard; the prince had fallen in a faint at orders so cruel. She perceived that with chagrin, in the fear that her chambermaids might discover her adventure; but the gods protective of innocence restored life to the prince.

As soon as he was able to begin to get up he put one knee on the ground and gazed at the princess with eyes wet with tears. "I will obey, Madame," he said, "and drag out a life so miserable that it will satisfy your vengeance."

After that he picked up his ring and disappeared in front of her in a moment, without her being able to see what had become of him. She remained in a strange surprise. She spent the night unable to sleep; the shame of having been seen in a state so little in conformity with her name and her humor rendered her inconsolable, and caused her to conceive projects of vengeance against the prince that gave her no repose. Daylight came, however, to calm her anxieties; a light sleep made her drowsy for a few hours.

As for Curious, he went to his apartment in an inconsolable despair. He had offended his princess without any hope of pardon, and it would not have taken much for him to curse the fay who had given him the means to see her for a moment only to lose her forever. He saw clearly that he could no longer appear before her after the prohibition she had imposed on him, but the proof that he had made of the ring enabled him to believe that he could remain in the court without being seen.

After having made his resolution he ordered his servants to go and wait for him on the border of Celusia, and only kept with him one squire, in whom he had confidence. He even remembered that the fay had predicted that he would never be happy until he was hated, and he hoped that this adventure might perhaps be the commencement of his happiness.

THE KNIGHTS ERRANT

Night had scarcely enveloped the earth with its darkness when a knight covered in black armor arrived on the banks of the Tagus. His helmet, which was charged with dead-leaf and white plumes, had the visor partly raised, allowing the sight of a visage on which dolor and beauty were painted. He bore on his arm a burnished steel shield, on which were visible a rose-bud and a grenadier[10] fallen to the ground, and the device: *By the same blow*. The horse on which he was mounted was as black as jet, but with a step so proud that it heightened further the good looks of its master.

After following the river for a few stadia, the knight plunged into a wood that was to his right, and having dismounted and given his helmet to his squire, he lay down on the grass in order to think about his misfortunes and his projects of vengeance against the man who was the cause of them.

A voice that he heard beside him obliged him to pause in those sad reflections. "Cease, Adelinde," said that voice, "to want to persuade me to live, and to seek to relieve my misfortunes; I ought no longer to expect anything but my despair."

Words more touching could not have struck the ears of the knight, who took back his helmet from the hands of his squire. He traversed the thicket in order to see the person who was lamenting.

He had not taken twenty paces when he perceived two women lying on the grass, one of whom, who did not appear to be more than fifteen years old, was of a beauty that could

---

[10] This reference is anachronistic, as grenadiers were only created as specialized soldiers during the reign of Louis XIV; they were usually the tallest and strongest men in a regiment, being the best equipped to throw long distances.

only be surpassed in the eyes of the knight by that of the person that he regretted at every moment of his life.

"Madame," he said, "the plaints that I have just heard emerging from your beautiful mouth cannot leave me in any doubt that you are overwhelmed by mortal chagrins, and I would be happy if, before finishing my sad life, I could destroy the enemies who are oppressing you; and to oblige you to have some confidence in my sincere procedure, I will tell you that I am Elmedor of Granada, Knight of the Deadly Sword, known throughout Spain for his amour for the admirable Alzayde.

"Sire," said the unknown woman, who had risen to her feet while Elmedor was speaking, "your name is known throughout the world, and it is sufficient to hear it pronounced to be convinced that nothing is impossible for your arm. Forgive me if the frightful misfortunes that are persecuting me force me to accept the generous offers that you are making me, but in order for you to know the enemies that you will have to combat, suffer that I tell you my adventures."

The Story of Princess Zamea and Prince Almanson

I am the daughter of Zamut, King of Fez, and Queen Zamare. The number of years that they were without children caused them to regard me as a gift of Heaven to whom they owed all their tenderness; the people followed her example, and I was the delight of the entire court.

The measure of beauty that the gods had given me, and the crown of Fez, obliged a number of the princes of Africa to come and render me homage, and to spare no effort to please me. The court of Fez had never been so brilliant; tourneys and horse races were seen there every day, for which I gave the prizes.

Among the large number of knights and princes who were attached to me, the Prince of Maroc, nicknamed the Terrible because of his extraordinary size and a grim gaze that renders him very disagreeable, was the one for whom my father destined me, and he had promised not to bring any obstacle to his amour if he could obtain consent to it. Promises so flattering redoubled the cares of Zoroaster—that was his name—but the more urgency he testified to me, the more hatred I had for him. I was in a mortal chagrin with regard to the amity that the king had for him, and I often said to the queen, my mother, from whom I had no secrets, that I would die rather than consent to marry him.

At that time, Zoroaster, in order to celebrate my birthday, had a tourney published, and invited knights, by means of challenges that he sent to all the courts of Spain and Africa, to come to admit that the Princess of Fez prevailed over all the beauties in the world. A challenge so outrageous for all the princesses that so many illustrious knights adored obliged them to render to Fez, and when the day of the tourney arrived, the King, the Queen and I were placed on platforms covered with rich blue velvet sheets embroidered with gold, which had been erected before the square destined for the diversion. The entire court, superbly ornamented, was at our feet, and, the judges of the camp having opened the barrier, Zoroaster appeared clad in golden armor enriched to the extremities with emeralds. What could be seen of his coat was green velvet embroidered with gold. His helmet was covered with a host of green and roseate plumes. He was wearing on his arm a buckler of the same metal on which a Venus giving me a golden apple was represented, and for the device: *I surrender*.

After having passed before the king and saluted us in a proud and arrogant manner, he went to set himself at the end of the career, in order to wait for whoever wanted to dispute the victory with him. He had not been there for a quarter of an hour when a knight presented himself, whose fine and noble features attracted the gazes of everyone, but his arm did not respond to his appearance, and Zoroaster had soon defeated that enemy. He was also victorious over several others, and he did not doubt that he would carry off the prize, which was my portrait surrounded by large diamonds, when a confused rumor that was heard among the people caused a new attention. It was caused by a knight who was asking to be received to combat.

Gods, what a sight for me, and how many tears that day has cost me! That handsome stranger was clad in a silver coat of mail enameled with blue; his coat was blue and silver; a quantity of plumes of the same color hung behind his head, and his shield, silver like the rest of his armor, had a ruby of extraordinary size in the middle, sculpted into a heart, and for a device the words: *For the most beautiful*. His horse was as white as snow, and it was so proud of bearing the most charming of all men that it was making the earth tremble beneath its feet.

The entire court could not help admiring the handsome stranger; but for myself, I confess that I had never felt such a great disturbance, nor more joy at seeing the terrible Zoroaster unhorsed at the second career. Everyone cried that he merited the prize, and, the judges of the camp having invited him to dismount, led him to the foot of the king's platform. He ordered me to give him my portrait. He received it in a manner so noble that he appeared to me to be even more lovable.

The races having finished, I went with the queen, my mother, to the palace. In the evening there was a magnificent ball, at which all the knights were present, except Zoroaster, who was so shaken by his combat that he was constrained to remain in bed for several days.

The stranger, whom we knew to be the Prince of Tunis, nicknamed the Knight of the Sun because he had always borne that star on his shield until the day of the tourney, came to it superbly dressed. He attracted the gazes of the entire assembly for a second time, and if he had appeared to us to be the God of War in combat, we took him for the God of Love in that new attire. My heart could not defend itself against so many charms, and no matter with what pride I tried to arm myself it was necessary to surrender to that young hero. My eyes had the same effect on his soul; for as long as the ball lasted he only looked at me, and I knew with pleasure that a similar fire was beginning to burn us both.

A few days passed after his arrival without him speaking to me except by means of his attentions and his gazes, but one afternoon I was alone with my chambermaids in my apartment. "Madame," he said to me, "this heart, which has been reserved until this moment for the most beautiful, has found what it was seeking; Princess Zamea can have no rivals who dare to dispute with her the prize for beauty, but I have reason to dread that this feeble homage might be rejected, and that she might render me the most unfortunate of all men."

"It is so pleasant," I said, smiling, "to carry off the glorious prize that you offer me, that you ought not to be apprehensive of being rejected."

"If I were fortunate enough for you to accept my prayers and my amour," said Almanson, I swear to you, my Princess, that no knight would ever love more constantly, and that I would employ every moment of my life giving you evidence of my gratitude."

"Not rejecting your homages," I said to him, in a more serious manner, "is not accepting your amour. Princesses like me can only receive for a knight the man who is offered to them by those who have the right to dispose of their destiny. It is for you to merit their choice, without expecting anything from me but a blind obedience to what they order me to do,"

"I beg your pardon, Madame," said Almanson, "for having interpreted your words too favorably; I ought to know that a confession so charming should cost years of trouble and suffering."

"Sire," I said, getting up in order to go to see the queen, who had just sent for me. "telling you that if you oblige the King, my father, to order me to listen to you, is telling you that one would be very glad to have that permission, and if that is not enough to render you happy, it is, at least, all that I can do for you."

I was so close to the queen's apartment when I finished speaking that Almanson could only respond by a profound reverence, which he made me as he quit my hand. I went into the queen's cabinet with an emotion on my face that she would easily have remarked, but the news she had to tell me caused her too much trouble to permit her to examine me.

"Zamea," she said to me, "the King, in spite of all that I could say to him, has ordered me to dispose you to marry the Prince of Maroc in eight days; he has given him his word and everything is arranged to complete that fatal marriage."

You can well imagine, generous knight, given that I had been apprehensive of that marriage when I only had an un-founded aversion, what despair it caused me at a time when my heart could only find Almanson worthy of my tenderness. I did not hide my dolor from my mother; she gave me sighs, but she told me that she could not do anything with regard to Zamut's mind, and that it was necessary for me to resolve to obey.

After those cruel words I retired to my room, from which I sent Adelinde to tell the Prince of Tunis what I had just learned, and that he should do what he thought appropriate in order to conserve me to his amour.

Beside himself with anger, the knight went to see my fa-ther and confessed to him the strong passion he had for me. Zamut received him very well, but he told him that, this word having been given to Zoroaster, he could not receive the honor that he wanted to do me.

It was a redoubling of dolor for my heart, which was very sensitive, when Adelinde came to tell me that cruel re-sponse. I spent the night lamenting, and in the morning I learned that the Prince of Tunis, having called out his rival, had wounded Zoroaster dangerously and disarmed him after a long and bloody combat; that he too was slightly wounded, and that he was a few stadia distant from Fez; that my father had had the Prince of Maroc bandaged with extreme care; that he had a terrible anger against Almanson; and that he had sent word to forbid him ever to appear at the court.

Such sad news caused me to fall almost lifeless into the arms of my chambermaids. The queen, having been informed of the accident, ran to me, and caused me to open my eyes by her tears and her cries, but it was to see me in such a pitiful state that she was inconsolable.

Zamut came to my room and fund me in tears. "I want to believe," he said, that Zoroaster's wounds are causing your dolor, unable to believe that you are so unaware of your duty and my will as to be shedding tears for the Prince of Tunis. The gods will render the Prince of Maroc to us, and I want you to marry him before the other leaves my kingdom, to punish him for the chagrin that his fatal valor has caused us. The king quit me after those cruel words, and the queen spent the rest of the day consoling me.

In the evening she sent secretly for news of Prince Almanson, and I had her give him compliments. The prince, charmed with the queen's good will, wrote to her to beg her to permit him to come to the palace the next day in disguise, his wounds being very slight. The queen granted him that favor, with the design of persuading him to quit the kingdom of Fez, for fear that the perfidious Zoroaster might have him assassinated.

Almanson did not fail to come at the appointed hour; after having given a quarter of an hour to the laments that our fate drew from us, we told him that an enchanter, a friend of the Prince of Maroc, had cured his wounds completely, but that the king, fearing a second duel, was having him guarded in the palace until he had married me, which he was to do in three days. Without giving him time to speak, the queen said to him that if he had any consideration or me he ought to leave Fez and not expose me to the mortal chagrin of being the cause of his death.

"If the princess consents to marry my rival, Madame," Almanson replied, "I will do as you advise, not to conserve me life but in order to end it far from her eyes."

"I will never consent to marry Zoroaster," I replied to him, "but you will be no more fortunate, since I cannot give myself to you without the consent of the king, my father, and the queen."

"But if Zamut forces you to complete your marriage," he said, "what means will you have of preventing it?"

"Death," I cried, "if my tears cannot touch him."

"Oh, Madame," he said to the queen, throwing himself at her feet, How many woes you can prevent, if you will permit me to abduct this charming princess. I promise you, on the faith of a knight, to put the crown of Tunis on her head as soon as we arrive there, and to have a blind obedience to her orders as long as I live."

Astonished by that bold proposition, the queen refused angrily, but in the end, she allowed herself to be touched by our tears. Almanson nearly died of joy at that welcome change of fortune, and after having assured the queen that she would never have reason to repent of her generosity, he withdrew in order to give orders for his departure.

The next day, at the appointed time, he came to fetch me, and it was not without a sharp dolor that I separated from such a good princess, but, amour prevailing over nature, I went with Almanson, only taking Adelinde. At the palace door we found one of the prince's squires, who had horses ready; we mounted up and we left Fez and the kingdom without any adventure.

One day, however, passing through a dark forest, we heard someone lamenting in the dense wood. Almanson took his horse in that direction and saw a rather beautiful woman who appeared very afflicted.

"Generous knight," she said, as soon as she perceived him, "come and deliver a princess from the hands of a monstrous giant, who is holding hr captive a stadium from here, in a castle where she is suffering insupportable torments; the gods have reserved that terrible adventure for your arm, and the Fay of Grandeurs has predicted it to me."

I arrived as the woman finished speaking, and I did what I could to turn Almanson away from the enterprise, but the desire to win that victory prevailed over my pleas; he begged me to wait for a moment as left with the woman.

I followed him in spite of him, and I saw that as soon as he reached the ditches of the castle the bridge was lowered, the gate opened, and when the unfortunate prince had entered with the unknown woman, the castle was sealed again.

No dolor ever equaled mine, when I did not see Almanson again; I called for him in vain for the rest of the day and the night; neither my cries not my tears were heeded. The prayers of Adelinde and my dear prince's squire but at day-break, a knight appeared beside me, who told me that I would only find an end to Almanson's misfortunes and my own on the banks of the Tagus, and disappeared after those words.

I followed his orders and I quit that deadly castle, where I left everything that could enable me to love life, in order to come to the banks of this river. I have been here for a year, without having seen the execution of the stranger's promises. May Heaven grant, generous knight, that it is for you that this adventure is reserved.

"Whether is it is for me or not," said Elmedor, as soon as the princess had finished speaking, "I shall not fail to attempt it as soon as you order me to depart. I shall be only too glad, charming Zamea, if I can return to you a prince so accomplished, who merits your tenderness so fully."

"As soon as daylight appears," said the Princess of Fez, "I will conduct you to the abode where the unfortunate Almanson resides, but as the night is not yet advanced, let us go and have a light meal and a few hours of repose in a cabin that I have made into my palace since I have lost my dear prince."

Elmedor dared not refuse Zamea, and for the first time since the death of Alzayde, he slept in a bed. He was not tranquil there; his mortal dolors kept him awake until dawn. Ashamed that it found him in bed, he got up, and having put on his armor and having found that Princess Zamea was ready, he helped her to mount up.

They rode all day without repose, but as their horses could not furnish their impatience, they stopped in a meadow irrigated by a stream, which was making an agreeable murmur.

They had not been there for an hour when they perceived a knight, whom Zamea recognized as Zoroaster. The fear of falling into his hands caused her to utter such a piercing cry that Elmedor asked her the cause of it, and, the princess having named the terrible knight, he remounted his horse, took his helmet and his lance from the hands of his squire, and went toward the Prince of Maroc, who had just recognized the beautiful Zamea.

"Knight," Elmedor said to him, "I have just learned that you are unworthy to bear that name, since you make use of force to possess a princess who does not love you."

"And who are you?" replied Zoroaster, proudly, "Who takes the side of an infidel that I am only seeking in order to punish for her crimes?"

"If I am the victor, I will tell you," said the Prince of Granada, "but let us not waste precious time in unnecessary discourse."

So saying, Elmedor struck him a blow with his lance that only caused him to stir in his saddle, while Zoroaster's broke against his enemy's coat of mail. They commenced to make their deadly swords shine.

Zamea, trembling for her defender, sent prayers to Heaven that he would not perish in the combat. Her dread was soon ended. Pierced by thrusts, Zoroaster fell at the feet of the invincible Knight of the Deadly Sword.

Zamea ran to the prince and asked him whether he was wounded; seeing blood flowing from a wound in his right arm, she stopped it with her beautiful hands, and what she had just seen him do enabled her to hope that he would soon deliver her dear Almanson.

They left the squire of the Prince of Maroc to take care of his body. The princess, before departing, wanted to have news of the queen, her mother, and what the king, her father, had said about her flight.

"When he learned of your departure, Madame," the squire told her, "the king, having no doubt that the queen was in collusion with you, by virtue of the aversion she had always had for the Prince, my master, made her a prisoner in her apartment, and maltreated her a great deal in order to make her say where you had gone with the Prince of Tunis The virtuous princess, seeing that she could not hide that you had gone with Almanson, and being afraid that your tracks might be followed, said that you had gone to seek a refuge with your aunt, the Queen of Granada. Zamut believed that, and sent men to the road to Granada in order to bring you back to Fez, where he destined the cruelest torments for you. Zoroaster, in despair at your flight, left Fez without waiting for the men sent after you to return, and for a year we have traveled all over Spain more than once. Finally, his evil destiny has brought him to this meadow, where that invincible knight has just found the end of his woes."

The Princess of Fez did not hear without tears about the chagrins that she had caused her mother, but, the prince having assured her that he would soon enable her to see her dear Almanson again, he mounted up again and commenced riding.

The agitation of the horse caused Elmedor's wound to bleed again; Zamea staunched the blood with a herb that she applied to the wound and constrained him to stop in a village they encountered on their route. The prince's squire went to look for a surgeon there, who, after having examined the wound, told him that it was necessary to stay in bed for at least three days, even though the wound was slight. The princess had all the difficulty in the world persuading the knight to take that short repose, and leaving him to go to bed, she retired to another room, where she spent the night.

The next day, having been informed that the prince was sleeping tranquilly, she only emerged from her room when she learned that he was awake, and went to seek information as to the state of his health.

"It is too good for an unfortunate man, Madame," he told her, "and Alzayde came to reproach me just now for the sleep that loss of blood caused me to take. I saw that admirable person in a chamber of the castle where Almanson is; she appeared to me in my dream covered in a veil of black gauze to reproach me for the scant care I have had in taking her out of the tomb and avenging her. I wanted to throw myself at her feet and tell her that the oath I had made to punish her enemies prevented me from following her, and that I had not lost a moment in searching for them, but the effort I made to embrace her knees woke me up."

"That dream," said the Princess of Fez, "appears mysterious to me. Alzayde is not dead; she is doubtless inhabiting the same prison as my dear prince."

"Oh, Madame," said Elmedor, shedding a few tears, "I cannot doubt Talmut, my squire, who saw her expiring and announced her last wishes to me."

"If I knew your story," said the princess, "and you had the same confidence in me that I have had in you, I would be able to speak to you with more assurance. Talmut could recount it to me while your wound is being dressed."

Elmedor could not refuse Zamea what she asked, and, the surgeon having come in, she went out with the squire and Adelinde, ordering Almanson's squire not to quit the prince. She went into a little wood behind the house and, having found a spot that was shaded from the sun, she sat down on the grass. Talmut, having sat down at her feet with Adelinde, commenced his master's story in these terms.

The Story of Prince Elmedor of Granada and Princess Alzayde

You doubtless know, Madame, that my master is the son of the King of Granada and Queen Ermendine, whose beauty and virtue are the delight of the court of Granada. The prince was named Elmedor, and later, by virtue of his glorious exploits, the Knight of the Deadly Sword. He began to be known by that name in the war the king, his father, fought against the Castilian Moors, where he did things so far above ordinary valor that he was regarded as the author of the peace those people were constrained to request of us.

After that victory he asked his father for permission to travel incognito throughout Spain; the king granted it, but the queen, who loved him tenderly, opposed it strongly because one of her friends, a magician named Zamat, had told her that the prince would run great dangers in that voyage. In order to protect him from them, however, he gave the queen an enchanted ring that had the power to destroy all enchantments when the point of a ruby heart that was mounted in it was directed upwards.

Seeing that she could not prevent her son from departing, the queen gave him the ring and made him promise always to carry it in the manner that the enchanter had indicated to her. Elmedor promised her that and left Granada, only accompanied by me.

After having spent a year seeing all the courts, we arrived in Leon on the day of a horse race, for which Princess Alzayde, the daughter of the King of Leon, was giving the prize, a sword garnished with extremely valuable rubies. My prince won it with a skill that attracted the gazes of the entre court to him, and he went to take it from the hands of the charming Alzayde.

If I had not seen you, Madame, I would say that the Princess of Leon was the most beautiful woman in all of Spain; never had so much majesty been accompanied by so much mildness. Her hair, which was a silvery brown, gave a surprising glint to her complexion, the bright and separate colors of which could only cede to the brilliance of her eyes; in sum, all the charms of beauty were found distributed throughout her person.

Elmedor, enchanted by so many attractions, remained beside himself for some time, and if the king, who had been told his name, had not obliged him to respond to the compliment he made him, he would not have emerged from the pleasant reverie that was occupying him for a long time.

When the races were over, everyone returned to the palace. The king having constrained the prince to take an apartment near to him own, he went to change his clothes, and came back to spend the evening in the queen's apartment, where he had the pleasure of conversing with the princess for more than two hours. What new graces he discovered in that conversation! Her intelligence even surpassed her beauty, and a mildness accompanied by a severe modesty reigned in all her actions, which, while inspiring a violent amour, forbade lamenting it. Elmedor felt that tyrannical power all too forcefully, and he retired to his apartment the most amorous of men. All the days that followed only served to redouble his chains and render them stronger than death—as time has made us know only too well.

I knew from one of the princess's maids, named Sancia, that the admirable person felt a tender penchant for the prince, which she was combating in vain, and that however severe her virtue was, she was not sorry to see that her beautiful eyes had made his conquest; but she hid her sentiments so well that Elmedor, only seeing a modest civility in her, doubted that she knew that he adored her.

"Divine Alzayde," he sometimes said, while gazing at her, "is it possible that my sighs and languid gazes have not told you that I am more amorous than all those who serve you? Can a fire so pure offend you?" At those moments he was ready to declare his amour, but respect and the fear of being banished by the amiable princess retained him.

In the meantime, the Prince of the Asturians declared war on the King of Leon. In order not to be surprised by his enemy, that prince assembled his troops and, putting himself at their head, marched for the frontier with Elmedor, who wanted to accompany him. He could only take his leave of the princess in the presence of the queen. She was afraid of not being able to hide from him the chagrin she felt in seeing him leave for a war that might be bloody. He was sharply touched by not being able to tell her that it was only to give her evidence that all his days were consecrated to her that he was going to fight the enemies of her father the king.

When we had arrived at the army's rendezvous, the King of Leon wanted to give the command, under him, to the Prince of Granada, but he refused, saying to him that he only wanted the honor of fighting by his side.

We went some time without finding a favorable occasion to deliver battle, but in the end, the Prince of the Asturians, who was stronger than us, presented it to us. It was terrible for both parties, and the victory seemed to be inclining toward the enemy, but my prince changed the face of the combat by killing the Prince of the Asturians. Instead of seeking to avenge him, his troops only thought of fleeing, and left the battlefield covered with the dying and the dead.

The campaign ended with that victory; the enemies retired over their frontier, and the king, after having given my master a thousand praises, returned to Leon.

The queen and the princess came to meet us. All the roads were full of people, who said loudly that in order to see the King of Leon master of a part of Spain, it was necessary to unite the Prince of Granada and Princess Alzayde. Elmedor, thinking the opportunity favorable to speak about his amour, approached Alzayde's carriage, where she was alone with Sancia.

"Madame," he said to her, "the gods sometimes explain themselves through the mouths of the people. Dare I hope that that oracle would not make the divine Alzayde unhappy? My heart, which her first gaze ignited with the most respectful passion that could ever be born, has only been waiting until this fatal moment to make itself known, if it can, without displeasing you; it is for you, charming Princess to condemn my amour to an eternal silence, or to permit me to call myself your knight."

"Sire," said Alzayde blushing, "if the gods want to unite the crown of Leon with that of Granada, I would try to prevent it in vain; but suffer that they explain themselves by means of less tumultuous voices; let me doubt at this moment their profound decrees, and do not constrain me to forget that we owe the victory to you, only to remember the offense you are causing me in speaking to me about an amour to which I ought only to listen on the orders of the king and the queen."

"If it only requires the orders of those sacred persons," the prince replied to her, "I have reason to believe that they will not be contrary to me, but if, as I can suspect, Madame, I have the misfortune of pleasing you, I will be able to punish this reckless heart, overfull of a culpable fire, since it is disavowed by the one who gave birth to it."

The king, who approached Alzayde's chariot, prevented her from responding to Elmedor, but whatever constraint she made to hide the tender penchant she had for him, she made him a sign to retire with such a tender gaze that he forgot the excessively severe words she had addressed to him.

From that day on Elmedor began to hope that he was not indifferent to the princess. He redoubled his attentions and his amour, with such a touching respect that the beautiful Alzayde confessed to him that if the king, her father, approved his passion, she would not be contrary to it.

At that time, Madame, the Prince of Maroc's challenge was brought to the court, and my master asked the permission of the king and the princess to go to fight in order to sustain her charms. Alzayde refused, by virtue of a modesty that rendered her even more worthy of the care that Elmedor wanted to take in order to win the victory for her, but the king, who loved her tenderly and was not sorry about the attachment that the Prince of Granada had for his daughter, permitted him to fight and to name himself her knight. He obliged the princess to give him a scarf that she was wearing that day, to hang on the sword that she had given him at the horse race when we arrived in Leon. The princess obeyed with a blush so obliging that my prince thought that with those marks of his good fortune he could vanquish Zoroaster and all the knights in the world. Taking his leave of the king, the queen and Alzayde, we took the road to Fez.

The first few days of our journey passed without adventures, but when we arrived on the banks of a river that it was necessary to cross in order to enter into Africa, we waited for some time for fishing boats that often fished in that vicinity. Finally, we saw one approaching, and Elmedor having said that it as a matter of reaching the other bank of the river, we entered the boat. But Madame, we were no sooner in the watercourse than we fell into a torpor from which we could not protect ourselves.

When we awoke we found ourselves in a magnificent palace built on an island in the African Sea. All that one could wish to render a place enchanted was there, whether in regard to the grandeur of the buildings, the sumptuousness of the furniture or the beauty of the gardens, and the quantity of fountains, which filled canals of marble and porphyry by means of different figures. The woods, by their admirable coolness, sheltered from the sun avenues of jasmine, orange trees and pomegranates, where birds with a thousand different plumages made a concert that delighted the heart and the ears. Finally, an eternal spring that always reigned in that admirable abode rendered it that of the gods.

Elmedor was surprised to find himself in such a beautiful place, and he was in the initial surprise that extraordinary things cause when he saw a young and beautiful woman enter, followed by several nymphs, all equally amiable.

"Elmedor," said the lady, "the gods, to who the lives of heroes like you are dear, have made it known to me that the journey of Fez would be fatal to you. Don't bear me a grudge for having distanced you from that place deadly to your days. The beauty of Alzayde cannot be disputed, and Zoroaster's challenge will not destroy her charms. As soon as the time of that dangerous diversion has passed, the same boat that brought you to this palace will return you by a much shorter route to the charming Princess of Leon, if you find nothing here that will stop you."

"Nothing can stop me far from my princess," the prince interjected, carried away by his passion, "and although I see

142

here everything that nature has of the most perfect, the gods would have given me more pleasure in letting me die fighting to sustain the charms of the divine Alzayde than making me languish far from her beautiful eyes."

"Time," said the lady, presenting her hand to him in order to descend into the gardens, "might perhaps enable you to change your sentiment."

After having made a few tours of a flower garden in which the most beautiful statues in the world were seen, she proposed a race against one of her nymphs in the great avenue of orange trees, telling him that all the knights that fortune brought to her lands were obliged to test their agility against Liriope—that was the nymph's name. Elmedor did not want to dispense with that playful custom, of which he did not know the mystery.

He set off at the same time as the nymph, and reached the end of the avenue more than twenty paces ahead of her, but he found himself so warmed by the exercise that he drank a great deal of the water of a spring that served as the runners' goal, although its color was blackened and its taste very agreeable.

He had no sooner drunk that water than he believed that he would never leave that place so long as he saw the light. Alzayde was effaced from his heart, but, his passion being no less strong, without remembering the one who had given birth to it, he believed that the fay Desirée was the object of it, and, approaching her in haste, he received the compliments that she gave him for having vanquished Liriope with an expression so tender that she applauded herself for having succeeded so well.

Night having fallen we returned to the palace, where a delicious supper was served. After leaving the table they spent the evening listening to a charming concert, and, the hour to retire having come, the prince was taken to his apartment, where, without thinking about the beautiful Alzayde, he slept tranquilly all night.

I have discovered since that the enchanted spring that caused such a prodigious change in Elmedor drew its source from the River Styx, and that the fay, by means of an extraordinary charm, had added to its natural virtue that of rendering herself the object of a knight's amour. I also found out from one of her nymphs, who had some benevolence toward me, that Desirée, having passed through Leon one day to collect herbs from the mountains surrounding that kingdom, had seen the Prince of Granada and conceived a tenderness for him so violent that she had resolved to draw him to her island. The opportunity of the tourney had seemed favorable to her, and she had sent us the fatal boat that had brought us to her palace.

Meanwhile, the prince, charmed by the fay's generosity, was spending the happiest moments in the world. Nothing opposed his desires; everything anticipated them, and by means of a thousand new diversions, the fay amused him agreeably. Sometimes, in little ebony chariots drawn by unicorns whiter than snow, the two lovers, accompanied by elegantly clad nymphs, went for excursions along the sea shore, and the fish of that terrible element, forced to obey Desirée's enchantments, came to run into the nets that the prince extended for them. At other times, mounted on horses whose agility equaled that of deer, they hunted the most cruel beasts, which, unable to avoid the fatal arrows that Elmedor launched at them, came to fall at his feet. Finally, savoring more tranquil pleasures, they amused themselves watching nymphs and fauns dance on fresh grass dotted with flowers. Even more frequently, however, content to explain their tenderness to one another, with no other witness than their amour, they spent entire days in the darkest places in the woods and the most remote from human commerce.

One day, when the prince, impatient to see his beautiful fay, whom he had not found in her apartment, went to look for her in a myrtle grove where she often went, he was approached by a man who had an air so majestic that he imposed respect and dread upon him.

"What are you doing, unfortunate Elmedor?" the stranger said to him. "You are languishing in slack idleness while the cruel Asmonade, having conquered the kingdom of Leon, is holding your princess captive. Do you no longer remember the amour you swore to the divine Alzayde? See whether your fay has anything approaching her beauty."

So saying, he gave him her portrait, and Elmedor, ashamed of his reproaches and struck by the features that he had adored for such a long time, remained beside himself for some while.

"Emerge from the enchantment that has rendered you a slave," the stranger continued. "Why have you forgotten to make use of the ring that the queen, your mother, gave you when you left Granada? Turn it in the direction that its fatality bears it, and you will see its divine virtue."

Elmedor, having recognized by his discourse the enchanter Zamat, looked at his finger and saw that his ring had the point downwards. He followed the advice of the sage magician and found himself as he had been in Leon.

He reddened with anger at the moments he had given to the fay Desirée. He wanted to ask Zamat how he could get away from the island, but no longer found him there. In haste to run after his princess, he ran to the palace to order me to prepare the horses.

As he was ready to leave, the fay, informed of his design, came to stop him, but without being touched by her plaints or her tears, we emerged from the palace and the enchanted isle. We found a vessel in the port ready to set sail to cross the arm of the sea that separated it from the mainland, and, mounting up again, we continued our journey.

One morning, as we were emerging from a dark forest, we saw a fully armed knight coming toward us mounted on a superb charger, who approached the prince.

"Elmedor," he said, "I am the Knight Avenger of Infidelities. What you have done to the fay Desirée can only be repaired by your death. I am her brother, as knowledgeable as her in enchantments, but, believing myself strong enough by

145

virtue of my valor to make you repent of the wrong you have done her, I shall only make use of my sword."

"Let us see, then, whether it is as dangerous as your charms," said Elmedor, drawing his own, "and whether I can find the place mortal to enchanters as well as that of other knights. As he spoke he turned his horse and fell upon the knight with an astonishing valor. Their combat was terrible, and the prince, seeing his blood flowing in abundance, redoubled his fury and cast his enemy down.

Putting his foot on his throat, he said: "Admit that your enchantments would have served you better than your sword."

"I admit," said the knight, "that you are more fortunate than me, and that my life is in your hands."

"Go," said Elmedor "I give it to you, to acquit myself of what I owe to Desirée." And, helping him to get up and mount his horse, he left him full of shame and chagrin.

However, we were constrained to stop at the first habitations we found, in order to staunch the blood of the prince's wounds and, putting him to bed in spite of the desire he had to see his princess, I went to fetch a surgeon, who told me that his wounds were very dangerous.

I confess to you, Madame, that that news touched me sensibly, but the gods, who reserved chagrins for that unfortunate prince more mortal than death, gave us help that I had not expected.

While Elmedor's wounds were being examined the master of the hut arrived. He approached my dear prince and, having seen the condition of his wounds, he went out and came back a moment later with his hands full of herbs. He crushed them, and having applied a compress soaked in the juice that he had extracted from them, he assured my master that he would be completely cured in two days.

What the shepherd said proved to be true; after having recompensed his charitable host, the prince took the road to Leon, and we learned from a man of quality we encountered about all the changes that had happened in the kingdom during our absence.

Asmonade, Prince of Estremadura, a cruel and evil magician, had fallen in love with the princess; he had asked the king for her, but that good prince had not wanted to sacrifice his daughter. To avenge himself, he had besieged Leon and, finding it defenseless, had rendered himself its master and had killed the king and queen. As for the princess, he was keeping her in the palace, and by means of attentions and presents he was attempting to make her forget his crimes; but the generous princess, scorning the evidence of his amour as well as that of his hatred, was spending her days very unhappily. We also learned that Alzayde had fallen ill a fortnight ago, and that the perfidious Asmonade did not seem alarmed by it.

Such sad news had a terrible effect on Elmedor's heart; he fell in a faint. His wound opened up, with a bad fever, which brought him to the brink of the tomb. His anxiety regarding the princess obliged me to go to Leon.

I found the palace full of confusion. The doors were unguarded. I went up to Alzayde's apartment without anyone recognizing me.

I went into her chamber, but gods, what a state I found her in! The colors of death were painted on her face. Her partly-closed eyes and her parted lips no longer seemed to give any sign of life. I was pierced by such a sharp dolor that I could not help uttering a cry. Sancia, who was in tears beside the dying beauty, turned her head and approached me.

"Sancia," I said, "Don't you recognize me?"

"Oh, Talmut," she said, "How fortunate the Prince of Granada is to be dead, if he still loved this unfortunate princess."

"My Prince isn't dead," I replied, "and he would be here but for Alzayde's illness, which has reduced him into great danger of his life."

"Great Heaven!" cried Sancia. "What fatality is attached to the unfortunate House of Leon?" The maid continued: "The Princess, had found great courage with which to brave all Asmonade's cruelties, but she could not resist the death of Elmedor, whom that perfidious individual told her had been killed in a single combat. From that moment on she has had no part of life. In vain I implore her to give me some sign that she still knows me; I can only get profound sighs from her. Asmonade, tranquil in our despair, gives us evidence of a malign joy, which redoubles our dolor. But let us see whether the news that you have just announced to me can recall her to life. Approach her, and speak to her on the part of the Prince."

"Madame," I said to the princess, taking one of her beautiful hands, which I squeezed in order to wake her, "Elmedor is not dead; he only breathes for you; do you want to abandon him?"

At that dear name Alzayde opened her eyes and, turning toward me, sought to recognize me,

"Madame," I continued, "I am Talmut, whom the Prince of Granada has sent to you, in order to know how he can assure you of his very respectful passion."

"Talmut," she said to me, "I no longer have any part in life, but tell your master that as I am dying for him, I want him to live in order to avenge me."

As she finished those words, which I could hardly hear, she fell unconscious again. Asmonade having come in, I withdrew; but I had not reached the staircase when I heard the cry: "The princess is dead!"

Penetrated by dolor, I returned to the prince. Not daring to tell him the truth, I told him that Alzayde was getting better; but, seeing on my face the traces of the tears I had shed, he did not doubt his misfortune.

Everything the fury can make one say and think, that unfortunate prince said and thought, and if I had not told him the order of the dying princess, he would not have survived that admirable person. "Yes, too unfortunate Alzayde," he said, "I swear it by all the amour that I have for your dear shade. I shall conserve my life until I have appeased your irritated Manes."

Since he made that resolution, forced to take care of his health instead of dying, he was able to quit his bed after a fortnight, and having given himself a little more time in order to be able to sustain the fatigues of riding, he sent me back to Leon to discover what had been done with the body of the princess and where Asmonade was. I could not learn anything of what he wanted to know exact from the people, who told me that the tyrant had taken Alzayde's body away with him, that Sancia had not wanted to quit her, and that the palace was closed. It was in vain that I tried to discover any more, and I was constrained to go and tell Elmedor that Asmonade was no longer in Leon. That increased the unfortunate prince's chagrin, but, having resolved to search for him all the way to the ends of the earth, we departed for Estremadura, believing that the perfidious individual, fearing that the people might rise up at the sight of the princess's body, had gone to give her a tomb in a foreign land; but we did not find him there.

Since that day, the unfortunate Elmedor has traveled throughout Spain without finding his enemy, no matter how hard we have tried, and for a year, the prince has spent his nights in the forests and his days in places where he hopes to satisfy his vengeance.

"I did not believe," said Princess Zamea, when the squire had finished his story, "that I could be sensible to other misfortunes than those that have overwhelmed me, but those of the Prince of Granada have touched me intensely. Let us return to him, in order to soothe him by the share that he will see us taking in his dolor."

At the same time, the princes stood up, and when she went into Elmedor's room she said to him: "Sire, you are not the only one shedding tears for your misfortunes; they have drawn them from my eyes."

"I ought to be able to tell you, Madame," said the prince, "that the compassion of a great princess like you softens my woes, but, lovely Zamea, they are of a nature that can only be soothed by death."

"I hope for a more fortunate end," said the Princess of Fez, "since I have heard your story. I no longer doubt that the admirable Alzayde is alive. Asmonade, fearing your presence, and knowing of your return, has doubtless abducted the Princess of Leon in the unconsciousness that caused your squire to believe her dead. The care he is taking to hide leaves no doubt of it, and as I told you this morning, he is holding her prisoner in the fatal castle from which you must extract the Prince of Tunis. That is what the enchanter Zamat wanted to make you understand by the dream you have had, and all we need, in order to end your misfortunes, is your health and the marvelous ring of which he made you a present."

"Alas, Madame," said the prince, "if our happiness is only founded on that fatal ring, how uncertain it is! I lost it during the combat with the Avenging Knight, and destiny has deprived me of that magical aid."

"Your valor," said the princess, "will take the place of everything for us; only think of healing yourself."

After those words, fearing that she had said too much, Zamea withdrew.

The following day she went for a walk in the little wood I mentioned, accompanied by Adelinde and the squire. She walked there for some time. but, the sun having constrained her to seek shade, she sat down in the same place where Elmedor's squire had told his story.

She had only been there for a moment when she heard a woman's voice, speaking rather loudly.

"I confess, Madame," said the unknown woman, "that the inconstancy of Prince Alinzor merits all your hatred, but I would like it to be more moderate and that, returning to the Canaries…"

"No, Phenice," said another woman, "Don't hope that I shall see the fortunate Canary Islands until I have punished the infidelity of the Prince of Numidia. The Fay of Grandeurs has predicted that I will find the end of my difficulties in the Kingdom of Granada. We are not far away from it. I shall not leave until I have washed away the mortal insult in his blood."

Curious to see the unknown woman, the sound of whose voice had something touching about it, Zamea got to her feet. When she advanced she saw two young knights sitting on the grass. The Princess of Fez, strongly suspecting, given what she had just heard, the subject that obliged the unknown woman to hide her sex, went toward her with open arms, charmed by her beauty and her youth.

"Charming Princess," she said, "do not be annoyed that hazard has enabled me to know that I can give you such tender proofs of the amity that one cannot help having for you as soon as one has seen you momentarily. I am an unfortunate woman accustomed to lamenting my woes; let us lament them together in order to soothe them."

"Whatever reason," said the Princess of the Canaries, "I might have for being annoyed at having been found out, I cannot be at such a fortunate encounter. The happiness of costing a person like you a few tears can soften many woes; but the one of which you have apparently heard me complaining is so outrageous that one the death of the man who caused it can cure it."

"The death of an enemy who has been dear to us," said Zamea, "and who often still is, although we do not believe him to be, is not always an assured remedy. But my Princess," she continued, "it is not time to dispute your vengeance; when a few days of acquaintance have attracted your amity to me, I shall be able to make you agree with what I am saying. Let us think presently of relieving you of your fatigues in a small habitation where the wounds of a great prince are retaining me for a few days."

Whatever desire the Princess of the Canaries had to continue her route, she could not resist the amities of the beautiful Zamea; they took the path to the hut together and went into the prince's bedroom.

Elmedor was astonished to see with the Princess of Fez a knight of such brilliant beauty, but, the charming Zamea having explained that adventure briefly, he offered the Princess of the Canaries his arm and his sword in order to avenge herself on her infidel.

"I only need my own hand to punish him, generous knight," she told him, "and if any arm other than mine caused his blood to flow, it would cost me tears."

"I told you, Madame," said Zamea, "that this ingrate was even dearer to you than you believed. You fear putting your vengeance in excessively reliable hands; you prefer to employ your own."

"Don't judge my hatred so poorly," replied the Princess of the Canaries. "If you had ever felt that cruel passion, you would agree that the pleasure of avenging oneself is so sensible that it can cost tears when one is deprived of it."

"I only see a disguised amour in everything you say, my beautiful princess," replied the Princess of Fez, "and if the excessively fortunate Alinzor appeared at your feet, his sighs and his repentance would extinguish your anger more surely than the loss of his life."

The prince's surgeon having come in at that moment, the princesses were obliged to go to their room, where, by means of a charming conversation, they got to know one another so well that, unable to find anything more amiable than one another, they loved one another tenderly.

Princess Zamea, having obliged the Princess of the Canaries to promise her only to depart with her, since they were both going to Granada, she begged her the next day to tell her about Alinzor's infidelities, and, forbidding anyone to interrupt them, the beautiful Canarian commenced in these terms.

The Story of Zalmayde, Princess of the Canaries, and the Prince of Numidia

You know already, Madame, that I am Zalmayde, the Princess of the Canaries, and according to all appearances, you are not unaware that, having lost my mother in giving birth to me, the prince, my father, followed her a few years later. I remained under the conduct of Princess Zantille, my mother's

152

sister, and to govern my Estate my father had chosen before dying the Prince of the Baleares.

He was a very prudent prince, very appropriate to rule a people as restless as ours. But amour, unfortunately for me, enabled him believe that of all benefits, the greatest was that of being loved by me. Princess Zantille made use of all her power, and represented to me incessantly that I had a hand too weak to sustain the scepter, that the Canarians, accustomed to the government of Zenore—that was his name—would see my crown shining on his head with joy.

All those arguments were not at all to my liking. Zenore displeased me greatly, and the reputation he had of being a great enchanter gave me an aversion for him that I had never been able to vanquish, even though he had served me throughout my life in a manner for which I ought to have been obliged to him.

The court of the Canaries was in that state when I wanted to go to a Temple of Diana that was built on the mainland. Princess Zantille could not make the voyage because she was ill, and Zenore had been summoned to soothe some uprising that had occurred in the city of Baleare. I therefore embarked with a maid, whom you see with me, and a few slaves, not wanting to be known in that petty pilgrimage.

Our crossing was very fortunate, and we descended to land without having had the slightest contrary wind. I mounted a carriage in order to go to the Temple. I walked for a long time under the long covered pathways that led to the portico, and when the hour of sacrifices arrived, I went into the Temple. During the ceremonies I perceived facing me a knight of admirable stature who was looking at me with an attention that made me blush. Finding a thousand charms in his face and throughout his person, however, I took as much care not to lose sight of him as to listen to the hymn that were being sung in honor of the goddess.

When the sacrifices were over, I emerged from the Temple, and my knight followed me into the pathways, where I made several detours. The stranger was my shadow; I always saw him beside me, and when his eyes encountered mine a fire emerged from them so intense that it went to my heart and began to burn me with a flame that would have been never-ending, even if the one to which I gave birth in his soul at the same moment had been one of the vestal flames that are never extinguished.

That effect of sympathy was so extraordinary that the Prince of Numidia—for it was him—could not help approaching and offering me his hand to help me climb into my carriage, and, without knowing whether I ought to accept that service from a man that I did not know, I could not refuse it.

"Madame," he said to me, "it is necessary that I am beloved by the goddess that is adored here to have inspired her vestal only to offer me sacrifices tomorrow, since that delay has permitted me to see the most admirable person that the gods have ever formed."

"That lady was not in the Temple, then," I said, not wanting to receive such flattering praise, "for I did not see any woman who arrested my gaze."

"That is because you could not see yourself, Madame", he bold Alinzor replied, "since you do not recognize yourself in that beautiful person, whose titanic empire I sense."

"Sire," I said, adopting a serious tone, "the customs of the realm you inhabit are doubtless different from ours, "as I cannot believe that such an accomplished knight could lack the respect he owes to my sex and my rank.

"If the laws of the pagans who have given birth to us," replied Alinzor, "dispense with shutting up in the presence of the adorable object of one's passion, I confess that the Numidians, of whom I am the sovereign, have an ardent and passionate temperament...."

"Say also inconstant," I said, laughing.

"I confess," said Alinzor, "that people charge us with the terrible fault. But charming stranger, your eyes cannot give chains that are not eternal, so you ought not to fear the moving sand of my fatherland."

"I fear maxims more than that," I said, "and for the few moments that hazard assembles us, forget them, I implore you. I am not in a humor to exchange your laws for ours, and as a knight, you are obliged to follow mine."

"With all my heart," said he prince, "I make a vow in your beautiful hands never to have any others."

"Begin, then," I relied, "this instant, by letting me climb back into my chariot and contenting yourself with a quarter of an hour's acquaintance, without wanting to accompany me any further."

I confess, Madame, that I would have been very sorry if he had obeyed me, and that it gave me great pleasure, after having put me into my carriage, to find him at the door again to help me to descend. I made him a few reproaches for it, but they were so feeble that they did not prevent him from escorting me to my chamber.

It was there that, having become bolder, I examined all his charms. If, like me, my beautiful princess, you knew that amiable infidel, you would excuse conduct so irregular in a person of my age, and if dark, flashing, well separated eyes full of a fire more dangerous than the one that departs from the arrows of Amour; a forehead formed to be the seat of majesty; a mouth in which the whiteness of teeth mingles with the incarnadine of lips makes the most beautiful effect in the world, a stature such as is credited to the valiant Achilles and a mind serious and playful by turns makes one find a species of enchantment in conversation against which one cannot defend oneself...if, I say, all those charms could serve as an excuse, I was doubtless very innocent, but nothing can excuse me but the sympathetic impulse that attracts to one's fellow, seeking to unite the two hearts in which it finds itself with an inevitable chain, in spite of all the efforts of reason. It is that fatal penchant that forced me to remain for the rest of the day and the following day, to be witness to the sacrifice that he offered to Diana, and that made us find one another again the following day in the avenue of the Temple.

As he had discovered from Phenice that I wanted to depart after the ceremony he had armed himself, in order to be ready to follow me. He wore a rose-colored coat that day, embroidered with silver and lemon yellow. His helmet was shaded by countless plumes of those two colors. He had a light buckler on his arm, on which one could see a flash of lightning emerging from a cloud drawn by an Amour and the words: *I am born; I die.*

As soon as he perceived me he came toward me and presented me with his hand to aid me to walk. We went into the Temple, where he took far more care to gaze at me than to implore the help of the goddess it was necessary to invoke. I made him a few reproaches on emerging from the sacrifice.

"Madame," he replied, "when I arrived in this place, I needed to consult Diana, "but my destiny is much changed from this moment on. It is in you that I find my altar and my gods, and your eyes are the witnesses that I need to consult. Do not reproach me then, for neglecting the daughter of Latona, since, more prompt to announce my destiny, it depends on you to render it fortunate or unfortunate."

"If your destiny," I replied, "depended on me, I would like to test whether one could only give birth in your heart to amour for it to die."

"Oh, Madame," he cried, trying to efface that device—which I prevented him from doing—"you have given birth in my heart to one that will never be subject to death. Immortal as the beauties that have given birth to it, it will burn eternally. But in order to live happily, charming Zalmayde, it is necessary not to regret having given birth to it."

"To have the glory of rendering a Numidian faithful," I said, laughing, "I want to grant you what you ask of me. But beware, Alinzor, of making me experience before sunset that the lightning has triumphed over the amour."

Alinzor swore to me a hundred times that nothing could change his sentiment. My feeble heart had faith in oaths as inconstant as the sands that are his dwelling; I let him know all the tenderness that he had inspired in me, before we had arrived at the port, which was to be the place of our separation I did not want him to come to the Canaries for fear that Princess Zantille would not approve of my conduct. But, unable to resolve to be separate from him for long, I told him to be on our island on the day when we celebrated the Festival of the Sun, which we worship.

Alinzor received that order with an extreme displeasure. After he had put me on the ship, I saw him turn away in order to hide his tears, and when the wind pushed us out into the open sea I saw him lift his arms again and fall into the arms of his squire. So much evidence of amour finished convincing me that only the Prince of Numidia was worthy of my tenderness, and occupied with that passion, I arrived in the Canaries very different from what I had been when I left.

The princess, my aunt, and Zenore came to meet me with a tender and obliging urgency, to which I only responded with words punctuated by sighs. Zantille made no reflection on that, but Zenore, by means of the science that he had, knew that he had a beloved rival, and that the rival in question as the Prince of Numidia. He felt a very sensible dolor, and accompanied me all the way to the palace without saying a word.

I sent the days there with Phenice, counting when the Festival of the Sun would arrive, and I was only occupied with designing a costume that would heighten the scant beauty that the gods had given me.

Perhaps you will not be sorry, Madame, to learn what happens in that festival. On the first day of summer, the ladies assemble, superbly adorned, on platforms that are set up along a great avenue of orange trees, which heads to the Temple of the Sun, where his statue can be seen, brilliant with precious stones, placed on a white marble altar. You can see by that, Madame that we do not worship the sun as the Persians once did, who claimed to be offering him illegitimate prayers if they were not offered to an uncovered sky.

At the door of the Temple is the marvelous tree whose leaves produce a sweet and agreeable dew incessantly, which falls into large porphyry vats, sufficiently for the entire island to irrigate fields and gardens and repair in an entirely miraculous manner the cruelty of nature, which has refused us the fresh water that she gives to the rest of the earth in abundance. It is to attract that necessary liquid that we hold the festival of which I speak. That year, the lot fell to me to present the offerings, and, charmed to be obliged to appear that day in an extraordinary adornment, I did not neglect anything at all that might give it splendor.

At daybreak I emerged from the palace, representing the goddess Flora, on a carriage ornamented with festoons of flowers, drawn by horses as white as snow. My garment was gauze with a background of silver, on which brightly and naturally colored flowers were sewn. A garland of roses and jasmines closed the top of my robe, and all my hair, in large curls, was attached with carnations and orange blossom. On my head was a crown of pomegranates and tuberoses, from which hung a veil of the same gauze as my garment, which came to be fastened to the left side of my robe; and I held in my hands a basket of flowers interlaced with their branches, which was an admirable bouquet.

Behind me appeared the entire retinue of the goddess I represented. Pomona and Vertumnus followed, carrying the most beautiful fruits of the season in magnificent baskets. In that order, accompanied by a rustic orchestra of shepherds and shepherdesses, we arrived at the dew-tree, where I descended from my carriage; and placing my bouquet on an altar erected expressly for that purpose, I allowed it to be refreshed by that divine water. Pomona and Vertumnus did the same, and, picking up our baskets again, we went into the Temple, where, on a little altar of rock crystal garnished with gold, we made the sacrifice of our flowers and fruits, while setting fire to the incense that was on a pyre of all kinds of scented wood, the smoke of which filled the Temple with a sweet and charming odor.

During that ceremony, the hymn to the Sun was sung, in order to beg him to receive our prayers and our offerings and to continue the divine dew for us. After that, we emerged from the Temple in the same order in which we had entered it, and I returned to the palace, not without looking to see whether the Prince of Numidia was there. I was anxious at not seeing him, but I thought he wanted to surprise me at the tourney that Zenore was holding in my honor.

I waited impatiently for the time destined for that diversion to arrive, and I nearly made all the ladies despair by obliging them to be on the platforms long before the lists were opened. Finally, the judges of the camp having opened the barriers, I saw a knight appear whose stature and manner greatly resembled the infidel Alinzor, and I had no doubt that it was him when I saw him vanquish all the others. I got ready to give him the prize, which was a gold, silver and blue scarf that I had worn all day with an incomprehensible joy. When he knelt down and raised the visor of his helmet, I realized that it was not Alinzor. I scarcely had the strength to present the scarf to him, and, penetrated by chagrin and anger, I returned to the palace. Phenice tried to make me understand that the Prince of Numidia was not as culpable as I thought; that some important affair had retained him involuntarily; but I could not listen to such feeble excuses.

Princess Zantille was astonished to see me in a dejection full of dolor. She could not understand the reason for my chagrin. But Zenore, knowing that I could never dispose myself to marry him so long as I loved Alinzor, tried to oblige me to make him the confidence of my tenderness.

"Madame," he said to me one day, "if I saw that my rival merited your amour, I would refrain from wanting to destroy him, but to tolerate that the most beautiful person in the world should suffer for an infidel who does not even remember having adored her, and, not content with that criminal forgetfulness, prefers a princess far less charming than her...."

"Oh, Zenore," I cried, without giving him time to finish what he was trying to say, "if you can make me see that the Prince of Numidia is inconstant, I promise you to hate him as much as I love him."

"It only depends on you, Madame," Zenore replied, "for your beautiful eyes to see him this very day at the feet of a beauty of his court."

You can believe, my beautiful princess, that I refrained from refusing an offer so in conformity with my jealous fury. As soon as night fell, the Prince of Baleare had me mount a chariot drawn by winged dragons with Phenice and him, which cleaved through the air with an astonishing velocity, to alight in the gardens of Alinzor's palace. It was illuminated by a thousand lamps; an admirable concert charmed the senses there, and the prince, without being occupied with the music, was at the feet of a young Numidian, who had nothing touching in my eyes.

Penetrated by a mortal dolor, I wanted to cry out, but the enchanter Zenore did not give me time. He made the dragons take off again, and I only just had time to let my portrait fall as close as I could to the infidel Prince of Numidia.

As soon as we had returned from that fatal voyage I shut myself in my cabinet with Phenice and I spend the days and nights complaining about Alinzor. The service that the Prince of Baleare had rendered me did not make him any more fortunate. On the contrary, the hatred of my feeble heart rebounded on him violently.

"It's you," I said to him, one day, "who is the cause of the state to which I'm reduced. If you had left me still ignorant of my misfortune, I would be less unfortunate."

Zenore only replied with sighs and unjust reproaches, and tried by means of complaisance to make me overcome my blindness.

One day, after spending the entire day lamenting, I descended in the evening into the gardens, only accompanied by Phenice, who was the only person I could tolerate. I saw a man at a bend in a path who was lying on a bed of grass and who was looking attentively at a portrait that he was holding in his hand. The scant curiosity that I had for what did not regard my tenderness caused me not to go any further, and I took another route; but the noise we made in walking drew the unknown man out of is reverie, and he recognized me.

"Why are you fleeing, my princess?" he cried, running toward me.

That voice, so dear, which I could not mistake, caused me to turn my head, and Alinzor—for it was him—came to throw himself at my knees and held them embraced for a long time, without me being able to free myself from his arms.

"My dear Zalmayde," he said to me, "It is permitted to me to see you again, then, and the gods have finally allowed my tears to touch them."

All the amour that appeared in his actions and the inconsequential discourse of the Prince of Numidia appeared to me to accord so little with what I had seen of his inconstancy that I could not get over my surprise. But eventually, convinced that the traitor had only come back to me in order better to deceive me, I said, sitting down on a grass seat behind me: "What have you come to seek here? Do you think that I am unaware of all your infidelities and that I am still feeble enough to give you evidence of a tenderness that you do not merit? No, Alinzor, my heart cannot be the prize of a cowardly return that my portrait, which I dropped in order to remind you of what you lost, has caused. Go away, let me finish forgetting you, without coming, by virtue of a cruelty unworthy of a knight, to raise an eternal obstacle to my repose."

"If I did not fear being interrupted in what I have to say," said Alinzor, "I would give you my justification so clearly that you would pity me rather than accusing me, if you still had any generosity toward me. But, ingrate princess, you are only criticizing me to make me forget that you prefer the Prince of Baleare to me; that is what you cannot deny, and if you care to give me an audience of an hour in your cabinet I will show you the fatal order that forbade me to come to the Festival of the Sun."

"You are telling me things that are so far from the truth," I said, getting to my feet because I perceived Zantille and Zenore coming toward us, "that in order to oblige you to admit your frivolity to me, I want Phenice to bring me to my apartment after everyone has retired. Leave me presently, and don't appear until I have spoken to you." After saying that, I went to meet my aunt, with a trouble that was easy to see.

The impatience to see whether my infidel could prove what he said caused me to retire earlier than usual. The sight of him had renewed the vivacity of my sentiments so much that I believed, without fathoming anything, that a prince so accomplished could not be inconstant, although I had seen it with my own eyes. To second my impatience, Phenice was at the place where I had told him to wait for my summons, but she waited in vain for part of the night and, unable to wait any longer, she came back to inform me of my misfortune. Gods, what became of me when I saw her enter, and she told me that he had not come to the rendezvous! Amour, jealousy and chagrin inspired in me a scorn so outrageous that I fainted, and only came to with a violent fever, which troubled my reason. I spoke to all those who approached me as if they were the perfidious Alinzor.

Zenore, in despair of my illness and fearing for my life, made me take a beverage so excellent that not only did it banish my fever but calmed my transports. I was still afflicted by the infidelity of the Prince of Numidia, but I was capable of making an effort on myself to forget him. By means of her sage advice, Zantille aided me to forget that fickle lover, and, wanting to hasten my cure by a change of place, made me consent to go to spend some time in the Baleare islands.

Charmed to see me in a land of which he was the sovereign, Zenore gave me elegant and magnificent fêtes every day. Everyone spoke to me about his amour and his constancy, and no lover was ever better able to make use of everything that might make him loved, but so much care could not banish the ingrate Alinzor from my heart. It is true that, more reasonable in my dolor, I was sometimes capable of wishing to be more sensitive for the unfortunate Prince of Baleare, but I could do nothing more to compensate his amour. What I had experienced of his science caused me to demand urgently to see the infidelities of my knight again, as a means of curing me of my tenderness; but what he had seen of the first complaisance he had had made him apprehensive that Alinzor's presence would only serve to increase my passion and my despair.

"How cruel you are, Madame," he said, when I pressed him to grant me that favor, "to want to constrain me to tighten your chains. Do you no longer remember that your hatred for me redoubled when you saw the Prince of Numidia again? Why, inhumane princess, did you want to punish me for the crime of my fortunate rival?"

"If your rival were infidel," I said to him, angrily, "you would not fear giving me profs of his inconstancy, which would finish curing me; but doubtless you know that he still loves me, and are rightly apprehensive that, convinced of his amour, I would prefer him."

"Well, Madame," said Zenore, "it is necessary to do as you ask, and give you the sad satisfaction that you demand; but at least, unjust Zalmayde, remember that you forced me to do it."

He quit me after that, and, coming back to find me after everyone had retired, he had me mount the same chariot in which I had made the voyage to Numidia. Having got in with me, we set forth through the air. I passed over mountains, valleys and seas, and we stopped on the island of the fay Desirée. Gods, what beauties I saw there, and if I had had less desire to find the traitor Alinzor I would have taken pleasure in admiring that surprising abode.

Pressing Zenore to take me to where the Prince of Numidia was, he made me stop above a flower-garden dotted with a thousand different flowers. A vividly and brilliantly beautiful nymph was making a garland of orange blossom and immortelles of various colors there and showing it to one of her companions.

"I want Alinzor's love," she said to her, "to last as long as this garland, which I have woven on a golden thread in order to give it the duration of that metal." As she said that, she perceived the traitor at the end of the flower-bed. "Come,

Prince," she said to him; "receive a new mark of my tenderness."

Alinzor, charmed by that charming rival, came to throw himself at her feet, and the nymph, putting the crown on his head, told him the effect she wanted it to have. My infidel kissed her hand and swore to her that nothing would destroy his amour.

You can imagine, Princess, the state that I was in. I asked Zenore a thousand times to let me descend from the chariot, in order to go and trouble such tender moments with my presence, but, inexorable to my pleas, he tore me away from that deadly place, saying that he could not remain there any longer without risking my life. Making his dragons fly, he took me back to my apartment.

Everything that I had felt the first time that I had known Alinzor's inconstancy did not approach what I suffered at that second proof of my misfortune. But, fearing that Zenore would no longer want to render such cruel services, I hid my despair and manifested more complaisance toward him. Charmed by the hope of curing me of an amour so contrary to his happiness, he did not cease giving me new diversions. But, unable to support the chagrin of being in a place where I was not the mistress of refusing the fêtes that were put on to please me, I returned to the Canaries, where, abandoning myself to all that jealousy has of the most terrible, I spent the nights in the same place where I had encountered the inconstant Prince of Numidia.

One day, when I was more depressed than usual, I wanted to go and offer a sacrifice to the Sun, in order to beg him to extinguish a flame that was conducting me to the tomb. As I went into the Temple I heard someone calling Phenice. Paying little heed to everything that did not regard my chagrin, I went on my way, and, when my prayers were finished I returned to the palace.

A short time later I was in my cabinet, where I had shut myself away, Phenice came in with an emotion on her face that astonished me. "What's the matter?" I said to her. "And who called to you this morning as we went into the Temple?"

"I don't know whether I dare tell you, Madame," the maid said to me, "after what you know about the Prince of Numidia's infidelities."

"What are you talking about?" I said to her, blushing. "Has that Prince anything in common with what I asked you?"

"More than you think, Madame," she said.

"But Phenice," I said, with a frightful agitation, "explain this mystery to me, if you don't want to displease me."

"It's necessary to obey you, then," she said, "and tell you, Madame that, while following you this morning I heard someone calling me when you were descending the avenue of orange trees. Curious to know what was wanted of me, I turned my head and I saw a knight whom I recognized easily as Alinzor. I slipped away from my companions and, seeing you enter the Temple, I followed the Prince under the trees, where he stopped.

"'Phenice,' he said to me, 'the anger of the Princess prevents me from appearing before her in a public place, but I can no longer live if she refuses to listen to me for a moment in private. Obtain me that favor, my dear Phenice, and if I cannot recall into her soul the memory of the benevolence she had for this unfortunate person at the Temple of Diana, I promise to deliver her of my odious presence by a death that will satisfy her irritated mind.'

"'Sire,' I replied, 'the Princess has so much reason to complain of you that I cannot promise you that I can persuade her to see you, but I will tell her that you want to speak to her. Be in the labyrinth at sunset, and I will inform her of your desire. In haste to return to you, Madame, I quit the Prince and came to ask you what you want me to do.'"

"Alas, Phenice," I said, "do I know myself? Too convinced of Alinzor's perfidies, I cannot belie my eyes, which have witnessed them; but in spite of such certain proofs, I cannot refuse myself the sad pleasure of reproaching him for them. Yes, Phenice, I will be in the labyrinth, and perhaps I will make him repent of bearing other chains than mine."

Guided by my evil genius, I flattered myself with that foolish hope. But scarcely had I taken a few steps along a winding path that led to the maze and one of the park's gates than I perceived the Prince of Numidia, who was mounted on a superb horse, with a young woman behind him, heading at top seed in the direction of the gate. I uttered a frightful scream at that fatal sight, but without turning his head, he left the park.

Outraged by fury and jealousy, I ran after him all the way to the sea shore, and without being able to prevent him, I saw him enter a ship that was apparently only waiting for their arrival in order to set sail.

At that certain evidence of Alinzor's scorn, I fell in a faint, and Phenice had me brought back to the palace. I spent a part of the night there without giving any sign of life, but the demonic enemy of my repose caused me to see the light again, in order to abandon myself to an inexpressible despair. My reason no longer being able to moderate my transports, I disguised myself as a knight and, having made my confidante do the same, in spite of the pleas she made me not to make a resolution so inappropriate to my birth and age, I left the palace and the island, without being perceived by anyone, in order to go in search of the perfidious Prince of Numidia and make him pay in blood for the woes he had made me suffer.

In order to discover where he was I consulted the Fay of Grandeurs, who, touched by my misfortune, told me that my difficulties would end in the kingdom of Granada. I set forth for it without thinking of any other joy than making my infidel prince perish, and without making use of any other retreat along my route but the forests and shepherds' huts.

I arrived yesterday in the little wood where Fortune, wanting to give me proof that she was softening in my favor, permitted me to encounter you.

"It is really me who ought to praise her," said the Princess of Fez, embracing the beautiful Zalmayde, "for having given me the pleasure of knowing you. How your adventures have touched me, and how much woe I would wish upon Alinzor if he were capable of loving any other beauty than yours."

"You know from my story," said the Princess of the Canaries, "that that Prince has never loved me, and that he has taken a cruel joy in rendering me the unhappiest person of my sex."

"By virtue of his appearing criminal," said Zamea, "I believe him to be innocent. His conduct is so extraordinary that I cannot help suspecting Zenore of being more culpable than him."

"Oh, Madame," Zalmayde interjected, "the Prince of Baleare has served me too well for me to believe him to be complicit with his rival."

"He might well," said Zamea, "without being in accord with Alinzor, have forced him to appear criminal to you. The Prince of Granada, taken to Desirée's island, spent years there at the feet of that fay, without being infidel to the beautiful and unfortunate Princess of Leon; your lover, by the same fatality, might have forgotten you without inconstancy."

"I understand so little of what you are saying to me," said Zalmayde, "that I cannot conceive how I can find Alinzor's justification in the fact of his crime, and what appears to be a very great one in what you tell me about the Prince of Granada."

"When I have the permission of that great Prince," replied the Princess of Fez, "to tell you about his misfortunes, you will know that you will have more reason to feel compassion for the destiny of the Prince of Numidia, if it is similar to Elmedor's, than to criticize him."

Adelinde came in at that moment and interrupted the two princesses to tell them that the Prince of Granada had sent her to ask whether they had had a good night, and that, having asked the squire about his wounds, he had told her that the surgeon had promised that he would be able to ride in three days.

The two princesses, having dressed with diligence, went into the Prince's room, and after a light meal they spent the rest of the day informing the Princess of the Canaries of Elmedor's most important adventures, particularly those which had given Zamea some reason to take the part of the Prince of Numidia.

Zalmayde, faithful to her hatred, did not listen to what the beautiful Princess of Fez told her in order to soothe her chagrins, and the latter had a great deal of difficulty obtaining from her that she would not leave except with them in order to go in search of an end to her troubles by means of the death of her infidel.

The Prince of Granada, even more eager than the two unfortunate princesses to finish the adventure of the castle that served as the prison of the Prince of Tunis, got out of bed that day, and two days later he mounted a horse, followed by Zamea and the Princess of the Canaries.

They rode all day without any obstacle, but in the evening, in a valley that commenced the dependency of the King of Granada, they encountered two knights, who were fighting with a great deal of animosity. Elmedor urged his horse forward rapidly in order to go and separate them, but one of them, who was wearing roseate and lemon yellow plumes, had felled his enemy before the prince had arrived.

That knight approached his enemy and, presenting the point of his sword to his throat, he said: "Admit to me, treacherous Zenore, what you have done with my princess."

"I'm looking for her, like you," the Prince of Baleare replied, "and I cannot give you any news of her."

"Here she is, infidel," cried Zalmayde, hurling a javelin at him that she was holding in her hand, and which pierced his thigh, "come to take your life, in order to punish you for your crimes."

The Prince of Numidia—for it was him—surprised by the sight and the fury of the princess, and weakened by the pain of his wound, fell unconscious alongside his enemy, and the irritated Zalmayde, believing that she had killed the amiable impostor, was in despair at having been able to avenge herself so well.

While Zamea was occupied in consoling the Princess of the Canaries, the Prince of Granada and his squire looked to see whether the unfortunate Alinzor was giving any signs of life, and the princesses' maids did everything they could to stem the blood that was emerging violently from the unfortunate Zenore's wounds.

"Cease trying to recall me to life," the latter said to them. "My crimes are too great not to be punished, and I only ask the gods for the time to confess them."

At that moment, the Prince of Numidia, recovering consciousness, searched with eyes in which death was painted for his beloved enemy. But the hatred of that princess having been reborn with the prince's strength, she was trying to withdraw from a place where two terrible passions were tearing her by turns, when the Prince of Baleare raised himself up slightly in order to stop her.

"Stay, Madame," he said, in a weak voice. "Stay in order to know to whom your hatred is owed; I alone have made the woes of your life, and if amour can serve as an excuse, when one is ready to render account to the gods, I will say that it has forced me to be culpable. It was amour that, rendering me jealous of my rival, caused me to forbid him on your part to appear before you at the Festival of the Sun. And when your portrait had retraced your charms for him, it was me again who transported him to the isle of the fay Desirée, where, forcing him to be infidel, I made you see him in that odious form. But the last of all my crimes is the one that has just constrained you to a vengeance so distant from your humor, that of having made him take away a phantom instead of you when you arranged to met him in the labyrinth, in the belief that he was removing you from my power. Heaven has caused me to find the punishment for my knavery today, at the point of the prince's sword, having so cruelly offended him. Live happily together; the gods, content with this wretched victim, will heap you with benefits, and for the final torture, are forcing me to announce it to you."

As he finished speaking, Zenore was allowed to fall unconscious once again, and died a moment later.

The princess, penetrated by a rightful dolor at having perhaps caused the death of her dear Alinzor, and knowing him to be innocent, approached him, weeping, and, helping the prince and Zamea to bandage his wounds, she washed them with her tears without daring to speak to him.

"Why oppose yourself to a death that is your work, Madame?" he said to her. "Can I have any more glorious than one I receive from your hand?"

"Oh, Alinzor, if you are innocent, how guilty I am! How can I repair what my jealous rage has made me do?"

"These marks of your tenderness," said the wounded prince, "are too precious to me to make anything you do a crime. It's me who is the criminal, since I appeared infidel to you."

"You are hardly in any state," said Zamea, "to speak with so much violence, which might do you more harm than a certain princess has done you. Suffer that we put you on this stretcher," she continued, seeing that the squires were brining one made of tree branches, "and that we take you to the huts that are ahead of us."

Having thanked the Princess of Fez for her foresight, Zalmayde begged Alinzor to allow himself to be taken, and the Prince of Granada having aided his squires to put him on it, they all mounted up again and arrived at a sufficiently comfortable habitation.

After orders had been given for a grave to be dug for the unfortunate Prince of Baleare, the wounded prince was laid in a bed such as the good people could give him, and, the owner of the place being one of the knowledgeable shepherds of which Spain is full, he examined Alinzor's wounds and assured him that he would apply a herb to them that would enable him to continue his journey in two days, provided that he was left to repose for the rest of the day and the night. Zamea made Zalmayde—who, trembling for the prince's life, did not want to quit him—consent to that.

As they came out of the little habitation, the two princesses encountered Alinzor's squire. Curious to know everything that had caused the unhappiness of her life, Zalmayde obliged the faithful domestic not to hide from her any of his master's adventures since she had seen him at the Temple of Diana, and, having sat down on the grass with the Prince of Granada, the squire, addressing the Princess of the Canaries, commenced his discourse thus.

The Story of the Prince of Numidia

After the Prince my master had quit you, Madame, he remained in a mortal chagrin, and, not daring to follow you, for fear of displeasing you, he went to spend the time of his exile in Numidia. How long the time was for his impatience! And how belated the summer appeared that year! Finally, those fortunate days drew near, and everything was prepared for your voyage when one morning, a knight came, bringing him a letter on your part. He opened it with an agitation that presaged his unhappiness, and he found these cruel words:

Zalmayde to the Prince of Numidia
Since my return to this island I have learned that the gods have threatened my kingdom with ruination if I give my people a king whose mores and customs are so different from ours. Let us forget, Prince, the feeble commencements of a passion contrary to my glory. I have resolved, or the god of my Estate, to give myself to Prince Zenore, whose splendid merit will sustain my crown. Do not, therefore, come to trouble with your presence the pleasure that I take in that alliance, no longer think about a princess who only wants to remember you in order to beg you never to see her again.

Zalmayde.

171

"Yes, ingrate princess," said the Prince, outraged by your scorn, "I will obey you, and I will not envy the fate of my unworthy rival." Speaking to the knight, he continued: "You can say that to your princess, and that I shall have as much joy in breaking my chains as I would have had in rendering them eternal if she had known the value of her conquest."

After those words, which chagrin drew from him, he dismissed the man who had bought that fatal letter, and, shutting himself in his cabinet, he abandoned himself to a despair that made me tremble for his days.

More than a month passed after that cruel news without him being able to make the resolution no longer to love you, but, finally ashamed of his weakness, he gave his attentions to a princess of his court. As if the marks of his amour were able to fly all the way to you, he only gave them to her in public. His heart, refusing to obey him, could not efface your charming depiction therefrom.

One evening, when he was giving a fête in the gardens of the palace and was with her, he saw something fall from the sky at his feet. He hastened to pick up the precious present, but imagine his astonishment when he saw that it was your portrait! Transported by a passion that all his reason had not been able to cure, he quit his princess, and, only listening to his amour, without remembering the prohibition that you had imposed, he departed for the Canaries.

You know, Madame, how he saw you in the gardens of your palace, but you do not know that, the Prince having remained in an arbor in order to wait for Phenice, he fell asleep there, and when he awoke he found himself on the isle of the fay Desirée, without having any memory of what had happened to him since he had been on earth, and without being astonished to be in such a beautiful place. He walked through the admirable gardens, and found a nymph there of a touching beauty, who approached him with an obliging smile, which gave him the desire to please her.

He returned her cares; she was no more insensible to them than the fay Desirée had been to the Prince of Granada. But Sire (he said, addressing that Prince) as soon as you had found the means of leaving that enchanted place, the fay conceived such a terrible aversion for all men that, no longer wanting to suffer them in her palace, she made them embark on a ship that took them to the mainland.

As soon as Alinzor had quit that pernicious abode, Madame, emerging from the lethargy in which he had been buried for such a long time, he remembered the rendezvous that you had given him, and, wanting to justify himself or die, he came to the Canaries a second time; he spoke to Phenice and went to the labyrinth.

He had not been there for an hour when he saw you arrive, your face covered in tears. "Alinzor," you said to him, "Since you departed, I have made the traitor Zenore confess that it was him who deceived you with a false letter; that in order to conceal that knowledge of his crime from me he abducted you to the isle of the fay Desirée; and, wanting to render us unhappy, he is forcing me to marry him. Save me from the horror of that monster and take me to your realm. When I am safe there, you can come to snatch my crown from him, and his life."

My Prince, charmed to see you disposed to follow him, not wanting to let such a fortunate moment escape after having promised to adore you for the rest of his days, untethered his horse, which he had attached to a tree, and, putting you on the rump, hastened to leave the park. He took you to his ship, and having made the crossing that separates your islands from the mainland, he continued his journey all the way to Numidia. As soon as he was in Numidia, however, you disappeared, Madame.

Alinzor, in despair, realized that Zenore, in order to get him away from you, had caused him to take away a phantom. Outraged by such a fatal destiny, he resumed the route to the Canaries, resolved to make you aware of his innocence and to constrain the perfidious Prince of Baleare to confess his crimes. I went with him on that journey, and I witnessed his fury when he learned that you had departed and that his rival had followed you. He left a place so fatal for him, and went to consult the Fay of Grandeurs in order to know where he might find you; she ordered him to come to Granada.

We took that route, and, having arrived in this valley, we encountered Zenore. Transported by fury, my Prince attacked him. You witnessed the end of that combat, when, following the impulses of your unjust anger, Madame, you thought of depriving yourself of the most faithful lover in the world.

"You see, my dear Zalmayde" said Zamea, as soon as the squire had stopped speaking, "that I was right to tell you that Alinzor, by dint of seeming criminal, appeared to me to be innocent."

"Don't reproach me any longer for my crime, my beautiful Princess," replied the Princess of the Canaries. "I have been punished for it enough by the mortal dread I have that my perfidious hand might have served me only too well."

"Have no fear for the Prince of Numidia," replied the Prince of Granada. "I have experienced the science of these shepherds on wounds less glorious but more dangerous than Alinzor's."

After those words, the illustrious adventurers, seeing that the night was advanced, went in search of a little repose.

The Princess of the Canaries was torn between too many different emotions to find any. The pleasure of knowing that Alinzor was faithful gave her a joy so sensible that it could only be balanced by the fear of losing him, and daylight appeared without her being able to decide to which of those two passions to abandon herself. Princess Zamea, who loved her tenderly, and whose own particular anxieties gave her scarcely any more tranquility, had kept her company.

Those two amiable persons having learned that the Prince of Granada was already with the wounded prince, went into his hut. Zalmayde entered it tremulously, and, approaching the bed, she asked him how he was.

"It is for you to tell me, divine Princess," he said, "my life only being secure if you assure me that you forgive me for everything that the jealousy of the wretched Zenore constrained me to do against my amour."

"Oh," Zalmayde said to him, "I am far more culpable than you, and if it were as easy to repair the harm that I have done you as to forget our past woes, I would no longer have any reason to shed tears."

"The wound that your beautiful hand has caused me," replied the invalid prince, "is so dear to me that I dread being cured of it."

The sage shepherd, fearing that such a passionate conversation might impede the effect of his remedy, obliged Elmedor and Zamea to intervene therein. They employed all day in that, and in the evening, in order to give him time to change the prince's dressings, they went for a walk along the bank of a river that flowed through the valley.

They had not gone very far when they saw a knight coming toward them, mounted on a horse whose lassitude made evident the scant care that its master had had to allow it to rest.

The knight was wearing armor of burnished steel enriched with gold thread. His helmet, the visor of which was raised, was charged with flax-gray plumes. What could be seen of his coat appeared to be silver and flax-gray, and on a heavy shield that was suspended from his saddle-bow the famous mountain could be seen that frightens its neighbors so frequently with the continual flames that emerge from its entrails, and for a device the words: *I burn endlessly.*

The handsome face of the unknown man, although it appeared very melancholy, made the beautiful princesses curious. Having become bolder by virtue of the presence of the Prince of Granada, they advanced toward him. After having saluted them, the knight went by without stopping, but, having cast his eyes on Elmedor's face, he uttered a cry and, leaping down from his horse, he ran toward him.

"Generous Knight," he said to him, "the Fay of Grandeurs is not deceptive in her promises, since I find you in the very place where she has ordered me to look for you. I cannot mistake the description that she made of you. You are the one who ought to extract my princess from the fatal enchantment in which the cruel Amerdin is retaining her in a castle a few days from here. I have tried in vain to liberate her from her irons; that glory is reserved for you, and everything must yield to the valor and the fidelity of the courageous Prince of Granada."

"Heaven would doubtless enable me to forget my woes," said Elmedor, "were they of a nature to be forgotten, if I were fortunate enough to render your princess to you, amiable stranger, while doing battle for the interests of the charming Zamea, for whom I am undertaking the adventure that you have just offered me, as soon as a prince who merits not being abandoned, is in a state to accompany us. Suffer that your felicity is delayed for a few days, and, to give us a desire to be of service to you, recount to the Princes of Fez and the Princess of the Canaries, whom you see, the subject of your difficulties. You could not, generous Knight, speak to anyone more disposed, by their own misfortunes, to sympathize with yours."

After having begged the pardon of the two princesses for not having rendered to them what he owed them, and after the illustrious company had sat down on the grass bordering the river, the stranger commenced the story of his adventures, addressing the Princess of Fez, in accordance with the indication given to him by the Princess of the Canaries.

The Story of the Prince of Mauretania and the Princess of Castile

The misfortunes of my life are so great, that I would hesitate to bore you with them if the Prince of Granada had not just assured me that yours have taught you to sympathize with those overwhelmed by misfortunate fate.

I will therefore tell you, Madame, that I am the son of the King of Mauretania, that my name is Zalmandor, and that, having spent the early years of my life like all princes of my age, seeing my father's kingdom peaceful, I slipped away from the court, accompanied by a squire in whom I had confidence. I sought to make myself known under the name of the Knight of the Ardent Sword.

I learned that the King of Castile was at war with one of his neighboring princes; I went to offer him my services, which he accepted with pleasure. There was a young knight with him, whose noble and majestic bearing attracted my gaze. I do not know whether he found something in me that merited his attention, but I noticed that he could not take his eyes off my face. Subsequently, however, that disposition we had to mutual esteem changed into a hatred that can only end with our lives.

We saw one another every day; when we were occupied in combats, we each sought to snatch the victory, or at least to merit equal praises. The King of Castile wanting to attach us to him, for fear that one of us, discontented, might go over to his enemies and balance out his conquests, heaped us with caresses. But, not having known until that day who we were, he pressed us with such good grace to tell him that we could not refuse.

I told him my name and my birth, and the other identified himself as the Prince of Aragon, Armande, known as the Knight of the Immortal Amour. That title made me understand that he was in love; I sought information and learned that it was with the Princess of Castile, that he had remained hidden in that court for several months, that he had sometimes seen Almandine—that was the name of the princess—but that, the king having strong reasons for only allowing her to marry one of his subjects, did not permit the foreign knights attached to him to serve her. He was having her raised in a palace separate from his own, from which she rarely emerged to show herself in public. A secret sentiment, of which I did not know the cause, made me annoyed that the Prince of Aragon loved the

Princess of Castile, and made me more determined to acquire the amity of the king.

I was fortunate enough to render him fairly considerable services in that war, and if they did not surpass those of the Knight of the Constant Amour, they could equal them. Finally, the campaign finished and we returned to Castile, without having been able to determine which of us had the greater share of the king's esteem. The queen and the majority of the ladies of the court came to meet us, and the king, presenting me to that princess, and singing my praises, told her that only the Prince of Aragon could dispute them with me.

The queen paid me a very honest compliment, and, already knowing The Knight of the Ardent Amour, made him a thousand caresses. We finally arrived at the palace, where the king wanted me to have an apartment, as well as Armande; and wanting to show the infinite esteem that he had for us, he invited the princess, his daughter, to come that evening.

I had never seen anything as charming as the beautiful Almandine. Everything that could form the most beautiful eyes in the world was in hers; a fire so bright that burns you at the first glance, and an attitude so mild and flattering permits you to bear the chains that they give you.

I sensed from that moment on that it was impossible to defend oneself against her charms, and although I saw that she responded kindly to the tender urgency of my rival, I abandoned myself to a violent penchant that forced me to love her, and I flattered myself that perhaps Armande was not so well-positioned with her that I could not at least oblige her to balance her esteem between the two of us.

You might think, Madame that I was very reckless, or very amorous, but in my experience, Amour has presentiments as well as Fortune. In order to make my design succeed, I took a different route from my rival. I hid my passion carefully, and, attaching myself to one of the most beautiful young women of the court, I gave her fêtes. I was in her favor in horse races, and neglected nothing of the fine gallantry that gives us the advantage over all the nations in the world.

The attentions that I rendered to Celdine—that was the amiable young woman's name—sometimes had the princess for a witness, the king suffering that she obtained pleasures for which she must not give any recompense. I perceived with a sensible joy that she was sometimes pensive there, and that, in spite of Armande's attachment, her eyes reproached me for bearing chains other than hers. I suffered in those moments, from not being able to make her aware of all the amour I had for her, but the fear of not yet being the stronger in her heart forced me to pretend until a more fortunate time.

However, I spent cruel hours; I knew that the Prince of Aragon, having bribed a maid that Amandine loved, sometimes got into her palace, and that in spite of the princess, he often spoke to her about his amour with no other witness than the confidante, and that if there was no tender response to his passion, at least she listened to him without anger. He even followed her to the Temple and during excursions, and he was always beside her as soon as she appeared in public.

The king began to get alarmed by that, and whatever amity he had for him, politics prevailed, and he asked him to leave his court.

Such a terrible command inflamed the Prince of Aragon's anger and constrained him no longer to appear at the palace. The king, believing himself to be secure and seeing me attached to Celdine, gave the princess more liberty. She appeared in public more often, and I was exposed to the danger of not being able to hide my passion for much longer. Sometimes my eyes betrayed me, and attached themselves to the adorable Almandine with such tender emotion that she blushed; but that amiable blush had nothing disobliging about it, and seemed evidence of modesty rather than anger.

One evening, when I was giving Celdine a ball in an arbor in the palace gardens, I went into a pathway to take a rest after having danced a great deal. I had only taken a few steps when I heard someone talking on the other side of the palisade.

"No, Phedime," said a person that I knew to be the princess, "No, I can't suffer any longer that Celdine is taking him away from me, and you can't comprehend the chagrin that the love Zalmandor has for her causes me."

"I confess, Madame," the maid replied, "that this bizarre chagrin astonishes me. Forgive me if I speak to you so boldly. You suffered without anger the attentions of the unfortunate Prince of Aragon; you let him hope that if anyone could please you, he would have the advantage over all his rivals, and since your father has forbidden him the palace, you do not seem sorry when, without you saying anything, I obtain him opportunities to tell you about all the dolor that a deeply touched heart feels when it does not have the liberty of seeing the object it adores. Why, then, Madame, if I dare ask, are you so interested in the attentions that the Prince of Mauretania renders to the beautiful Celdine? What does it matter to you into whose hands a heart might fall that you do not want to receive?"

"As, until now, I have not revealed my veritable sentiments," said the princess, "you have reason to be astonished by my anxiety. But Phedime, my soul is too afflicted not to seek the sad pleasure of lamentation. Learn, then, that Armande has never had a part of my tenderness. The eccentricity of my father, who, under the pretext of I know not what prediction, will not allow me to live like other princesses of my rank, gave me the desire to find a protector who could defend me against being sacrificed to a prince who is a subject of the crown that I ought to wear one day.

"The Prince of Aragon seemed to me to be appropriate to my design. Master of his Estates, as of his person, I believed that I could not make a better choice. I received his attentions benevolently, and even thought that I might be able to love him, but I had not seen Zalmandor. As soon as he appeared, I no longer had anything but indifference for Armande. I flattered myself that I would conquer him in a matter of days, and my heart was already flying toward its prayers when the fêtes he gave Celdine informed me that I was mistaken.

"Oh, Phedime, if you knew all that a proud and glorious princess can suffer, who believes herself to merit being loved and who sees the incense that ought to be destined for her borne elsewhere; I confess to you that there is no torture more frightful. I wanted to see whether I could not forget in Armande's amour the insult that the Prince of Mauretania has offered to my charms. I even affected, in those cruel fêtes in which I was the witness to my rival's triumph, to listen more favorably to the Prince of Aragon.

"I confess to you that I sometimes thought that Zalmandor had some chagrin in consequence, and I have often surprised him gazing at me as one gazes at someone when one loves them. This very evening, my dear Phedime, occupied as he seemed to be with the fortunate Celdine, his eyes, full of a fire to which only amour can give birth, attached themselves to mine with a languor so eloquent that I could not sustain their gaze. However, he loves my rival; I cannot doubt it."

"Oh, Madame," I said, no longer able to hide myself, "my dear Princess, I do not love Celdine; you alone have filled my heart with that fire, which you eyes alone can ignore. Learn in your turn that I have only feigned love in order to deceive your father and—dare I confess it?—to give you the desire to make my conquest in spite of the esteem you had for my rival. How I have suffered from that cruel constraint! How many times have I been ready to kill him! But, retaining such just transports for fear of letting my passion burst forth, I returned to Celdine. Today, Destiny, in accord with Amour, has led me into this pathway. Do not be annoyed, my adorable princess, by what they enabled me to hear. Let us cease our constraint; accept a heart that has never borne any other chains than yours, without any longer conserving my rival."

"Zalmandor," said the princess, "I cannot deny my weakness, since you have heard it. But in order to merit that I make a vow to you and sacrifice the Prince of Aragon for you, it is necessary to give me proof that you do not love my rival, and heap as much scorn upon her as you have enabled her to triumph in my eyes. When, by a disavowal as spectacular as your amour for her has been, I can no longer doubt your sincerity, perhaps I will forget the unfortunate Armande."

"Oh, Madame," I cried, "you love my rival more than you think, since you are hesitating to dismiss him, and your vanity has a greater share than your heart in the favorable things I have heard."

"What you say might well be true," said the princess, with an expression of chagrin; "but after all, you know the condition that I put on my esteem; it is up to you to do it, if you want to oblige me to anything more."

After saying that she returned to the ball, and, wanting to show her that I was able to obey her, I did not approach Celdine, and was one of the first to leave the assembly, in order not to be obliged to give her my hand to escort her to her apartment. Wanting to speak for a moment more to the charming Almandine, however, before I went back into the palace I waited for her in a large flower bed that was under the windows of her apartment.

I had not been here for a hour when I perceived my rival, and Phedime, quitting the princess, came to talk to him. I could not hear what she said to him, because I was hidden behind a honeysuckle bush, but a moment later, I saw the window of the cabinet open, and the Prince of Aragon, having approached, talked for more than half an hour to a woman whom I assumed to be the princess.

All the respect I had for her nearly yielded twenty times over to my jealous fury, but in the end, I waited for Armande to leave the palace and having caught up with him outside the city as he was about to mount his horse, I said to him: "Knight, you cannot contravene the king's orders without having a mortal enemy in me and without me forcing you to obey him."

"I did not think," said Armande, "that princes like you served as spies for the King of Castile, and that person can only be pardonable in Zalmandor for being the lover of Princess Almandine."

"Whether as the lover of the princess," I replied, drawing my sword, "or as the friend of the king, I will not suffer that you remain in this place any longer."

"Let's see," he said, putting himself in a stance to receive me, "whether you can execute that generous design."

With those words, we commenced a combat that might have been fatal for me if the Prince of Aragon's sword had not broken; and, his squires having arrived, I withdrew without a wound. Armande had a rather considerable one in the thigh, but, not wanting to be found in that place, he had himself cried a few miles from the city, where he had chosen his retreat.

As our combat had only had domestics for witnesses, it remained secret for some time, and was, to begin with, from the Princess, who learned about it from Phedime, whom Armande had informed. She made me a few reproaches the first time she saw me, but as that recklessness was evidence of my passion, she pardoned me, without wanting to promise me to banish my rival.

However, the affectation I had in avoiding Celdine, for whom I had been seen to have so much enthusiasm, was remarked by the entire court, and as she was a relative of the queen, the latter testified some chagrin to me in consequence. I told her that the orders I had received not long ago from my father, who did not approve of that alliance, had obliged me to conceal the sentiments I had for the beautiful young woman, for fear that he might order me to return to him.

As Celdine, whom I had had the misfortune of not displeasing, was proud, and had flattered herself that she might one day be Queen of Mauretania, she did not listen to such feeble excuses, and she soon divined the veritable reason for my change. She conceived such a great chagrin in consequence that she told the king that the Prince of Aragon had not left the realm, that he had the design of abducting the princess, that I was his rival and that we had fought on the day of the ball. She knew about that adventure from one of my domestics, whom she had bribed, and who rendered her a faithful account of all my actions.

The king, alarmed at that news, sent men to take the unfortunate Armande prisoner and take him to a castle overlooking the city. He ordered the queen not to let the princess leave her palace any longer, the guard of which was doubled. As for me, he dared not say anything to me, fearing that he might need my arm in the war, which had only been deferred by a truce of one year, but he set spies to watch me, who told him everything I did.

All those changes caused me a mortal dolor. I was in despair at having caused my rival's misfortune by my imprudent anger and of having lost the liberty I had had of sometimes seeing the adorable Almandine. But as Amour is ingenuous, I found the means of entering a small wood that extended under the window of her apartment, and where she often went for a walk. I did not encounter her for two days, but one evening, when it was very warm, she came to savor the fresh air, only accompanied by Phedime. I appeared before her and tried to beg her pardon for my boldness, but the princess did not give me time to speak.

"Zalmandor," she said, "you ought to be content with the harm you have done me, without coming to try to do more. To what extremity would the king's anger not go if he knew that you had come into his palace, at an hour when it is only permitted for my women to approach me. What right have you, who know so well how to obey, to scorn his orders?"

"If your heart, Madame," I said, "were not prejudiced toward my fortunate rival, you would not make it a crime for me to have been unable to suffer his good fortune without making him purchase it with his blood, and you would find, in a little generosity for me, the excuse for what I am doing today. But, cruel princess, the care I took to attract the hatred of Celdine, by virtue of the indifference I have for you, has not been able to touch you. You only wanted that striking evidence of the effect of your charms, without any concern for the person who gave it to you."

"You are quite unjust to make me that reproach, Zalmandor," Almandine said. "You do not know me if you believe that sacrifices can be agreeable to me, if the hand that offers them to me is not dear to me. That is what makes me support my prison without a murmur. Be faithful, and rely on me for the recompense.

"I confess that the misfortunes of the Prince of Aragon touch me; that I am sorry to see him in my father's irons, and that I would like with all my heart to render him liberty, but it would not be to receive his amour. Determined to share your chains, I can no longer listen to his sighs. Help me to break the irons with which my father in afflicting him, and I promise you to forbid him to carry mine."

"Whatever danger there is in obeying you, Madame," I replied. "I will employ everything in my power to do that. But divine princess, remember that this prince...."

"I will only remember the tender penchant that you know I have for you," she told me, "if you are able to serve me as I wish to be served."

After that, without wanting to allow me to say any more, she ordered me to withdraw, but she did so without forbidding me to return, and I was able to profit so well for that indulgence that I saw her every evening, with no other witness than Phedime.

Gods, how many new charms I discovered in those private conversations, and how I blessed Heaven for my good fortune! In those transports I did not forget to employ myself for my rival, but all my pleas were futile; the king did not want to hear talk of his liberty; and although the queen, who loved that prince, made use of all her credit, she did not obtain anything more.

However, Armande, his wounds having healed, found the invention of escaping through a window of his room that overlooked open country, and over which it had not been thought necessary to put bars because of the impossibility of making use of it. The first usage he made of his liberty was to try to see the princess. He spoke to Phedime and the maid, who had always favored him, hid him in one of Almandine's

cabinets, and when there was no one in the princess's apartment but her, he took him to her bedroom.

Her astonishment was great when she saw that prince,
and her first emotion was to be glad to see him out of the
king's hands; but, reflecting on the further misfortunes that
might happen to him if he were caught, she said: "Armande,
the gods are my witness to the extent that your imprisonment
touched me and what I would have done to liberate you from
it. Heaven has seconded my prayers; don't fall back, by virtue
of your obstinacy in remaining in a place so fatal to your repose, into a danger more to be feared than the first. Return to
Aragon, and if you have some amity for me, give to the esteem that I have for you the forgetfulness of the offense that
my father has caused you and don't think of avenging yourself
for it."

"To be sure of my obedience, Madame," Armande replied, "it is necessary not to send me away. So long as I can
see my princess I cannot hate the man to whom she owes her
birth, no matter how unjust he has been; but I cannot guarantee, if you have the cruelty to banish me, that I will not remember the ill-treatment he has meted out to me."

"You cannot stay here any longer without being discovered," said Almandine, and I can no longer see you without
risk of being the most unfortunate person of my sex."

"Oh, Madame," the Prince of Aragon interjected, "you
would not have those anticipatory fears unless you had some
benevolence for me. Doubtless Zalmandor, with whom the
combat has made me see only too well that he is my rival...."

"Armande," said the princess, without giving him time to
finish what he wanted to say, "the Prince of Mauretania has no
part in the plea that I am making; only my duty and the fear of
being the cause of your doom obliges me to make it, although,
in order not to hide anything from you, that prince is dear
enough to me to prefer him to the whole earth."

"I have no more to do, then, than to die," said Armande,
"since you have announced my death sentence."

At the same time, the furious prince drew his sword, and would have passed it through his heart if Phedime and the princess had not snatched it away from him violently.

Overwhelmed by despair, he left Almandine's apartment and went to spend the night in an isolated house.

He sent me a challenge in the morning and identified the place where he would be. I went there with no other accompaniment than the squire that you see, and without asking him the reason for that second combat, we commenced like men who feared that they might not have time to finish.

I was fortunate enough to be victorious, and the Prince of Aragon, weakened by the loss of the blood that was flowing from two large wounds, fell unconscious. My squire and I carried him to the nearest habitation, and having sent for a surgeon from the city, where everything was in rumor at his flight, I had him bandaged. The wounds were large, but not dangerous, and as soon as he had recovered consciousness I approached his bed.

"Generous prince," I said, "the fate of arms has given me a victory that you merit more than I do. Suffer that I make you know, by the care that I shall take in this place where everyone is your enemy, to give you all the necessary help, that if you cannot love me, since the amour we both have for the Princess of Castile prevents us from doing so, at least I merit your esteem."

"Valiant Zalmandor," he said, "I ought, in order to recognize your generosity, to cede our divine princess to you, but I cannot promise you that. Thus, to rid yourself of an enemy whose life is incompatible with yours, let me end my misfortunate days. You have stolen the heart of the ingrate Almandine from me; do not have the cruelty to make me witness your happiness."

"I do not know," I said to him, "whether or not you have a greater share than me in the esteem of that princess, but whichever one of us she chooses, let us await her choice, without taking away from her by our combats two faithful friends. If it is true that you love her, do not dispose without her orders of a life that ought to be hers."

Armande yielded to my arguments, and promised me to suffer everything that was necessary for his cure. After that I returned to the city, for fear of rendering myself suspect.

I found the king in a frightful wrath at the escape of the Prince of Aragon. He gave orders so precise to capture him wherever he might be, that, fearing that he might be discovered, I went in the evening to beg the princess to send him a command to allow himself to be taken to Aragon. Phedime took it, because she was not sure that she could confide in anyone else. He resisted Almandine's plea for a long time, but finally consented to it.

I had a stretcher made, and I had him transported all the way to his realm, not daring to accompany him myself for fear of harming him.

In the meantime, the king fell ill and died after a week; the queen, touched by his loss, followed a month later. The princess, overwhelmed by so many chagrins, did not want to survive people so dear to her, although the king had caused her to pass sad moments, and without the benevolence she had for me, she would not have wiped away her tears so soon, but she yielded to my prayers and the urgency of her people, who recognized her as queen with a joy that marked their tenderness.

Celdine, whose hatred had not diminished, seeing no obstacle to your happiness, had recourse to the traitor Amerdin. It cannot be that you do not know that formidable enemy of the human race, who only makes use of his science to do harm, without having any other interest than making tears flow, of which he forms a stream and with which he masks his cruel enchantments.

That perfidious individual, delighted to have a new opportunity to exercise his rage, abducted the princess one day and took her to the fatal castle where, for a century, he has kept so many princes and princesses enchanted, making her suffer a thousand different tortures.

No dolor was ever equal to mine, when I found myself separated from my dear Almandine. I wanted to make Celdine pay with her life for her cruel vengeance, but, thinking it shameful to steep my hands in the blood of a woman, I ran after my princess, and I arrived at the fatal castle. I was there for several days without my cries or my threats obliging anyone to respond to me. Finally, despairing of my fate, I went in search of the adorable fay who makes at a pleasure to help all the unfortunate. She ordered me to come and wait in this place, and assured me that you alone reserve the power to punish the perfidious Amerdin and render liberty to so many illustrious unfortunates.

The Prince of Mauretania finished his discourse with a sigh so touching that Elmedor promised him again to risk his life in order to render the lovable Almandine to him. The princesses, rose to their feet after having thanked him for taking the trouble to tell them about his adventures, and they all retired together to the Prince of Numidia, to whom they introduced the Prince of Mauretania.

The sage shepherd having cured Alinzor of his wounds in two days, as he had promised, all hose illustrious persons took the road to Amerdin's castle, after having recompensed their charitable host liberally, and at the first town the Princess of the Canaries resumed female attire, along with Phenice, having no more reasons that obliged her to conceal her sex.

They continued their journey for several days without any adventure arriving, but one morning, when they had all descended from their horses on the bank of a river in order to rest, they saw a boat in the form of a small galley coming toward them conducted by elegantly dressed oarsmen. A nymph clad like those of Diana appeared there, sitting on cushions of green and gold velvet, and gazing attentively at the bank.

Such an agreeable spectacle arrested the gazes of the princesses, and they saw the nymph advance to the side of the galley as soon as it was close to them. Addressing Elmedor, she said "Prince of Granada, the Fay of Grandeurs, whose abode is not far from here, has sent me to tell you that she would like to see you, and all your amiable troop, before you attempt the adventure of Amerdin's castle. She can return to you the fatal ring that you lost, and which Zamat confided to her as he died. It is by that means alone that you can break the enchantment of the cruel magician and enjoy a happiness for which you have not hoped."

Seeing that he was uncertain as to what he ought to do, she went on: "Have no fear that this is an artifice of the fay Desirée; the one who sent me only has need of her beauty to make herself loved, and only wants to see you in order to render you happy."

Ashamed of that reproach, the Prince offered his hand to the Princess of the Canaries, who was the first to climb into the galley, and, the whole charming troop having embarked with Elmedor, it set forth for the isle of the Fay of Grandeurs.

They soon arrived, and were astonished by the magnificence that they encountered. Everything was glittering with gold and precious stones, and the simplest habitations were made of marble and porphyry. All the inhabitants of that fortunate place reflected the grandeur of their sovereign, and nothing appeared that was not superb, but it was impossible to support the glare of the palace, which was built of rock crystal, ornamented at intervals by golden columns. The apartments of that magnificent edifice responded to the beauty outside, and the fay's was so brilliant with precious stones of every color that the Sun's could not surpass it.

That adorable princess came to meet them at the door of her chamber. Without borrowing anything from art to enhance her beauty she appeared to be a masterpiece of Nature. Her stature was beyond that of a mortal woman, and all her facial features were so perfect that it was impossible to depict them without taking away something from their charms. A majesty accompanied by a charming mildness completed rendering her adorable, and the Princesses of Fez and the Canaries rendered her without difficulty the homage that one renders to goddesses, prostrating themselves at her feet.

She lifted them up benevolently, and, having embraced them, she told the Prince of Granada that she had so much esteem for his virtue that she had wanted to return to him the ring that Zamat had confided to her, and that before he rendered her a considerable service in the destruction of Amerdin's castle, it was only just that she should ask him to do it herself.

"I should no longer regret my sad days," Elmedor said to her, "if they are of some use to you, and the unfortunate Alzayde could not complain that I am delaying her vengeance if I am fortunate enough to show you my profound respect."

"You will avenge Alzayde in serving me," said the fay, "and you will rediscover that lovable person in the same place where you will punish the cruel Asmonade."

"Oh, Madame," cried the amorous Prince of Granada, "what are you telling me? My princess is not dead, and I can hope to see her beautiful eyes announcing my good fortune again?"

"Perhaps my oracles are not sure," replied the Fay of Grandeurs, smiling.

"Oh, Madame," said Elmedor, "I shall certainly refrain from doubting them. They promise me a wealth too precious not to hope for it."

After those words, the fay, fearing that the princesses might need repose, took them into an apartment, where they found nymphs who presented them with magnificent garments, of which the Fay of Grandeurs was making them a gift. They put them on in order to please her, and in order not to wound her eyes by their negligence.

How the Prince of Numidia congratulated himself for the choice he had made of the Princess of the Canaries when he saw her enter the fay's chamber with that superb attire, and how beautiful he found her! The Fay of Grandeurs gave her and Princess Zamea abundant flattering praise, and after spending the day in charming conversation, the adorable sovereign conducted them to the gardens where everything that art, in combination with Nature, could form of the admirable was to be found.

They strolled there for a long time, and paused to repose in an arbor of myrtles and pomegranates. There was a round fountain in the middle, where there was a statue of Juno holding several crowns, from which threads of water were emerging from every fleuron, were lost in the air and fell back into the basin with a confused murmur.

When the fay had invited the princesses to sit down next to her they heard an enchanted concert, which surprised them agreeably. Having listened to that admirable music for half a hour, the fay recommenced talking to Elmedor about the adventure that he was about to undertake, and gave him such precious lessons on everything that he had to do that he and the rest of that illustrious company knew that she had a secret interest in it.

Zamea, bolder than the others, told her that she was convinced that the Prince of Granada would carry the perilous enterprise through, but that, in order not to neglect anything that might render it unfailing, she ought to have the goodness not to hide from him the part she was playing in it. Zalmayde joined her voice with the Princess of Fez in order to obtain that favor, and the princes, by their respectful silence, marked well enough that they had no less desire to know than the beautiful princesses.

The Fay of Grandeurs granted them, with an amiable blush, what they were requesting with so much eagerness, but, unable to resolve to be present at her story, she stood up and ordered Celine, one of her nymphs, to satisfy their curiosity. Celine, obeying her charming sovereign, commenced speaking as soon as she had drawn some distance away, addressing Zamea, the Princess of the Canaries having instructed her to do so.

The Story of the Fay of Grandeurs and Prince Salmacis

You doubtless know, Madame, that the Fay of Grandeurs is a daughter of Venus and King Poliandre, and that one sees in her face the beauty of the goddess, her mother, with the air of majesty and grandeur of the king, her father. His tenderness for her was so great that he wanted her to be a sovereign as soon as her hand could carry a scepter. He gave her this island, and Venus heaped her with gifts, rendering her the most savant and the most powerful fay in Europe. Only making use of her science to spread happiness, she soon had the adoration of the entire world, and the unfortunate came from all over the world in search of her.

In her court there was a prince named Salmacis, whose merit was unequaled; his beauty, intelligence and courage seemed to dispute the advantage of making the admiration of all those who knew him, and if Fortune refused him the crown that his forefathers had worn, he merited it so clearly that no one perceived that blindness on Fortune's part.

Such as I have described him, and even more charming, it is not astonishing that he made the conquest of all the nymphs of that brilliant court, but his glory could not rise any higher than being regarded favorably by our divine fay. She felt a penchant for him that she had difficulty hiding, but her pride told her that, being the daughter of Venus and the great King Poliandre, and the queen of a flourishing empire, she could only regard Salmacis as her foremost subject.

Undoubtedly the grandeur of the fay prevented the prince from raising his sights as far as her, and caused him to find charms in a young nymph possessed of a brilliant beauty, whose name was Ismire. He did not sigh for long without being heard. Ismire, flattered by the vanity of having prevailed over all our beauties, loved as much as she was loved, and, making a glory of her conquest, did not hide her tenderness.

At the peak of felicity, Salmacis could not live for a moment without his charming nymph; everything appeared insupportable without her, and, the obligations of paying his court to the fay taking him away from her for precious hours, he was no longer seen in public except to accompany Ismire. Every day he invented fêtes to amuse her, and every evening, when she had retired, he spent a part of the night giving her concerts of all the best musicians in Europe.

So much amour wounded the queen's eyes. If she had not been able to vanquish the penchant she had for Salmacis, she had been able to conceal it as long as he had not loved anyone, but as soon as jealousy was mingled with her tenderness she became pensive, anxious and chagrined, and as no one knew what was passing in her heart, there was not a moment when she did not hear talk about her rival. Finally, unable to enclose so many cruel passions in her soul, she talked about them one day to me.

"Celine," she said to me, "is it true that Salmacis loves Ismire so tenderly?"

"Madame, I said to her, already having perceived that the prince was not indifferent to her, "Ismire is only loved by Prince Salmacis because he dares not look at what there is in this court more beautiful than her."

"And who do you find more lovable that that nymph?" the fay asked me.

"If you will permit me to say so, Madame," I said, "I will tell you that the Fay of Grandeurs is even further above her in beauty as by birth."

"Alas, Celine, how little you know of the power of amour if you think it is born in a heart by virtue of the counsel of reason. Salmacis sees nothing more perfect than the fortunate Ismire, and I am sure that his eyes would prefer her to the goddess my mother."

"I do not know whether he finds her more beautiful than Venus," I replied, "but I know full well that all the amour he

194

has for that nymph does not prevent him from praising you ardently, and I can guarantee, Madame, that he has only attached himself to Ismire to protect him from the misfortunate fate of finding you too worthy of his adorations."

"Oh, Celine," the queen said to me, "how little that misfortunate fellow would have to fear for himself, and how much pleasure I would take in making him know that if his birth distances him from my throne, his merit brings him close to my heart. But why flatter my dolor with that deceptive idea when I see him full of my rival? Rather paint him for me with all the blackest colors of ingratitude; tell me that in spite of all the benevolence I have for him, he has only wanted to hear it in order to make a sacrifice of it to Ismire, and that, having no crown to offer, he will make her triumph over all the penchant that I have for him. I would rather pardon him for that kind of crime than for having gazed at me so scantly as to be entirely ignorant of what is passing in my heart. It is for that cruel indifference that I would punish him severely, because for that of sacrificing me to my rival I could blame Amour. That blind child disposes of us with so much power that he only lets us know of wealth what he offers us; however precious the man is that he causes to neglect us, he cannot have charms for eyes enlightened by his fatal torch."

"Even if I must render Salmacis even more culpable," I said. "I cannot help believing that your power has closed his eyes to everything you have of perfection. Dazzled by the glare of your throne, he has not dared to approach it, and if he had been able to perceive a few favorable gazes he would have been careful not to heed them, for fear of rendering himself criminal."

"How ignorant you are of the mysteries of the god my brother," replied the fay. "If Salmacis had for me the tender penchant that is making all the misfortune of my life, he would have forgotten that I am his sovereign, and the long line of kings from which he takes his origin would have made him believe that he is worth as much as the greatest king, and, Amour having rendered him reckless, he would have sighed loudly enough to be heard. He would have dared to interpret my gazes, and would have been charmed by having seen there the same fire that was burning in his heart. But Celine, the good fortune of teaching him such a charming language is only reserved for Ismire. What happy moments they are passing! Nothing troubles their tenderness.

"Wait, too fortunate lovers," the queen continued, "to name your fate adorable, until I have decided mine. Perhaps, carried away by my jealousy, I will take pleasure in rendering you as unhappy as I am; you might answer to me for the undignified sighs that my feeble heart is uttering incessantly, and your tears might flow in order to dry mine up.

"But to what extent are you allowing yourself to be carried away, unfortunate princess? For what crime do you want to punish them? What complaint do you have against your rival? Is she not unaware of your amour? And ought insensible Salmacis to have heard you? And even if he had heard you, do you not know from your own experience that one is not the master of retracting from one's heart an object that pleases us? Why do you want them to do what you have not been able to do? Have you less virtue than the lovers? Let them love one another, since they can do so with innocence, and to punish you for having been able to think of separating them, be the witness of their pleasures."

At that moment someone came to inform the queen that foreign princes had come to consult her. She ordered that they be allowed to enter, and I left her cabinet. I went for a walk in the gardens, and I met the prince there. The expression of languor that I had on my face, and the profound reverie in which I was buried, obliged Salmacis to ask me what was wrong, and whether amour was the cause of my melancholy.

"That god undoubtedly has a part in it," I said to him, laughing, "and I was thinking about the bizarre effects that he takes pleasure in making people suffer in his empire."

"To know whether you have reason to criticize him," said the prince, "it would be necessary to tell me what complaint you have against him."

"You have more reason to complain of him than I do, Sire," I said to him, looking at him intently. "If he had not put a blindfold over your eyes, there would have been few princes more fortunate than you; and I doubt that the favors with which he heaps you in the company of Ismire can equal those he is causing you to lose."

"Celine," the prince said to me, with an embarrassed expression, "it is not without mystery that you are speaking to me as you are. Explain yourself, I implore you, or you might make me commit crimes that would cost me my life."

"Sire," I told him, "princes like you can do anything, even if they extend their desires as far as goddesses. Venus loved Anchises, who was only a Trojan prince, and visible divinities cannot be any more difficult."

With those words I quit him to go to join the queen, whom I saw appearing at the end of the path that we were on. After that conversation, Salmacis, who had understood me very well, was more assiduous with regard to the fay. He was nonplussed and pensive, and Ismire had fewer charms for him. He no longer gave her fêtes, his visits were less frequent, and everyone perceived that change. The nymph was sensibly chagrined in consequence, but she resolved to discover who her rival was before talking about it to her lover.

Meanwhile, the fay, remarking the prince's assiduities, suspected that I had talked to him. "Celine," she said to me, "you have betrayed me. Salmacis knows something of my weakness; his sighs and gazes tell me so; and if you had not said something to him, he would not be so bold as to make himself heard."

"Madame," I said to her, "it is Amour that is rendering him bold, not my discourse; the god must have informed him of the tender penchant that forces you to hold him in sufficient esteem to judge him worthy of bearing your chains."

"But Celine, the prince dos not love me; Ismire is still the object of his tenderness, and Amour cannot tell him what is happening in my heart until he has told me."

"Perhaps, Madame," I replied, "he has only ever loved that nymph because he was seeking, as I have already told you, to defend himself against the misfortune of finding you too lovable, and a few of your gazes have told him that he ought no longer to constrain himself."

The prince, who came in as I was speaking, caused the queen to blush in such a manner that he was confused; but, wanting to give them the means of explaining themselves, I said: "The prince can tender you an account more exactly than I can of what you are asking me."

"May I be fortunate enough to know, Madame," said Salmacis, "what can merit your curiosity?"

"Celine," said the fay, blushing again, "is sometimes so unreasonable that is necessary not to listen to what she says, and what I was asking her is not worthy of a greater clarification."

"As it will give you a little confidence in what I have the honor of telling you," I said, "permit me, Madame to explain to the prince the bagatelle that caused our dispute."

"Celine," said the queen, "I would rather believe you than have you take Salmacis for a second."

"I am content, Madame, and the prince ought to be too, if you do not doubt my words."

"Celine has always had too much amity for me," said Salmacis, who understood by virtue of the queen's embarrassment, that we were talking about him, "for me to doubt, after what she has just said, that I ought to thank you for wanting to add faith to her discourse. There are situations in which the profound respect that we have for the persons whom we adore force us to the cruel necessity of keeping quiet, and without the favorable help of a tender friend, we would die rather than admit that which is taking us to the tomb."

"You see, Madame," I said, laughing, "that Amour is taking care of explaining my enigmas, and that the prince...."

"Shut up," said the fay, who prefer to quarrel with me rather than her lover, "and do not force the prince to say what he does not think. I ought to punish you for his temerity; without you, he would not have offended either me or Ismire."

"Oh, Madame," said Salmacis, "forgive Celine for the pity she has had on an unfortunate prince. If it is a crime to adore you, as one adores the goddess your mother, it is me that it is necessary to punish. No mortal has ever been more criminal. Burned by a fire that I hid with care, believing the flames unworthy of the one who had given birth to them, I spend my misfortunate days lamenting that Heaven had made you so perfect that no man could dare to love you without temerity. I am not talking about the rank where the gods have placed you; perhaps, if that were the reason, I would not be so distant from the throne that your eyes could not look at me without descending too low; but Madame, who could dare, without being criminal, to adore you, with the accumulation of virtues and beauties that give you the advantage over the goddess Venus?"

"Salmacis," said the fay, "you are doubtless forgetting that you are talking to me, or you believe me to be very indulgent. Cease trying to persuade me of something you do not think, and do not force me to banish you for temerity or deceit. Do you hope that I am the only person in my court unaware of your love for Ismire? How do you expect me to receive an incense so profaned?"

"I have not profaned my incense, Madame," the prince replied, "and I offer it to you as pure as that which is burned on the altar of the Mother of Amours. Do not reproach me for the attentions I have rendered to Ismire; it is you, divine fay, who has forced me to do that. Desperate at sensing in myself a passion that I named sacrilegious, I sought in the company of that nymph for the means to disengage myself from such a dangerous chain. I believed for some time that I had found in her generosity the help that was necessary to me, but one of your glances, perhaps cast without design, troubled once again all the happiness of my life. No longer having any amour except for my divine queen, I can only love for her.

"Yes, Madame," he continued, throwing himself at her feet, "it is for you to order my fate, and to spare you the trouble of punishing me if my prayers are illegitimate, I will pierce thus unfortunate heart, which constrains me to offend you, before your eyes."

"Salmacis," said the fay, lifting him up, "do not try to infringe my rights; leave me the care of choosing the punishment that you merit, without attempting your life. The goddess my mother has not made me crueler than her; her altars have never been bloodied; she has other means of avenging herself, which she wanted me to learn. As an equitable judge, I want to examine your crime, and its temerity will merit a torture milder than treason."

Having said that, she dismissed the prince, without wanting to hear any more. When we were alone she made me a few reproaches, but I knew very well that they departed from her modesty, and that her heart had no part in them.

From that day on the prince became bolder, and not a day passed without him speaking to the fay about his amour. He was so well able to convince her that he did not love Ismire that she permitted him to sigh and to hope that his sighs might be recompensed.

A fate so far above a mortal ought to have made Salmacis forget Ismire, whatever charms he found in that lovable person, but the reproaches of the nymph, who finally knew the redoubtable rival who had stolen her lover's heart, troubled him sensibly. He still saw her, and tried to persuade her that the interest of his fortune constrained him to attach himself to the queen, but Ismire, not being in a state to feign, and not content with that feeble excuse, and also knowing the power that she had over him, told him that she could not stand to witness the happiness of her rival and that she was going to withdraw to a palace she had at the extremity of the isle.

Troubled by that resolution, the prince swore a thousand oaths only to love her, in order to prevent her from going away. The adroit nymph pretended to cede to that discourse, but at dawn the fooling day she departed, knowing full well that as long as the prince saw the queen, she would succumb to that dangerous rival, and that, rather than be far away from her, the prince would not fail to come in search of her.

She was not mistaken. As soon as Salmacis learned of her departure, he ran to her. What, cruel Ismire," he said, "you're abandoning me? You want to break the chains that you have sworn to me a hundred times would be eternal?"

"Sire," the nymph replied, shedding a few tears, "it is not me who is breaking the irons that I take so much pleasure in sharing; you know, unjust prince, all that I have done to render them light for you. How many times, charmed by the tender happiness of loving as much as you were loved, did you prefer your fate to that of the gods! That charming time is no more; the brilliant glare of the crown has surprised your tenderness; you have only been able to find satisfaction with a mistress who can combine fortune with amour; follow, follow that blind divinity, and allow me to conserve the memory of exceedingly happy times. Faithful to my tenderness, I shall only remember the moments when you merited it so well, and I shall forget that you betrayed it, for fear that such a cruel idea, by igniting my anger, might weaken my amour."

"Oh, my dear Ismire," said the prince, throwing himself at her feet, "what is it necessary to do to repair my crime?"

"No longer to love anyone but me, Sire," replied Ismire, "and to make me know that I hold you instead of another, by remaining in this palace."

"Yes, lovable nymph," Salmacis said to her, "yes, I only love you; I am only too glad to renounce the fortune that the bounty of the fay promises me, to prove to you that my amour is as violent as in the first days that you gave birth to it."

While the prince forgot with so much imprudence what he owed to the queen, that charming fay had a sensible chagrin at that preference for a person so far inferior to her in beauty and birth. At first, her anger could not find a torture rude enough to expiate such a cruel offense. Her first transports represented the pleasure of avenging herself with so much charm that she was quick to invent an enchantment in which those criminals would cause their despair to burst forth by turns. But amour, replacing fury, constrained her to be content to shed tears.

"Oh, Celine," she said to me, "how much I ought to resent you for having flattered my tenderness. Without you, I would not have savored the deadly pleasure of being loved by the prince; I would always have seen him at the feet of my rival, and in the end, that terrible object would have made me hate him; but, poisoned by his deceptive tenderness, I made a sweet necessity of being loved by him all my life." Shedding tears, she went on: "What remedies, cruel maid, can you bring to the woes that you have caused me?"

"Madame," I said to her, penetrated by dolor, "if my death could spare one of our tears, I would suffer it with pleasure. I confess that I was wrong to talk to you about the perfidious Prince Salmacis; he was unworthy of your generosity, since he has been able to forgotten it, and you ought to punish him, if he is not yet dear enough for the punishment to rebound on you; but if that ingrate is necessary to your repose, forget, my princess, an aberration in which his heart has no part. The cunning Ismire feared your charms, and she is holding him far from your eyes by virtue of the habitude he has of finding her lovable. Appear, Madame, in that deadly place; go to extract a slave too honored by your chains from the hands of your enemy, and I'll answer for his fidelity."

"Oh, Celine," the queen said to me, "Although I sense clearly that I cannot live without being loved by the prince, I cannot resolve to take a step that would cover me with shame, and might perhaps only serve to redouble my rival's triumph."

"Well, Madame," I said to her, don't leave your palace, and have the tourneys published that you hold every year on your birthday. Offer a glorious prize that will flatter the vanity of the weak Salmacis. Sensible to his glory, he will quit his nymph for a time, and, provided that he sees you for a moment, I'll answer for his repentance."

After having hesitated for a while, the fay determined to follow my advice and had the tourney announced, promising for the prize a golden crown enriched with rubies, which he victor could wear at all ceremonies when he found himself on our island.

The hope of that recompense had the effect that I expected. Salmacis could not resist the desire to be honored by such a particular distinction. He departed, in spite of Ismire, and arrived on the eve of the tourney. The offense he had given the queen prevented him from appearing before her.

The day of the celebration having arrived, the fay, magnificently clad, placed herself on a platform with her entire court, and, the judges of the camp having performed the customary ceremonies, the prince presented himself at the barrier first. His armor was glittering with gems; his plumes were white, and his coat a silver fabric heightened on the arms by carbuncles and rubies. On his buckler, an Amour was seen, who, trying to pierce three hearts, could not succeed fully, his arrow being too short, and for the device: *Too many for one*.

He had never been so charming, and the son of Venus, who could not see anyone more worthy to bear his chains than that prince and the fay, had taken care to animate their natural beauty with his charms.

In making a tour of the camp, Salmacis passed before the queen, saluted her with the shame of his crime painted on his visage, and, surprised that he had been able to prefer Ismire to that admirable fay, was unable to take his eyes off that divine object for a quarter of an hour.

Eventually, a knight having presented himself for the combat, he set about meriting the prize. He was victorious not only against that adversary but all those who wanted to dispute it with him, and having been declared the winner, he was led to the queen's platform in order to be crowned by her hand.

The tourney having finished, she retired to her cabinet without wanting to permit entry to anyone, but the prince, unable to resist the desire to obtain his pardon, came to find me.

"Celine," he said to me, "either give me death or obtain from the queen that I throw myself at her feet. I know that I am unworthy of her bounty, after what a blind passion made me do, but if an ardent repentance and a fidelity to any proofs that she wants do demand of me can find mercy from her, oh, Celine, I would be able to repair my weakness by so much amour that she would be constrained to refasten my chains."

"Sire," I said, "I cannot promise you that the queen will listen to you. Doubtless anticipating that you might want to see her, she has shut herself away and forbidden anyone to interrupt her."

"Celine," said the Prince, "I am not unaware that her prohibitions do not apply to you. Accord me the favor that I ask of you, or I shall believe that you have never been my friend."

Finally vanquished by Salmacis' prayers and believing that it would not displease the queen, I presented myself at the door of her cabinet, but I was astonished when she ordered me to go away without listening to what I had to say about the prince's repentance. I went to render him that cruel response. He almost died of dolor, and withdrew to his apartment without speaking to anyone.

Several days went by without him finding a favorable opportunity, the fay having prohibited him from him appearing before her, but one evening, when she was walking on the sea shore, only accompanied by her maids, he came to throw himself at her feet, and made his eyes and his sighs speak so eloquently that the fay promised to forget his crime if he abandoned Ismire. The prince accepted that condition without difficulty, and from that moment on, he only gave evidence of a constant amour.

Ismire employed all her charms to recall him, and in order to banish him from her heart she quit the island and married a prince who had loved her for some years.

Meanwhile, rumor of the good fortune of Salmacis, causing a thousand jealousies, spread all the way to the court of King Poliandre. Finding it very bad that a subject dared to love the fay, he sent for the famous magician Amerdin, and ordered him to kidnap the prince and enchant him in his fatal castle. That cruel minister, ever ready to make the tears flow with which he makes his pernicious charms, surprised

Salmacis while he was hunting and took him to his deadly abode.

The queen, in despair at her misfortune, consulted her books in order to discover who could render her lover to her, but she discovered that you alone, generous prince (Celine addressed herself to Elmedor) could destroy the enchantment of the castle where, for a century, so many illustrious unfortunates have been suffering pains unknown to the rest of mortals. The queen saw, with chagrin, that you had lost the ring to which the success of that great adventure was attached, but Zamat, whose science had no limits, handed that treasure so precious to her tenderness to her as he died, recommending her to return it to you in order to advance her happiness.

She conducted your sure steps to the banks of the Tagus where, on her orders, without her being aware of it, the beautiful Princess of Fez was waiting for you; and, knowing that you were ready to run such great peril with no other aid than your valor, she went me to you this morning, wanting to return that constellated ring to you on which the change of her fortune and yours depends, since you will find your charming princess there, still constant to our memory.

Asmonade, knowing of your return from the island of the fay Desirée, and fearing that you would come to snatch Alzayde from him, abducted her during the faint in which your squire believed her to have died. He left Leon, only taking Sancia with her. He stayed at Amerdin's castle, where the fay Desirée, delighted to avenge herself on you, told him that she would make that lovable person love him, but he learned that enchantments could not have any effect upon her heart. Still faithful to her dear Prince of Granada, she spends her days regretting your loss.

As for you, beautiful Zamea, your knight, deceived by your resemblance, is savoring pleasures that make him bless his fate, and Almandine, in order to satisfy the hatred of the vindictive Celdine, is sometimes regretting the death of the Prince of Mauritania with a deluge of tears, and sometimes lamenting the fact that those of the Prince of Aragon have ended. As for Salmacis, he has no other torture than that of being distant from his adorable fay, but as he believes that her absence will never end, he has no less to lament than all those who inhabit that terrible abode.

Celine ended her discourse thus, and gave the Prince of Granada such a strong desire to be at Amerdin's castle that he could hardly wait until the next day to leave the isle of the Fay of Grandeurs. The joy of knowing that his princess was alive occupied his mind so much that he did not thank Celine for the story she had just told them. Zalmayde and Zamea did that in his stead, and went to rejoin the queen in her apartment.

The evening was spent begging the fay to aid them with her advice, which she did, as an interested person, and the next day, at sunrise, the amiable troop left the island in the same galley that had brought them. On the shore they found a magnificent carriage for the princesses, and fay horses for the princes, which could never tire or be injured.

A dwarf presented Elmedor with golden armor enriched with rubies and pearls, and on his shield, which was gold like the armor, the prince was depicted holding expiring monsters beneath his feet. Elmedor accepted such a precious present, and was armed by the dwarf, who informed him of the power of the arms in question. After that they took the road to Amerdin's castle.

They rode all day without having felt the slightest inconvenience, and when night approached they found themselves in a hamlet built on the banks of a stream, the huts of which were white and red marble. Shepherds and shepherdesses clad in fabrics of the same colors, whose crooks were silver with crimson enamel, came to offer them dwellings for the night. The princesses, surprised to find so much gentility among the shepherds, asked them on whom he depended, and the shepherds replied that they were subjects of the Fay of Grandeurs, who had ordered them to receive them kindly. At that name, so dear to the illustrious troop, they recognized the generosity of the adorable fay and dismounted.

They found the huts as comfortable as they were solidly built. All the furniture was upholstered in silver and roseate fabrics; the tables of red and green porphyry were covered with large alabaster vases filled with a thousand different flowers, which exhaled a perfume by which the senses were enchanted.

After having admired the pleasant place, the princesses lay down on soft beds and were served a delicious supper. During the meal, the shepherds played flutes and bagpipe, and as soon as they had finished eating the princess were left at liberty to go to sleep.

The next day, at dawn, the beautiful adventuresses, followed by the knights, climbed into their carriage again, and after having heaped their amiable hostesses with caresses, they resumed their journey.

The end of the day was as charming for them as the one they had spent in the marble hamlet. They found themselves in a great forest, pierced by roads as far as the eye could see, of which the one they were following seemed to end at a brilliant and translucent castle. The princes, who had gone on ahead by a short distance, saw that the walls were white agate and the cornices and the roofs flame-colored porcelain.

A nymph of divine beauty clad in gold and green gauze was at the door, and she addressed the Prince of Granada. "Generous prince," she said, "the Fay of Grandeurs has ordered me to receive you in this place; have your charming princesses advance, and assure them that they will be mistresses here."

After having responded to the nymph's compliments, Elmedor was joined by Zalmayde and Zamea, and they all arrived at the castle together. The princesses embraced their beautiful hostess, who took them to a hall of gate, like the walls of the castle, sustained by twelve flame-colored porcelain columns. All the furniture was upholstered in green velvet with a gold background. As soon as they were seated the nymph presented them baskets full of fruits and preserves.

When they had finished the meal, they went for a walk in a forest of pomegranates of extraordinary height. Jets of water between the trees fell back into porcelain basins of the nymph's favorite color, and had the most beautiful effect in the world. Zalmayde and Zamea were so delighted with such a beautiful abode that they could not resolve to emerge from it, but the nymph led them gradually to a part of the forest where they found a magnificent repast. During the super, voices, theorbos and violins made an admirable concert, disappearing when the princesses got up from the table; from all the paths ending at that place, Moors and Mooresses emerged, who danced a ballet.

A part of the night passed in that diversion, and the princesses, thinking that they ought to get up early, retired to the palace. The next day, lazier than usual, they only got up two hours after the sun. Their charming hostess escorted them to their carriage and as she took her leave of them she gave a dog of extraordinary form to the Prince of Granada, telling him to follow it if she wanted to arrive at the fatal castle. Elmedor thanked her a thousand times, as did he beautiful adventuresses, and they left the enchanted palace, following the miraculous dog along a high road through the forest.

They had not been on the road for three hours when they perceived Amerdin's castle. The Prince of Granada felt a joy that he could not express, and, having made the princesses stop and asked the other princes to remain with them to guard them, he advanced alone to the gate of the infernal place.

A knight emerged from it after he had made the customary signal, who came with his lance raised to fight him. Having recognized him as Almanson, Elmedor did not want to make use of his arms against him; he presented his ring to him, and the knight, emerging from the enchantment that had deceived him for so long, lowered his lance and threw himself at the King of Granada's feet.

He lifted him up and embraced him. "Amiable knight," he said to him, "receive from me your liberty and your princess." He indicated the carriage where she was.

Transported by joy, Almanson ran to his dear princess, while a second adversary emerged from the castle, whose device made him recognizable as Salmacis. The respect that he had for the princess prevented Elmedor from reddening his sword with his blood, and, lowering its point, he caused the fatal ring to shine in his eyes. Ashamed of the design that had caused him to emerge from his prison, the knight came to his liberator with open arms.

"Prince," the Prince of Granada said to him, "the Fay of Grandeurs, whom you have always loved tenderly, has delivered you from your chains, in order no longer to bear any but hers."

"Oh, generous knight," said Salmacis, "what happiness are you announcing to me? Is it possible that I can see that charming fay again?"

"Yes," said Elmedor. "You will see her still beautiful and faithful, but let me finish my adventure. Very dear interests press me to test all the enemies that the cruel Amerdin wants to send me. Go and wait for me with the princesses, and protect your heart from their charms."

The knight obeyed him, and Elmedor, having seen a third enemy emerge, advanced with his sword high.

"Who are you, reckless youth, who comes to seek death in this place?" said the unknown man.

"I am Elmedor of Granada," said the price, "who, favored by the gods, has come to punish the party of the traitor Amerdin and deliver Princess Alzayde from the hands of her enemy."

"Here he is," said Asmonade—for it was him—"who will make you repent of your audacity."

With those words, without further ado, the two competitors delivered blows so terrible that they made the princesses tremble for their valiant defender; and the princes, no longer remembering that they were not permitted to mingle in that adventure, ran to his aid; but when they arrived beside him, he had already felled the proud Asmonade, who was rendering his soul to Hell through a gaping wound in his side.

Rid of his rival, Elmedor thanked the generous knights and begged them to return to the princesses. They went, very annoyed at not being able to second him.

As soon as Asmonade had rendered his last sigh, a roaring lion emerged from the castle, which came to attack the prince, but without being astonished or making use of the ring, of which he had turned the point so that it was no use to him, he waited for the cruel beast, and after an hour's combat, laid it lifeless beside Asmonade.

The lion having been defeated, a knight mounted on a griffin appeared over the drawbridge. His visor was raised, and rolling haggard eyes full of fury, he said: "Don't think, Prince of Granada that you have come to the end of your enterprise for having been victorious so many times. You cannot escape my vengeance, and even though I am forced by Destiny to test your deadly valor, I have no fear of being vanquished."

"Let's see," said Elmedor, "whether you are any more invulnerable than your defenders. You doubtless thought that you could tire my arm by so many combats, but learn that my strength is redoubled by my victories."

Amerdin, driven by his evil genius, commenced to measure his sword against that of the invincible knight, and, making his griffin prance, gave Elmedor a great deal of trouble, but after defending himself for a long time, the latter delivered such a furious riposte to his adversary's arm, that he caused it to fall, with the sword. The magician, seeing that he could no longer defend himself, caused the griffin to take flight and soon vanished from his vanquisher's sight. From his poisonous blood, a host of dragons and serpents was born, which turned their murderous tongues against the prince. Seeing that valor could not defend him against so many enemies, he turned his ring again, and, passing through their midst without them approaching him, he entered the castle.

Two bears of enormous size guarded the entrance to the vestibule. They wanted to hurl themselves upon him, but, constraining them by means of the virtue of his fatal ring, he drove them away. The vestibule opened and a knight of noble appearance advanced to forbid him entry thereto. Elmedor, not wanting to sacrifice a prince so accomplished, told him not to force him to test his arms, but the unknown man, whom, the magician had told as he left that someone was coming to steal Almandine from him, did not listen to such sage advice and gave him a blow to his helmet with his sword. Irritated, Elmedor, disdaining the force of his ring, fought with his own valor, and although there was no knight in the world more valiant than the Prince of Aragon, he laid him dead at his feet.

Impatient to find his princess, he generous prince continued on his way, and after traversing several apartments, each more frightful than he last, he arrived at a tower that had neither a door nor windows, and from that place he heard the plaints of the unfortunates who were imprisoned therein. He thought he could discern the voice of his princess. Moved by her plaintive tone, he took his battle hammer, of which he remembered that the Fay of Grandeurs had told him to make use, and, attaching the magic ring to it, he struck he wall of the tower violently, which split, forming an opening large enough to give him passage.

He entered the place precipitately, and found it full of ladies of a charming beauty, whose tears, which were flowing in abundance, formed a stream that ran through an opening in the tower.

He searched for his Alzayde, and found her next to a tomb, which she was watering with her tears. Elmedor saw himself so well represented therein that he was astonished by such a marvelous resemblance, but, dying of the desire to make her sighs cease, he presented the enchanted ring to her, and the tomb disappeared instantly. The walls of the tower changed into a magnificent triumphal arch, and the names of Elmedor and Alzayde were written on it in letters of diamond, sustained by amours.

All the ladies and knights, emerging from the enchantment in which the cruel Amerdin had held them for a century, came to throw themselves at the feet of the Prince of Granada.

He lifted them up so nobly and so politely that they felt a new joy at being delivered by such a generous knight. Knowing the impatience he had to converse with his princess, they retired to the far end of the chamber.

The prince, wanting to profit from their complaisance, said: "Oh, my dear Princess, how much veritable chagrin your false death has caused me! The gods doubtless permitted the order that you gave me to preserve my life in order to avenge you. Without the blind obedience I had to you, I would have sacrificed myself to my despair."

"Prince," said Alzayde, with a flattering expression, "you can see by the torture that the perfidious Asmonade chose for me that he knew that nothing was dearer to me than you, since to punish me for the scorn I had for him, he condemned me to weep for you for as long as I lived. But what favorable demon led you to this castle and saved you from the cruel hands of Amerdin and your rival?"

"My rival," said the prince, "has paid with his life for the harm he has done us, and the perfidious magician, no longer being in a state to defend himself, vanished into the clouds before my eyes."

He was about to tell her about his adventures at length when Alzayde suggested to him that the presence of so many illustrious unfortunates, who were listening to them, did not permit them a longer conversation.

"Let's get out of such a baleful place," she continued, "and be sure that Alzayde is for the Prince of Granada everything that she was when you left Leon."

After that favorable assurance, the princess approached the ladies, who recommenced praising the generosity of the prince.

"I confess," said Alzayde, "that we owe him a great deal, but in order to complete his work, it is necessary for us to get out of this frightful prison."

"I will obey you whenever it pleases you," said Elmedor, "if you care to introduce me to whichever of the amiable persons I see is named Almandine."

The beautiful Princess of Castile came forward as soon as she heard her name pronounced, and the prince told her that he wanted to beg her pardon for having been obliged to kill Prince Armande.

The princess blushed and sighed at that sad news, and Elmedor, wanting to enable her sighs to cease, said: "If I have been unfortunate enough, Madame, to take one illustrious lover away from you, I can, in order to repair my fault, render you Zalmandor."

"Oh, Sire," said Almandine, "are you not giving me a false hope to console me for a true misfortune?"

"You will know very shortly" said the prince, "that I do not make promises I cannot keep."

As he spoke, he offered his hand to the adorable Alzayde, and all the ladies followed her, conducted by the knights who were in the tower.

As they passed through the vestibule, the Princess of Castile perceived the corpse of the unfortunate Prince of Aragon. That sight drew tears from her, and Armande's squire, throwing himself at Almandine's feet, said: "Oh, Madame, suffer that I render the last duties to my illustrious master, and that I build him a tomb in the place where you have caused him to lose his life. After being cured of his wounds, he abandoned his kingdom, and when he learned that you had been abducted to this castle, he came to search for you here. The cruel Amerdin received him, and promised him that if he could defend this fatal place from the valor of the Prince of Granada, he would return you to his hands, in order to take you back to Castile. My Prince accepted that condition, and has ended his sad days here."

"Cleon," said Almandine, "the gods are my witnesses to how sensible I am to the misfortune of your illustrious master, and I wish that I could, at the price of my crown, render him life; but since that is impossible, let us render to his shade that which it expects of us. Prepare the pyre, and give him a tomb worthy of a perfect knight."

"Cleon," said Elmedor, "commence that work, and I will send you everything necessary for such a just enterprise."

After that, the prince, impatient to rejoin his admirable troop, emerged from the castle with his numerous following; but he had only taken a few steps over the bridge when the sky seemed to catch fire, only giving illumination in flashes of lightning, followed by terrible thunder, and frightful screams caused him to look toward the castle. He saw a host of demons emerge therefrom, which could not be counted, and which, after destroying that deadly palace, took flight into the air, causing the storm and lightning, in order to mark the end of the enchantment.

The princesses trembled not knowing what to do, but daylight, reappearing more brightly than before the tempest, came to calm their dread, and enabled them to see the most beautiful object in the world. That castle, where everything that Hell had of the most frightful had reigned for so long, had been changed into a magnificent palace. The eyes could not sustain the glare of the precious stones of which it was built, and on the frontispiece, in a huge cartouche made of a single carbuncle, words written in diamond letters could be seen:

This enchanted palace, this superb edifice
Was embellished by artifice
To immortalize the valiant Elmedor,
The honor of knights, the glory and the model,
The animated portrait of the famous Almanzor,[11]
Of the amorous Empire, the most faithful lover.

---

[11] The warrior known in Christendom as Almanzor (Muhammad ibn Abi Aamir, c932-1002) was the effective ruler of Moorish Spain for a quarter of a century, and won numerous victories against Christian armies, but when the Caliphate fractured after his death the tables were turned conclusively and the Moorish kingdoms went into a long gradual decline.

A lady of majestic beauty appeared at the door, approached Alzayde and said: "The Fay of Grandeurs, Madame, wanting to leave to posterity an eternal mark of the valor of your illustrious lover, has elevated this palace on the ruins of the one that has just been destroyed by his heroic courage. Come and honor it with your gaze, and in a Temple dedicated to Constancy, consecrate the mysterious ring that has caused your liberty. You have no more need of its magical aid; nothing can any longer trouble your felicity; your days will be counted by Amour and ended by pleasures.

"For you, Prince," she said to Elmedor, "learn that nothing can equal your glory. Possessor of a great empire and one of the most beautiful and virtuous princesses in the world, you will surpass the greatest heroes of antiquity, and to complete your prayers, a son will be born to you who will make himself known from here to the most distant Poles."

Elmedor and Alzayde were so surprised by the happiness that the savant fay announced to them that they were still unable to reply to her when the Princesses Zalmayde and Zamea, and all the knights who accompanied them, having seen the end of the enchantment, came to express their joy to them.

The Prince of Granada, taking Zalmandor by the hand, while the princesses embraced Alzayde, presented the beautiful Almandine to him.

"You see, Madame," he said to her, "that I acquit my promises."

Without replying, the princess extended her hand to her lover, and received the marks of his amour with an extreme satisfaction.

The obliging fay, after having given a few moments to the first transports of all those adorable persons, obliged them to enter the new palace. How many beauties they found there! Everything was brilliant with gold, silver and gems, and in the middle of the courtyard there was a trophy elevated from the debris of the old castle, to the honor of the Prince of Granada.

After having admired that new edifice, the fay conducted them into a Turquoise Temple. Constancy could be seen there on an altar of the same stone, the base of which was gold. Alzayde took the prince's ring, laid it at the feet of the goddess, and after having prayed to her to reign over Elmedor's heart, she was about to go out when the fay took her by the hand.

"Let us, Madame," she said to her, "appease the shade of the Prince of Aragon by means of a few tears on the part of the Princess of Castile, of which Zalmandor will not be jealous. The Prince of Granada wanted him to have a tomb in this place; the Fay of Grandeurs, who wants to mark her gratitude to him, has erected one near this Temple."

As she spoke, the fay marched to a pyramid of flax-gray marble, where all the deeds that Amour had caused the unfortunate Armande to perform were represented in bas-reliefs, and on the apex of the pyramid the figure of the prince, with the same arms that he wore in combat, was so well depicted that the eyes were deceived by it. On his shield the cruel goddess who destroys all things was represented holding a heart from which flames emerged, and for a device, the words: *In spite of death*.

Almandine could not see an object so sad without uttering sighs and shedding few tears. Zalmandor even accompanied her in that lugubrious exercise, but the fay, who only wanted to give pleasures to all those illustrious persons, constrained them to quit the tomb and pass into superb apartments, where she left all those lovers happy in liberty to converse with their charming princesses.

Only Salmacis was not tranquil. The joy that he saw the princes savoring was giving him a sharp impatience to enjoy the same pleasures when a sound of drums, trumpets and oboes drew him out of his reverie. He ran to the window, in order to see where it was coming from; but what was is joy when he perceived, in a chariot drawn by unicorns whiter than the horses of the Sun, his charming fay, followed by all her nymphs, in smaller chariots. He was at her feet before she had descended, and by transports in which amour alone appeared, he expressed his tender passion to her. She lifted him up benevolently, and made him see in her eyes a languor so touching that he nearly died of pleasure and tenderness.

At the same time, the princes and the princesses arrived before the queen and, delighted to see her, they believed that nothing could any longer trouble their happiness. The Fay of Grandeurs embraced all those lovable heroines, and, turning to the Prince of Granada, she said to him: "It is only just, generous Elmedor, that I come to thank you for the care you have taken to spare the blood of Salmacis and render him faithfully to me. In order to recompense you, I want to complete your happiness in this palace consecrated to your victory. In a short time we shall have news of the king, your father, and I have taken care to inform all the princes whose consent is necessary to complete the adventures of all those who accompany you. Savor, in the meantime, the sweetness of knowing how much you are loved by your beautiful princess.

"And you, amiable Fay of Pleasures," she said to the fay who had appeared at the door of the new palace, "spare no effort to enable us to spend happy days while awaiting the one on which so many illustrious marriages will be celebrated."

After the queen had finished speaking, she gave her hand to the Prince of Granada and entered the apartment that had been prepared for her. All the walls were lined with white agate with green and flame-colored lines. The furniture was upholstered in golden fabric embroidered with pearls, rubies and emeralds, and beneath an awning sustained by four turquoise Amours a crown of interlaced hearts was visible. A throne of the same agate as the walls was elevated by six steps covered with a magnificent carpet, where the queen placed herself, and all the princesses sat down on the two sides of the throne, on rich cushions.

Never had anything so beautiful appeared as what was seen in that chamber, and never had so many beautiful women been assembled in the same place. Alzayde shone there with so many charms that everyone gave her the prize, after the Fay of Grandeurs, without discord having the power to animate the other beauties against her, so they had no reason to complain.

They had so much reason to praise the graces that Nature had given them that it was necessary to see Alzayde next to them to believe that there was anything more perfect than what they each possessed in particular.

A part of the day had already passed in such great events, when the Fay of Grandeurs, fearing that the praise with which the adorable Princess of Leon was being heaped might eventually give some small chagrin to the other princesses, told the Fay of Pleasures that they could not ignore any longer the adventures that had changed their days destined to joy into a long sadness, and begged her to inform them before the amiable company.

The charming fay obeyed the sovereign, and commenced her story, addressing the queen, in these terms.

The Story of the Fay of Pleasures and the Cruel Amerdin

You know, Madame, that I am the daughter of a savant fay, who held her court in an island near yours, which is called the Isle of Happiness. One day, my mother was walking along the sea shore when she saw Venus emerging from the waves, followed by the God of Pleasures, who, on perceiving her, quit the goddess in order to come and testify to her the amour that she had just inspired in him. The fay was not insensible to his passion, and their union procured me the light of day.

My mother, charmed to see me resemble so perfectly the god, my father, heaped me with all the gifts that were in her power; but, consulting her books with regard to my destiny she knew that I was threatened with a great misfortune if I were loved by a prince who know the magic art. In order to avoid that misfortune, she built a palace in this fatal place, filled with everything that could please, and gave me for company the most amiable persons of both sexes. My father, wanting to make me know that I was dear to him, enclosed the

Pleasures there, young children of divine beauty, who always give by their presence an atmosphere of you to the most tedious things, permitting them to leave the palace every day in order to show themselves to mortals, but commanding them to come back every evening into my delightful prison. That is why humans are so soon deprived of their amiable presence.

The approach to that palace was defended by monsters, and a dense cloud rendered it invisible. I spent happy days in that charming retreat; everything favored my desires. Amour had even given birth to a prince destined for me, five years older than me, who, by a tender and constant passion, enabled me to find new pleasure even in the most ordinary pleasures. His name was Constant, and no lover ever merited the name more. But what can all the precautions of prudence serve, against the order of cruel Destiny?

One day, when I was walking on a terrace above the palace I perceived a man mounted on a griffin cleaving through the air. That novelty caused me to utter a cry, which caused the stranger to stop. He approached the ground gently, and, after having gazed at me for some time, he resumed his flight and was lost in the air. Frightened by that adventure, I returned to my apartment. The next day, when I was in the garden, the same stranger came to land nearby. I had never seen a man so disagreeable and appropriate to inspire hatred and terror.

"Don't be astonished to see me again, beautiful princess," he said. "One cannot have seen you for a moment without wanting to spend one's life with you. I have quit voluntarily my power of making the whole earth tremble under my power in order to persuade you that nothing can approach the love I have for you. You could not make a more glorious conquest. I am as redoubtable as the gods, and Heaven and earth are obedient to my voice."

"Sire," I said, "my ambition will not enable me to desire the good fortune of please you. Content to reign in this palace and over the heart of Prince Constant, I ask no more. Take your heart to some beauty who can recognize its value, and let me enjoy a repose that your mere presence can trouble."

As I finished speaking I attempted to quit him in order to go to Constant, whom I could see at the end of a pathway, but stopping me by grabbing my dress he said: "Princess, you can no longer have any happiness except by responding to my passion. I will not suffer that you prefer a young Adonis to me. If you are wise, accept the offer of my heart, or fear that I will punish you for having made me know a tenderness so contrary to my nature. I can do anything I wish, as I told you; beware of forcing me to hate you as much as I love you. To-morrow I will come to learn your resolution and regulate your fate and in."

As he finished those cruel words he remounted his griffin, and having lost sight of him, I ran to tell Constant about our misfortune.

We spent the night lamenting, and the next day the cruel Amerdin—for it was him, Madame—appeared in my chamber. "Well, Princess," he said to me, with a visage in which fury and amour were painted, "have you reflected upon the glory that I have offered you? Are you disposed to receive a heart that has only ever sighed for you?"

"Sire," I said, "one does not dispose of one's tenderness as one wishes. I admit that you merit that of the greatest princesses on earth, but Amour has not reserved that fortunate fate for me. I belong entirely to Prince Constant; I have loved him since my most tender childhood; do not trouble such sweet chains. They cannot offend you; I did not know you when I received his prayers; why would you want to constrain me to break such beautiful bonds?"

"I shall certainly refrain from breaking them," replied the perfidious Amerdin. "It is necessary that they serve to make your greatest torment. It is done; my heart, unaccustomed to love, has returned to hatred, which is natural to it. Tremble, unfortunate princess, tremble for the sighs you have made me utter. They have prepared misfortune for you, which will be all the more terrible because they will not cost you your life."

At the same time he struck this palace with a wand that he was holding in his hand, and it changed into a frightful prison, and, taking Prince Constant, who tried to defend me, he imprisoned him in a tower that had no entrance or exit. He expelled all the Pleasures; and, redoubling the love I had for the prince, I spent the days circling his prison trying for find an entrance.

From that moment on, the perfidious Amerdin, the enemy of all fortunate lovers, has sought to trouble their pleasures and to fill that fatal tower with all those he has been able to have in his power, inventing new torments to make their tears flow, of which he formed a stream that he received in a black marble basin. With those warm waters of dolor he made the most terrible enchantments.

One day, having consulted his books, he learned that a prince cherished by Heaven would come to destroy his power. Desperate at that order of Destiny, he sought to attract into his castle all the knights that had a reputation for courage and valor. He distributed demons in the forest and on the high roads with the faces of beautiful women, who asked for help against him. It was by one of those phantoms that Prince Almanson was brought here, and it was under the deceptive promise of rendering the beautiful Almandine to him that the unfortunate Prince of Aragon lost his life.

Finally, the Prince of Granada, under your glorious auspices, Madame, came to break our chains, and has returned my dear prince to me, as faithful as before our misfortunes. At the same time I received your orders to elevate this new palace of the glory of our invincible protector. I employed in that, all the power that the fay my mother has given me, and Prince Constant has departed in order to bring back to this happy abode the Pleasures that the cruel magician had expelled from it.

The fay had not finished her story when Prince Constant was seen entering the chamber, with those amiable children so necessary to the happiness of life. They came to prostrate themselves at the feet of the adorable queen, and to tell her that they would accompany all her steps henceforth, The Fay of Grandeurs received their homage with an air of joy to which their presence alone could give birth, and, the night already being very advanced, after a magnificent repast, the queen retired to her apartment, and all the princesses, having bid their lovers good night, went to bed.

All the following days were employed in merry fêtes, and, the ambassadors of the Kings of Granada, Tunis and Mauretania and the Queen of Fez having arrived, the Fay of Grandeurs wanted to unite all those heroic lovers with an eternal bond. She had the Fay of Pleasures consent to the happiness of Prince Constant, and ordered the Pleasures to prepare the celebration.

Salmacis would have liked to be one of those fortunate lovers, but the queen told him that, in the just apprehension she had that his natural inconstancy might enable him to find the distaste so commonplace in marriage, she wanted him to remain a lover for a few more years. She accompanied that harsh law with such flattering promises always to love him that he was only too glad to expiate his fickleness by means of such a fond hope.

The day so desired by our princes, and perhaps our princesses, having arrived, Alzayde conducted by Elmedor, the Fay of Pleasures by Prince Constant, Zalmayde by Alinzor, Amandine by Zalmandor, and Zamea by Almanson, appeared in the Temple of Constancy, where the Fay of Grandeurs was waiting for them with Salmacis, more brilliant that Aurora when she quits the bed of her old husband.

A charming orchestra commenced the ceremony and conducted them back to the palace again when it was over. A sumptuous meal awaited them there. After the dinner, a theater appeared at the back of the hall, where the Pleasures danced a ballet, which represented the destruction of the enchanter Amerdin. In the evening there was a ball, where the queen wanted the Princess of Leon to take her place, and when the night was ready to cede to the day she conducted the fortunate lovers to their apartments, where they compensated one another for all the pains they had suffered in the course of their amours.

Salmacis was not tranquil in that happy night. He waited with impatience for the Fay of Grandeurs to wake up, in order to make reproaches to her, but the amiable majesty that was always spread over her visage prevented him from complaining, and he contented himself with marking by his sighs that he merited a more perfect happiness. The fay took care to console him by means of tender and passionate gazes, and the promise she gave him that she would never be anyone's but his.

Those happy days having passed, the queen, wanting to return to her island, departed from the Palace of Pleasures with her illustrious court. She slept in the porcelain castle, and Zamea and Zalmayde were astonished that it disappeared as soon as they had left; that told them that the charming fay had only placed it on their route as evidence of her generosity. That same evening she arrived at the huts, where she spent the evening in a thousand agreeable games, and the following day she arrived on her island.

There the queen told Elmedor and all the princesses that the fay Desirée, in despair at the happiness if the Prince of Granada, had destroyed her enchanted palace and had retired to a desert near Granada in order sometimes to see the prince, whom she could not forget, although she would have tried if the Spring of Forgetfulness had been as faithful for her as for those she had obliged to drink from it.

After that news, and having heaped the princes and princesses with gifts, the Fay of Grandeurs gave them magnificent and comfortable equipages to take them to their realms.

It was not without tears that the royal troop separated from that adorable queen. She promised them always to honor them with her protection, and saw them leave her palace and her island.

All our heroes and heroines separated from one another a few days from the Isle of Grandeurs. The princesses embraced one another and swore an eternal amity, and the princes promised one another to unite against all the kings who wanted to attack them, and to send one another their news as soon as they arrived.

Elmedor was the first to reach his realm. The King and Queen of Granada, charmed to see again a son who had cost them so many tears, lavished caresses upon him, as well as his charming wife. Elmedor, always content with the virtues he found in her, savored a thousand pleasures when he learned that all the princes who had been companions in his fortune were peaceful possessors of their crowns and their lovable princesses; that the Queen of Fez had had Zamea crowned, and Almanson, after the death of the king her father; that the Prince of Numidia had wanted to remain in the Canaries, for fear that the sand of his homeland might make him inconstant in spite of himself; that Zalmandor, in order to be closer to Granada, was in Castile, and that the Fay of Pleasures had arrived on the Isle of Happiness.

So much joy was augmented by a son whom the beautiful Alzayde brought into the world a year after their marriage, who left them in no doubt subsequently that he was the prince famous for his exploits predicted by the Fay of Pleasures.

THE FAMILIAR SPIRIT

Persian Tales translated from the Arabic

A young Persian woman of surprising beauty was reading a book one day about sylphs and sylphides, and, regarding with pleasure the complaisance of those aerial lovers, wished ardently to have one, in order to distract her from the frightful solitude in which the jealousy of her husband forced her to live. She prayed to her false prophet to allow her that grace, and without that flattering idea quitting her for a moment she went to bed in the hope of being as fortunate as those women whose stories she had read, without being frightened by the punishments that they inflicted upon the infidel.

In the middle of the night she heard a rather loud noise. A secret joy took possession of her heart; she did not doubt that it was what she had wished for with so much urgency. In order to clarify the matter she opened her curtain, and saw by the light of a lamp that a chair was being drawn across her bedroom.

"If you are a sylph," she said, without being frightened, "show yourself to me, I implore you, for I feel capable of loving you constantly, is you are as amiable as you are depicted."

After the beautiful Persian had said all that, there was no response, and the noise ceased. As she despaired of seeing the sylph, she perceived a thread that was attached to the awning of her bed, from which a key was suspended, which came to touch her face but returned to the foot of the bed as soon as she put her hand out to it.

Curious to see whether she was mistaken, she got up in order to bring a lamp next to her, and returned to the same position as before. The game of the key continued, and lasted for more than an hour, without anyone showing themselves, in spite of all the pleas she could utter. Finally, the ends of the awning were seized, and after it was shaken violently, something was thrown on top of it. For the rest of the night, she did not see anything more.

She got up at dawn in order to go into her dressing-room to think freely about her adventure. As she leaned over her table, thoughtfully, she perceived a piece of paper covered with an unknown handwriting, which she picked up, and read:

I am the sylph you requested, beautiful Zaïde. I have been waiting for this happy moment for more than a year. I will love you with a constancy that you have not found among men, but I want to be loved in the same way. For that reason, I shall test your fidelity before showing myself. In the meantime, I shall take care to distract you by means of tender conversation. If your heart is able to appreciate the difference of our amour from that of mortals, I will render you the happiest woman in all Persia.

"Yes, charming Sylph, yes," cried the amiable Zaïde; you will find me delicate and tender, and you will never have reason to repent of the benevolence you have for me."

She spent the rest of the day in an intense impatience for the night to arrive. She went to bed early, in the hope that her lover might come to see her. She was not mistaken.

Scarcely had the slaves retired than she heard a voice that said to her: "It is just, amiable Zaïde, that I recompense you for the care you have taken to get rid of everything that might impede our conversations. I have come to assure you of an eternal amour, a complaisance proof against anything, and that whatever is in my power will be within yours. That is very little. We can do anything we want, and we find nothing impossible to please the person we love, but as I wrote to you, we are jealous and delicate; the slightest infidelity offends us, and we punish as severely as we love. Our amour is the measure of our hatred. It is up to you to decide whether you are capable of such a dangerous engagement."

"Oh, my dear," replied the tender Persian, "have no fear that my sentiments will displease you; my heart will only never be yours; I shall only think of that which might please you, and I am certain that my constancy will equal yours."

"I wish that more than you do," said the sylph, but the inconstancy of your sex is so well known to us that, in order not to be constrained to punish the only person who can make my happiness, I want to test whether you are what you think you are. I will talk to you at all the times that you are at liberty. I shall tell you all the most beautiful adventures, in order to give you an occupation worthy of a woman whom I want to render perfect; and in order for you to rest from that difficult labor, I will inform you of all the most hidden things that are happening in the various parts of the world; but you will only see me when I have nothing more to fear of your heart. And to commence to give you proof that I am seeking everything that might please you, know that the charming sister for whom you weep every day is not dead."

"Oh, my dear sylph," cried Zaïde, "what are you telling me? Istherie was saved from the terrible shipwreck that caused all those who were with her to perish, without our ever being able to discover what had become of her? Oh, if it is true that you love me, enable me to see her once more in my life and tell her all that her false death has cost me in tears."

"I cannot give you that evidence of obedience right away," said the sylph, "but in order not to leave you in ignorance of everything that has happened to her since your separation, I can tell you that, if you have no need of repose."

"Sleep," said Zaïde, "cannot give me a pleasure as sensible as the one you are promising me, so I implore you not to delay a moment in giving it to me."

Without responding, the sylph commenced the story of Istherie in these terms.

The Story of Istherie

You know with what joy Istherie was awaited by the Prince of Sogdiana, and that the beautiful young woman, sensibly touched by his merit, only felt at her departure the chagrin of being separated from you. You saw her embark with a favorable wind, but that calm did not last long. In the evening, a tempest blew up so violent that at daybreak it caused the ship to break up on a rock that formed a little island, to which the beautiful Istherie escaped with the aid of a few planks. All the rest of those who had accompanied her were engulfed by the waves.

As soon as Istherie had recovered from the dread that such great peril had caused her, she thanked Heaven for having conserved her, but when she found herself alone on an uninhabited island, exposed to wild beasts and without the hope of getting away from it, she regretted not being among the number of those she saw lying on the sand.

She spent the day and the night in that cruel situation, but dawn enabled her to conceive some hope. She perceived a ship in the open sea, and, climbing to the highest point of a rock, she made so many signs that she was perceived. A small boat was launched, which came to collect that beautiful person, but she soon realized that she had only escaped one misfortune to fall into a greater one, since her protectors were Turks and the war that there was between the Shah and the Great Sultan caused her to judge that she was going to be a slave, her clothing having identified her as Persian and a person of very high birth.

She was not mistaken in her conjectures; she was taken to the Pacha, who was a cruel man with a grim gaze. He scarcely looked at her, and without saying a word he ordered that she be put with the other slaves.

"Sire," said a man in his retinue, "this young woman is Persian; she ought not to be treated like the other slaves."

At those words the Pacha raised his eyes, and, finding himself dazzled by that supernatural beauty, he made a sign that she be taken to one of the most beautiful cabins on the ship, that she be given slaves to serve her, and that she be carefully guarded. Istherie suffered that latest misfortune with the same constancy with which she had suffered the approach of death.

The next day, the Pacha, whose name as Acmar, came to see her as soon as he knew that she was awake. "Beautiful person," he said to her, "although fate has rendered you my slave, I have come to tell you that I am more enslaved than you are, and that I cannot live without being loved. Think hard about the happiness I am offering you; I will break your chains and make you the mistress of all that I possess."

"Sire," the beautiful Persian replied to him, "I am very obliged for your offers, but, prejudiced by a passion for one of the most amiable princes in all of Persia, I am incapable of changing."

"Ishterie," said Acmar, "it was sufficient to tell me that you cannot respond to my tenderness, without giving me a cruel excuse. The hope of vanquishing your insensibility would have constrained me to suffer without complaint, but since a beloved rival is the cause of my misfortune, I ought to regard you as my enemy and on that basis overwhelm you with all my hatred."

"Your hatred, Sire," Istherie said, "is far less fearful to me than your amour."

"Well," the desperate Pacha replied, "we shall see whether your constancy will not cost you a few tears."

Having said that he left the cabin, with eyes in which fury was depicted, and left the beautiful Persian very afflicted by that new misfortune."

For as long as the navigation lasted, the amorous Acmar, without remembering the resolutions he had made, did not quit her. Sometimes submissive and sometimes furious, he tried in vain to shake her constancy.

Finally, she arrived in Alexandria, of which he was the Sultan. He had her taken to the most beautiful apartment in his seraglio, and gave her an infinite number of slaves to serve her, magnificent garments and jewels of an inestimable value. All that did not touch your lovely sister. The moments when she was alone were all employed in lamenting being separated forever from the Prince of Sogdiana.

One day, when she was more depressed than usual, she avenged herself for that on the unfortunate Pacha; outraged by her scorn, he left her chamber swearing no longer to employ pleas and prayers when he could do anything he wished.

A young slave approached her. "Madame," she said, "be careful of the Pacha if you love the prince; he is in the same chains as you and even more unhappy."

"Oh, Fatima," cried Istherie, "what are you telling me? My dear prince is in this palace? The same fate has overtaken both of us? No, that isn't possible, and you're telling me something I can't believe."

"The same storm that put you in the Pacha's power," said the slave, "put us in his chains. I had the good fortune to be one of the maids chosen to serve you. The place where you were found, your garments, and the beauty that is only encountered so perfectly in your visage, left me in no doubt that you were Istherie. I informed the unfortunate prince, but I hid the Pacha's amour from him, for fear of augmenting his chagrin. I was able to speak to him for as long as the navigation lasted, but since we have been in the palace I was only able to obtain news of him yesterday, when, passing the new flower garden, I recognized the prince, who was tracing a design with a cord in his hand.

"Fatima," he said to me, "what is Istherie doing? Is she still faithful to an unfortunate, and have the grandeurs with which my rival is heaping her not changed her?"

"Sire," I said, "since you know that the cruel Acmar loves Istherie, you ought not to be unaware of the cruelties by which she is afflicted. Her constancy is unshaken either by threats or kindness."

"If it is true that my dear Istherie has such advantageous sentiments, Fatima, you can give me the pleasure of seeing her tomorrow. I shall be tracing a flower bed under the windows of her apartment. The Sultan commanded me to do it this morning. I have the good fortune of pleasing him; he is content with my work, and we might perhaps find an opportunity to escape from slavery. Go, Fatima, and ask the charming Istherie for a moment of conversation. After those words, Madame, I quit the prince and came to acquit my commission."

"Oh, Fatima," said Istherie, "how I wish you harm for having hidden that the prince was so close to me!"

"I was afraid," said the slave, "that a careless word might let the Pacha know of an adventure so dangerous for him, of which the prince would be the victim. That was what obliged me to keep quiet. But Madame, without reproaching the past, what resolution do you have for the present?"

"That I shall see the prince, and in order to have more liberty to do that, I shall treat Acmar less harshly, and allow him to hope that his constancy might oblige me to some return."

As she finished speaking the Pacha came in. Penetrated with the fear of having displeased her, he had come to beg her pardon for his anger. In the hope that a little mildness might allow her to see her lover, Istherie received his apology with less arrogance, and the credulous lover, charmed, told her that he had a slave who had a particular genius for flowered beds, whom he would order to trace one under her windows.

"I would like very much to see that man work," said Istherie, "and you would give me pleasure by allowing me the liberty."

"You are free throughout the interior of the palace, Madame," said the amorous Pacha, and everything here is under your law. Command anything you please, without fear that anything will be refused, except the liberty of abandoning me." As he finished speaking he presented his hand to the lovely Persian, in order to descend into the gardens, and conducted her to where the prince was working.

If Fatima had not run to inform him of his good fortune, the prince would not have been able to help giving evidence of his joy, but the clever slave, having gone ahead of her mistress, had had time to warn him.

"Soliman," the Pacha said to him, "this is the sovereign of this palace; obey her in everything she cares to order you to do."

"Sire," the prince replied, without daring to look at Istherie, "I make it my unique concern to please you, and since you order me to obey this lady, I am ready to sacrifice my life for her."

"I shall not request such violent services from you," said the lovely Persian. "That of tracing under my apartment a flower-bed similar to those of the Shah's seraglio will be the most difficult in which I shall employ you."

"I hope that I will succeed well enough in the first order that you have had the kindness to give me," said the fake Soliman, "to merit a little praise."

After that, Istherie asked the Sultan to continue walking, for fear that a longer conversation might enable some suspicion, and after having praised the magnificence of the beautiful place highly, she returned to her apartment.

She did not spend the night there without speaking to Fatima about her lover, and in the morning, as soon as the sun had risen, she opened her windows and saw the prince, already occupied in his labor. As he was alone in that place, because it was so early that one could scarcely distinguish the light in the darkness, Istherie made him a sign to advance, and while the faithful Fatima watched the approaches to the apartment in order not to be surprised, the two lovers said to one another everything tender that Amour causes to be felt in hearts deeply penetrated by his arrows.

After giving a few moments to their initial transports, they thought about how they might be able to get out of the hands of the cruel Pacha. They decided that Soliman would give money to one of his servants to purchase his liberty, with orders to alert them to the first merchant ship ready to set sail for Persia; that the beautiful Istherie would go for a walk that day on the edge of the sea, which extended around a large terrace at one end of the gardens, and at the favorable moment, they would descend with the aid of a rope-ladder, which Soliman would take care to obtain.

Fatima came at that moment to warn them that a few slaves were approaching, and their conversation ceased.

Impatient to advance his happiness, the prince searched among the men who had been taken into slavery with him for the one he thought most capable of carrying out his design. Everything succeeded as the lovers wished, and they escaped from the barbaric hands of the Pacha a fortnight after their conversation.

Scarcely had they savored the pleasure of being at liberty, however, when their ship was attacked by corsairs, who, being much stronger than them, in spite of the generous resistance of the prince, forced them to surrender and put them in irons again.

Istherie's beauty gave the mercenaries the desire to take her to Constantinople to present her to the Great Sultan. That made them scorn the propositions that the unfortunate prince made them to pay them whatever ransom they wanted for that beautiful person and himself. They did not change their plan, and after a long voyage your lovely sister was imprisoned in the Great Sultan's seraglio, without the hope of ever seeing her dear prince again. She spent her misfortunate days lamenting him, while her unfortunate lover, who had been sold to the Grand Vizier, sought in vain for the means to see her once again in his lifetime.

I have not mentioned the rage of the Pacha when he learned about Istherie's flight; I thought that you could easily comprehend it and that I would give you more pleasure by not leaving you ignorant any longer of the place that the unfortunate Persian was living.

"Thank you," said Zaïde. "At another time, I would be more sensible to such cruel adventures, but I confess that the pleasure of knowing that a sister for whom everyone has been weeping for such a long time renders me incapable for the moment of sighing for her misfortunes. I am interested in everything agreeable or disagreeable that might happen in Constantinople, and I will be grateful if you can tell me everything that is happening there in secret."

"I can satisfy you," said the obliging sylph, "and the dethronement of the Great Sultan will provide me with sad material.

The Story of the Valide Sultan

The youth of the Great Sultan, when he was recognized as sovereign, having given a great deal of authority to the Sultana, his mother, who was a princess of ambitious mentality, she gave far more thought to conserving her power when the prince was of an age to govern his Estate than to giving him the lessons necessary for a glorious reign.

She searched throughout the world for the most beautiful women to fill his seraglio, and in that great number of young beauties she chose the one whose intelligence seemed to her most suitable to that vast design. She took care to instruct her in everything that might give her an absolute power over the young sultan, and, speaking often to her son about the charms of that beautiful slave, she gave him a desire to see her. Her eyes had the effect that she expected; the Great Sultan loved her tenderly and declared her the favorite Sultana.

As soon as the Valide Sultan found herself, by that means, the mistress of her son's mind, she also wanted to be united in her interests with the Grand Vizier, and, sparing no effort to subjugate him, she became inseparable from that principal minister of the Ottoman Empire. Only the janissaries gave her umbrage; their bellicose humor could not easily adapt to the soft and effeminate life that she was making the Sultan lead, and the government of a woman could not suit those generous troops. They complained loudly about not seeing their prince bear the Crescent into enemy lands.

"Are we to remain idle, then," he said, "while all Europe is at war, and we have only to present ourselves in order to make the conquest of Hungary. The malcontents are waiting for us and that crown will only cost us the trouble of going to seek it. Let the Sultan lead us to it, or we will chose a prince worthy to command us."

Such dangerous murmurs frightened the Valide Sultan. She advised the Great Sultan to quit Constantinople, and to put himself in security in Andrinople while the Muftis appeased that nascent disorder, not being able to remedy it in the usual fashion, which was to double their pay, the treasury of the Empire having been employed by the princess and the Grand Vizier to buy hirelings.

The Sultan, therefore, set forth on that journey, so secretly that no one learned of his departure until it was too late to prevent it; but that augmented the sedition instead of extinguishing it. The spahis joined the janissaries, and went in good order to find the Mufti, to tell him that if the Great Sultan did not return to his seraglio to lead them against their enemies, and did not give them the heads of the Valide Sultan, the Grand Vizier and the great Testedere, they would go lay siege to him in Andrinople and elect his brother Selim in his place.

In order to save himself from their fury, the Mufti promised them everything they wanted and dispatched a man in their presence to the Great Sultan; but without waiting for the response the troops, animated against the bad government, changed all the officers in command in the city and after leaving as many soldiers as they thought necessary to guard it, they marched directly to Andrinople.

Meanwhile, the Mufti's courier alarmed the Sultan greatly. He lamented, but too late, having believed his mother's advice. In such a great extremity, he wanted to show that he was the master, and to go with him to complain to the troops about their insolence; but the tears of the Sultana stopped him, the advice of the Valide Sultan and the Grand Vizier was heeded again. They sent an officer on behalf of the prince to say that the Great Sultan was willing to forget their revolt and to give them double pay if they returned to their dwellings, and that he would go as soon as them to Constantinople, where it would be decided whether it was in the interests of the Empire to go into Hungary.

The janissaries did not give that envoy the time to complete his commission; they killed him, sent word to have the young Ottoman prince released from prison, whom they recognized as Sultan at the head of the army, and who set forth on the road to Andrinople at top speed.

That was the final blow of misfortune for the Great Sultan. He sent them the heads of the Grand Vizier and the Testedere and promised to have the Valide Sultan imprisoned permanently. But those victims were immolated to late, their woes did not appease the mutineers; they continued their march and approached the city. That is the condition of the seraglio, which might perhaps serve for the good fortune of your sister.

"Oh, my dear sylph," Zaïde said to him, "could you not help the unfortunate Prince of Sogdiana to break his irons and those of the unfortunate Istherie? What proof of amour could you give me that would touch me more sensibly?"

"It is necessary to satisfy you," said the sylph, and I shall tell you tomorrow what I have done." He dropped a sheaf of paper on to the bed. "There," he added, is something to amuse you during my absence, and substitute for me while I am away from you for an entire day."

Zaïde wanted to reply to him, but she knew that he was no longer there. She gave the rest of the night to sleep, and the next day, she went into her cabinet and opened the manuscript that her lover had left her, in which she found this tale:

Princess Patientine in the Forest of Erimente

There was an ogre named Insacio who made his dwelling in a lair into which the sun's rays had never penetrated. He was cruel and devoid of justice, and the Furies of Hell, which had presided over his birth, having spread the foam of Cerberus over his tongue, it was so penetrated by it permanently that as soon as he touched a woman with his tongue she was doomed to die, without any remedy being able to save her. To possesses all the wealth of the earth was the sole passion that occupied his heart; neither amour nor amity had ever found any place there. The devouring avidity by which he was tormented to amass riches gave him an anxiety that never allowed him any repose.

He had two sisters who were similar to him in humor. They lived with him. The elder was named Aigredouce; she had beauty and some mildness in her temperament; that sometimes made her take the part of the unfortunates whom the ogre tormented cruelly; in particular, she often stopped him from touching with his piercing tongue those who were unfortunate enough to enter his lair. But with that benevolence she nevertheless had a bitterness in her facial expression and all her words which was very displeasing. The younger, whose name was Bizarrine, had a humor so capricious, so imperious and so chagrined that no one could invent torments more insupportable than to oblige someone to live with her. Her amity was no less to be dreaded than her hatred, giving no more repose to those she loved than to her enemies.

The ogre often went to take lessons from the goddess Avarice, whose dwelling was not far from his lair. When he consulted her one day regarding his destiny, she told him that if he could make himself loved by a princess named Patientine, the daughter of Lycaon, and have her in his power, he would be the richest of all the ogres of his era. He thanked Avarice for her good advice, and, returning home, he disposed his equipage with diligence. He quit his natural form for fear of frightening Patientine. He took that of a well made young

237

man with good manners, and changed his bristling hair into the most beautiful blond hair in the world.

Under that new metamorphosis he appeared at the court of the Queen of Lydia, Patientine's mother, who had been a widow for some years. He was received there under the name of the Prince of Thrace, and was able to disguise himself so well that he won the hearts of the queen and the princess in a very short time.

Patientine had a very strong amity for a young woman of her court named Espritée. She held the first place in her heart, as she held it by her rank with regard to the queen, and she did not hide anything from her. She confided to her the nascent tenderness she had for Insacio.

Espritée, who, by virtue of a presentiment of whose cause she was unaware, feared that the princess might be unfortunate if she married the false Prince of Thrace, tried to turn her away from that alliance, but eventually, seeing that the queen wanted it as much as Patientine, she no longer opposed it. The marriage was therefore concluded in a matter of days, and that amiable princess, whose beauty, sweetness and virtue had made all the neighboring princes sigh, was delivered to the barbaric Insacio.

The ogre, impatient to return to his lair with his prey and get out of a court whose magnificence wounded his humor so much, departed with his wife and Espritée, who did not want to quite Patientine, no matter what opposition Insacio raised.

After a few days' travel, the princess arrived in the Forest of Erimente, and a short time later at the terrible lair. She found Aigredouce and Bizarrine there, who attempted to please her by means of urgent attentions. How can the astonishment of the princess, on finding herself in such a frightful place, be described? She nearly died of dolor, and all the influence that Espritée had over her mind could not console her.

The ogre, who had resumed his ordinary form and his natural cruelty, was not touched by Patientine's tears, Aigredouce tried to make her understand that she was wrong to be afflicted by being united with Insacio, that all princesses would envy her good fortune if they knew about it; and that if, by her complaisance, she could win his heart, nothing would be lacking to her happiness. Bizarrine, who happened to be in a compassionate mood, believing that her presence might soothe Patientine's chagrins, did not quit her, and made her so impatient with the advice she gave her regarding her conduct, that she augmented the princess's dolor greatly.

Espritée employed all the intelligence that the gods had given her to win the amity of the ogre and that of his sisters, in order to diminish Patientine's chagrin. She thought she had succeeded in that, but she realized subsequently that nothing touched that heart insensible to pity.

Meanwhile, Insacio, wanting to take advantage of the good fortune of having Patientine in his power, in order to become rich, began to put Avarice's lessons into practice. He made the unfortunate princess get up before dawn and forced her to go into the forest in search of herbs, which he made her put into huge cauldrons over the fire in order to extract the juice from them. Then he made her carry them into the animal sheds to give them to the monsters that he kept there. Fattened on the juice of those herbs, the beasts were infinitely valuable, and worth a great deal of money. The merchants of Thrace and Bosna often came to buy them from him.

When Patientine came back from such a difficult employment, in order to relax, she was given a distaff and made to spin wool in order to make the crimson fabric in which all the kings of the Orient dressed themselves. She was only allowed to rest when she had filled several spindles. At other times, she employed her sad days searching in the nearby mountains for the marvelous seed from which the crimson dye was made, and she was made to spend every evening making the dye. The poor princess did not have a moment's rest. If she had been able to win the ogre's cruel heart with so much hard labor, she would have been consoled, but Insacio, always tormented by the desire or sordid gain, never thought that she worked hard enough, and scolded her incessantly for not doing more.

The princess suffered all those reproaches and obeyed him with a meekness that would have touched anyone but Insacio. Aigredouce told him sometimes that he ought to be content with Patientine, but Bizarrine said that her brother did very well not to be sensible to the unhappiness of his wife, that it was necessary to profit from the opportunity to enrich himself, and that if any relief were given to Patientine, she would find her more insupportable work.

"At least," said Aigredouce, "I could give her nourishment that might sustain her in such hard employments, for she can't live on acorn-bread and the little piece of goat's cheese that you give her for the whole day. You ought to remember that she hasn't been brought up with so much harshness, and you ought to fear that she might soon succumb to those fatigues."

"My sister," said the ogre, angrily, "you've already corrupted that girl, nourished in a superb court, but I shall certainly refrain from following such pernicious advice. I don't intend to eat in one day, in overly delicate fare, everything that I've accumulated with so much difficulty."

Insacio's natural anxiety did not permit him a longer conversation; he quit his sister and went into the mountains to see whether he could find Patientine there collecting seeds. He found her lying at the foot of a tree conversing with her dear Espritée, The furious Ogre vomited all the most horrible insults at the unfortunate princess and swore to take away the only consolation she had by sending Espritée away. He would have done so right away had it not been for the fear that the young woman might tell the queen about all her daughter's woes.

Without responding to the barbarian with a single word, Patientine wiped away her tears and, having finished stripping the earth in that area of its precious seeds, returned to the lair. She found Bizarrine there, who made a crime of her sadness, and Aigredouce, wanting to console her, told her that with an affected air that she thought she was driving her patience to an extreme.

All the ogre's subjects experienced his cruelty, and in order to content the insatiable thirst he had for riches he made them work night and day digging in the soil in a valley near his lair, where Avarice had told him that he might finds a treasure. That was a further misfortune for Patientine. He wanted her to be with those unfortunate diggers incessantly, in order to prevent them taking a moment's rest. That new employment did not dispense the poor princess from her spinning; she took her distaff with her, and, sometimes burned by an ardent sun and sometime pierced by rain and fog, she remained exposed to the insults of the weather all day long. What heart would not have been sensible to impulses of pity on seeing the evils that the young princess suffered?

One day, when she was with the workers, Courageous, the Prince of Bosna, who had seen her at the court of the Queen of Lydia and who had always had an inclination for her, which all his reason had had difficulty vanquishing, passed close to her. Surprised by such an unexpected encounter, he dismounted from his horse and approached her urgently. He found her beautiful, in spite of the change that so many misfortunes had brought about in her charms, and testified to her in respectful terms the pleasure he had in seeing her again.

The princess, ashamed of being found in a state so different from the one in which the prince had seen her before, did not say anything for some time, but the fear of being found with him by Insacio caused her to speak in order to beg him to go away.

As she finished speaking a furious lion emerged from the forest and came to hurl itself upon Patientine. The prince drew his sword and set himself to defend her; by means of a menacing cry and a blow he struck the lion at the same time, he obliged the furious beast to turn its rage against him. Courageous defended himself for a long time, but not without receiving a large wound in the belly from the lion's claws, and if the diggers had not run to his aid he might have perished in the combat, but they overwhelmed the lion with so many blows that it fell dead at Patientine's feet.

Insacio, attracted by the screams of the princess, arrived as the prince, losing consciousness because of his wound, let himself fall on to the grass. Touched by pity for the first time in his life, he had him carried to his somber abode, and ordered that his wounds should be dressed. Penetrated by gratitude, Patientine bandaged him with her beautiful hands and took the trouble to go with Espritée to look for simples to put on the wounds.

How sensible Prince Courageous was to the benevolence of the princess! His amour acquired new force; he could not express sufficiently how appreciative he was of the evidence of her gratitude, and praised a hundred times a day the two wounds he had received in saving her life.

In the meantime, the ogre was obliged to go away with his sisters for a few days. Courageous took advantage of those fortunate moments to tell the princess everything he felt for her, but Patientine, whatever reasons she had to be discontented with her cruel husband, responded to him with so much discretion that she fully merited the prince's tenderness.

Insacio came back sooner than expected, and finding his wife with the invalid, he entered in a fury and heaped her with outrageous reproaches. He repented of having Courageous brought to his home, and, his avarice combining with his jealousy, he forbade Patientine to furnish the prince any longer with the necessities of life, and told her that she was not to enter the cave that he was in again. Patientine received that order dolorously, but did not murmur in protest, and recommenced her hard labors.

The amorous prince suffered the misfortunes of the princess with impatience. His cave was so close to the ogre's that he heard all he ill-treatment that the latter meted out to the beautiful Patientine, and, not wanting to augment it, as soon as he could ride a horse, he took care to depart from a place that was so dear to him. That was not without having consulted with Espritée as to what he could do to extract the princess from such a hard slavery. First of all they made the resolution to inform the Queen of Lydia, but Espritée told him that she did not have the power to break her daughter's chains, and that it was necessary for her to go and find a fay who was a close relative of Patientine, who, by means of her science, could give them the means to remove the princess from the ogre's cruel hands. She said that she would leave with him the next day at dawn in order to find the fay, without telling the princess, who would not want to consent to her happiness.

After having made all their preparation, Courageous took his leave of Insacio and the charming Patientine, and departed the next day with Espritée. The princess did not learn about her friend's departure without chagrin, and could not understand what had obliged her to leave her, knowing the tender amity that she had for her.

While Courageous and Espritée were making their journey, a very powerful prince arrived with his wife in a castle near the Forest of Erimente. His name was Entreprenant and his wife was named Froidine. The ogre was told by the goddess Avarice that he would need Entreprenant's help to preserve him from a great misfortune that was menacing him, and as he knew of no misfortune except those regarding the loss of wealth, he followed the advice of the goddess; he went to see the newcomer and took Patientine with him. Emerging from her natural humor, Froidine received the beautiful princess very well, and Entreprenant was unable to see without paying for the pleasure of gazing at her with the loss of his heart. He made the ogre a thousand amities, in order to have the liberty of seeing his lovely wife, in spite of the natal aversion that he conceived for him at first sight.

Entreprenant often went to Insacio's home and, not being able to hide his passion for long, talked about it to Patientine. That beautiful person, abandoned to the ogre's furies, listened without anger to a declaration that she would not have wanted in better times, in order to assure herself of an aid against Insacio's cruelties, and the prince, charmed not to be rejected, obliged Froidine to visit Patientine often, and to testify amity to her; but the ogre, seeing that it took Patientine away from

243

her ordinary labors, ordered her not to go see Froidine so frequently, and made a crime of what he had ordered her to do.

He searched for new work for her, and the princess, with her usual meekness, obeyed him. Entreprenant often surprised her breaking reeds, from which she extracted a cotton that was very rare in the region, which served to make cloth with which she dressed herself. She would have liked to hide from everyone the ill-treatment she received from the ogre, but, that not being possible, she tried to excuse it. Entreprenant wasted no time in trying to make Patientine comprehend that her husband did not merit that tenderness. His concern was futile; the virtuous person replied that, the gods having given her Insacio for a husband, it was her duty to obey him and to love him with the same fidelity as if he were the best of all men.

Bizarrine often came to interrupt these conversations, and warned the ogre about them. She put him in such a bad humor that, in spite of the advice of Avarice, he quarreled with Entreprenant and Froidine and shut the princess in his lair, not allowing her to go out into the forest any longer. His fury did not stop there; he no longer gave Patientine any rest, and every day was employed in furnishing her with new torments, which the amiable person suffered with an admirable patience.

Insacio, fearful of losing Patientine, not because of any sentiment of amity, but because of the great wealth that she amassed by her labor, surrounded his lair with clouds so dense that he rendered it invisible to everyone, and, changing his two sisters into monsters, he put them at the entrance to the cavern in order to forbid entry to anyone who might penetrate the enveloping cloud. Having taken his precautions so well to take away the anxiety of losing Patientine he savored some tranquility.

Meanwhile, Prince Courageous and Espritée arrived at the palace of the fay Clementine, and were received by her with the air of benevolence that made everyone love her. She took them into her cabinet, and, having invited them to sit down beside her, she said: "I know the purpose of your journey, charming Espritée; Patientine needs my help; she is at the extremity of misfortune, and the gods, who wanted to give a model to humans by the example of her virtue, will extract her by means of my art from the tyranny of the cruel ogre. It will need a few days or me to prepare for the journey; spend them here in all the pleasures that can be obtained in this palace."

After those few words, he fay dismissed the prince as Espritée; he found in the hall a troop of nymphs, who came toward them and conducted hem to a superbly furnished apartment. After they had rested there for a few hours, the nymphs had Espritée pass into a cabinet, where they dressed her in a silver and pink garment and decocted her head with a feather capeline of the same color. In that new apparel they brought her to Prince Courageous's room, and served them a light meal of fruits and preserves. After the collation they took them into a garden, which responded to the beauty of the palace, and, leaving them in an arbor of jasmine and pomegranate, they gave them the liberty of listening to a charming orchestra, which was in a myrtle arbor next to theirs.

Courageous and Espritée gave a few moments to the pleasure of such a pleasant symphony, but as nothing could prevent them from thinking about the woes of Patientine, they talked about that beautiful person for such a long time that it was night when they returned to the palace. The time having come to repose, Courageous left Espritée in her apartment.

The next day, at dawn, the nymphs came to wake the amiable Espritée in order to take her to the fay's park. They gave her a very elegant hunting costume and took her into the courtyard of the palace. There she found a small ebony chariot with golden suns, drawn by four tigers, into which she climbed. The nymphs followed her in other chariots of a similar beauty, and Prince Courageous, mounted on a superbly harnessed black horse, came to join them at the rendezvous.

The whole day passed as agreeably as possible; the deer only ran for as long as was required to provide pleasure without fatiguing the ladies, and when night constrained them to return to the palace they arrived there with all the joy that such a charming amusement had inspired in them. Afterwards, the fay sent word to Espritée and Courageous to come to see her, which they did urgently.

"Espritée," she said, "my charms are ready; it requires no less power than mine to extract Patientine from Insacio's irons. He has employed all the art of Hell to form an enchantment that renders her invisible to our eyes; Avarice has given him advice, but I shall render his power useless and render the princess to you. Let us depart right away, in order to arrive at his tenebrous abode at sunrise. And you, Prince Courageous, forget your valor, and without using your arms to vanquish the monsters—they would be impotent against them—leave me the care of breaking Patientine's chains."

Without waiting for a response, the fay presented her hand to the prince, and, telling Espritée to pick up a small bottle that was on her table and follow her, she went on to a large terrace that was at the end of her apartment, where they found a chariot drawn by eagles. The fay, having placed herself therein, had the prince and Espritée enter it, and, the eagles having flown into the air, they arrived with the first ray of sunlight at the cloud that hid the ogre's lair.

Clementine told Espritée to spread a few drops of the essence in the bottle over the cloud, and it dissipated immediately, allowing Espritée and the prince to see the entrance to the lair, guarded by the two monsters.

"Remember," the fay said to Courageous, seeing him already putting his hand on his sword, "that to combat the princess's guardians, your sword is useless, and only my power will suffice to destroy the enchantment."

The prince, ashamed of having disobeyed the fay's command, stopped, and presented his hand to Clementine to help her descend from her winged chariot. Espritée followed her, impatient to see the princess again. Approaching the monsters, the fay touched them with her enchanted wand, which constrained them to resume their natural form, and, fearful of the presence of Clementine, to flee into the forest. The fay, scornful of objects unworthy of her anger, went into the cavern, and, expelling the obscurity by her presence, she saw the beautiful Patientine, who was removing a cauldron full of herbs from above the fire.

Ashamed to be surprised in an exercise so unbefitting to her birth, and dazzled by the fay's splendor, she dropped the cauldron. No sooner had the water and herbs it contained touched the ground than the cavern was seen to be full of brilliant gold instead of what had been in the cauldron. More astonished than ever, Patientine uttered a loud cry.

The ogre, who was in his animal shed, heard Patientine scream and ran to see what had happened to her. Charmed to see his cavern full of a metal that was so dear to him, without perceiving the Fay, the prince or Espritée, who was holding the princess in her arms, he bent down precipitately to pick up that precious gold, but as he touched it, it became once again what it had been before. The water, running through his avid hands, formed a stream in the cavern. The ogre's astonishment at such an extraordinary sight is inexpressible, and, raising his haggard eyes, he saw the fay, who said to him, with a severe expression:

"Tremble, unfortunate Insacio, and recognize the justice of the gods by the torments to which they condemn you. You will lose this unfortunate princess, whom you have rendered yourself unworthy of possessing by the evils that your avarice has made her suffer. I want to take her back to her realm, where she will find the recompense for her virtues, while you will employ your misfortunate days in amassing riches that will disappear from your hands as soon as you have touched them, without you being able to correct your desire to amass them by the experience that you will cumulate, at every moment of your life, of being unable to possess them.

"You will serve as an example to all those who see your torture, and to take away the only pleasure that might remain to you, in making use of your poisoned tongue to avenge yourself on those who approach you, you shall no longer have that dangerous power; it will only be possible to spread that venom over those who resemble you. The evil that your tongue pronounces against mortals will not do them any harm, and will only serve to add a new splendor to the innocence that you have oppressed."

The cruel ogre trembled with rage at the fay's discourse, but, the gold taking the place of the stream again, without remembering his torture, he bent down to pick it up.

Clementine made use of that moment to take Patientine away, and, making her enter her chariot with Courageous, and Espritée, she sat down next to her. The eagles having resumed their flight, they were soon far away from the fatal lair.

While they made their voyage through the air, the ogre, without remembering Patientine, was occupied in picking up the liquid gold; but, the fay's enchantment taking effect, it changed its nature as soon as he had touched it, and flowed away as it had the first time, becoming gold again as soon as it was on the floor of the cavern.

Since that terrible moment the ogre has experienced a torture in conformity with the frightful vices that had led him to commit so many crimes. Without giving himself a moment's repose, he spends his misfortunate days in a continuous rage, like the unlucky Tantalus in Hell, persecuted by a continuous thirst that he cannot slake, unable to approach the water that recoils when he tries to drink it. All his neighbors and subjects, charmed by such a just torment, come to see it every day, and make him know, by the lack of power that the venom of his tongue over those of which he wishes to avenge himself, that the fay's words were veritable.

Meanwhile, Clementine and the beautiful Patientine arrived in Lydia and descended into the courtyard of the Palace of Sardis, surprising the queen agreeably by her presence. She embraced her dear daughter a thousand times, and threw herself at the feet of the fay to thank her for having liberate Patientine from the cruel yoke of Insacio. She heaped Espritée with caresses, and assured Courageous of an eternal esteem.

After having heaped the charming Patientine with benefits, the fay returned to her palace. Courageous remained at the court of the Queen of Lydia, and, adapting his passion to the virtue of the princess, adored her in secret. Espritée shared the fay's gifts with Patientine, and, charmed to have her with her, knew no greater happiness than being loved by Clementine and her dear princess.

CLASSIC FRENCH FANTASY

Honoré de Balzac. *The Last Fay*
Gabrielle-Suzanne Barbot de Villeneuve. *The Naiads * Beauty and The Beast*
Chevalier de Béthune. *The World of Mercury*
Jean Carrère. *The End of Atlantis*
Charlotte-Rose Caumont de La Force. *The Land of Delights*
Félicien Champsaur. *Pharaoh's Wife*
Jacques Collin de Plancy. *Voyage to the Center of the Earth*
Gaston Danville. *The Perfume of Lust*
Paul Féval. *Anne of the Isles*
Charles de Fieux. *Lamékis*
Judith Gautier. *Isoline and the Serpent-Flower*
Nathalie Henneberg. *The Green Gods*
Gustave Kahn. *The Tale of Gold and Silence*
Edmond Haraucourrt. *Dieudonat*
Marie-Jeanne L'Héritier de Villandon. *The Robe of Sincerity*
André Lichtenberger. *The Centaurs; The Children of the Crab*
J-M. & Randy Lofficier. *The French Fantasy Treasury 1-3*
Charles Lomon & P.-B. Gheuzi. *The Last Days of Atlantis*
Marie-Madeleine de Lubert. *Princess Camion*
Maurice Magre. *The Marvelous Story of Claire d'Amour; The Call of the Beast; Priscilla of Alexandria; The Angel of Lust; The Mystery of the Tiger; The Poison of Goa; Lucifer; The Blood of Toulouse; The Albigensian Treasure; Jean de Fodoas; Melusine; The Brothers of the Virgin Gold*
Marie-Madeleine de Lubert. *Princess Camion.*
Camille Mauclair. *The Virgin Orient*
Hippolyte Mettais. *Paris Before the Deluge*
Victor-Emile Michelet. *Superhuman Tales*
Henriette-Julie de Murat. *The Palace of Vengeance*
Charles Nodier. *Trilby * The Crumb Fairy*
Edgar Quinet. *The Enchanter Merlin*
Henri de Régnier. *A Surfeit of Mirrors*

Restif de la Bretonne. *The Fay Ouroucoucou* (2 vols.)
J.-H. Rosny Aîné. *Pan's Flute*
Marie-Anne de Roumier-Robert. *The Voyage of Lord Seaton to the Seven Planets*
Nicolas Ségur. *Penelope's Secret*
Kiurt Steiner. *Ortog*
C.-F. Tiphaigne de La Roche. *Amilec * Giphantia*
Simon Tyssot de Patot. *The Strange Voyages of Jacques Massé and Pierre de Mésange*